BROKEN PROMISES

MARIANNE DELAFORCE

Published by Marianne Delaforce

Copyright © Marianne Delaforce 2018

The moral right of the author has been asserted in accordance with the Copyright Amendment (Moral Rights) Act 2000.

National Library of Australia. Cataloging-in-Publication Data

Broken Promises

The Promises Series

Delaforce, Marianne (1964–)

ISBNs: 978-0-6486334-3-3 (ebook)

978-0-6486334-4-0 (paperback)

Cover design by Marianne Delaforce

Cover layout by Ally Mosher

Images from AdobeStock.com

DEDICATION

This book is dedicated to all the women, men and children who have been touched by domestic violence. Do not suffer in silence if you or anyone you know is being abused. Please ask for help.

There are many organisations who can help in so many ways, you are not alone. Have faith and believe in yourself. There is a better life out there, one that you deserve. If these services and support had been available many years ago, Rose's life would have been very different.

Her journey was a long road to happiness, yours doesn't have to be.

Sending love out to you all, Marianne. XXX

CHAPTER 1

MARIA RIVER

DECEMBER 1960

Her father was not going to be happy that she had gone against his wishes, as her mother pulled the car into the driveway Rose's joy at finding out she was pregnant turned to dread, her mother turned the engine off and they sat in silence in front of the house.

"You know you have a choice Rose? You need to think long and hard about what you are going to do. If you have this child it means you won't be able to have your career, you will have to stay at home and take care of the child."

Rose started to speak. Loretta held her hand up.

"Let me finish. There is another option. You can have the child and adopt it out or you can have an abortion, think about it, you don't have to decide right now. Just know that whatever you decide, I will be right beside you, all the way supporting you." Loretta had tears in her eyes. This is not what she had hoped for her daughter, she had wanted her to have a chance to be whatever she wanted to be. To grow up to be a strong, independent woman, not tied down at fifteen to a husband and a child. Heavens, at fifteen Rose was still a child herself. The world was changing, there were so many more opportunities out there for women these days. She took her daughter's hand and smiled. "Ready?" Rose nodded. "Well then" she sighed, "let's go and tell your father."

Martin was out in the backyard chopping wood. He looked up as they came out the backdoor and smiled. "Hello girls, why so gloomy?"

"Martin, you need to come and sit down." Loretta calmly said. "There is something we need to tell you. You're not going to be happy about it either my love so put the axe down and come inside."

Once they were all seated at the kitchen table, Loretta took Martin's hands in hers. She knew he was going to get angry and more than anything he would be disappointed with Rose. She felt for him but she also had to stand by her daughter.

"What's going on? What's happened?" Martin did not like the silence, he could see that Rose was close to tears and she wouldn't even look at him, he knew whatever it was it was not going to be good news.

"Martin. There's no easy way to tell you this, so I'm getting straight to the point. Rose is pregnant." Loretta held his hands tightly.

"What? What do you mean pregnant? You can't be serious!" He stared at Rose with disbelief. "Did you not promise me you would not do that? Didn't you? How can this be?" He pulled his hands from Loretta and stood up so fast that the chair was knocked over backwards hitting the floor hard with a loud crash. He turned his back to them, Rose could see his whole body shaking, she knew, she had disappointed her father. The room was silent.

"Dad."

"Don't say a word Rose, not one word." He held his finger up to silence her, he needed a moment to collect his thoughts. "Give me a minute, just stay there." He stormed outside slamming the door on the way out.

Rose had tears streaming down her face, the elation she had felt discovering she was having Jimmy's baby had turned to sadness and disappointment at the pain she was causing her parents. She was scared and felt so bad for letting her father down. They sat in silence until Martin returned.

"Well Rose you have made your bed and you will have to lie in it. You need to seriously think about what you are going to do now. Does Jimmy know?"

"No, we came straight from the doctors to tell you." Rose said softly.

"Rose, you will need to ask him to come over tonight so we can discuss this together, as a family." Loretta tried to remain calm, she knew she had to keep her family together, she could not let this cause any kind of rift between them. Family meant everything to her.

"Okay Dad. But I'm keeping the baby. I'm not giving it away. I know Jimmy loves me and he will marry me." She sounded convincing but deep down she was starting to have doubts. After all she had not really known Jimmy that long, but she could tell he loved her.

Jimmy arrived just after he'd finished milking the cows. Rose heard his car pull up outside and she ran out to meet him. She needed to tell him before they spoke to her parents.

"Hi beautiful. What's going on?"

"Oh Jimmy." She threw her arms around him. "I have wonderful news, well I hope you think it is wonderful."

"What news?" He kissed her on the forehead and held her close.

"I'm pregnant!"

His body stiffened in her arms and he pushed her to arm's length to look at her in the eyes. "What you're pregnant? But we only did it once."

"Yes I know, but that's all it takes."

"Okay. I guess we have to talk about what we are going to do then. I suppose I had better face the music with your parents. I bet your dad's not happy with me right now."

"No he's not, Mum is upset too but she will support me, whatever I decide. I'm keeping the baby whether you stay with me or not." Rose stood defiantly in front of him.

He pulled her back into his arms. "I asked you to marry me Rose and I meant it. That hasn't changed. We will have this baby together. I promise you, I will always take care of you and I'll never hurt you."

Loretta and Martin were waiting for them in the lounge room. Jimmy was holding Rose's hand as they entered, he could feel the tension in the room and he knew that he had to stand up as a man. "Before you say anything Sir, I love your daughter and our unborn child and I will stand by them and take care of them both. I have already asked Rose to marry me and she said yes so we are going to get married as soon as possible."

Martin's expression was dark and gloomy "Okay then, sit down Jimmy!" He commanded. "I hope you understand the commitment you are both making. You do realise the gravity of this situation and that you will have a wife and child to support?" Are you ready for that?

"Yes Sir I am."

"We'd better make plans for a wedding then." Martin glanced at Loretta and sighed there was nothing he could do now but stand beside his daughter and hope that this marriage worked.

.

CHAPTER 2

The Uniting Church in South Kempsey was small and quaint. It sat on the top of the hill overlooking the valley. It wasn't a grand church by any means, built from local hardwood, painted white and had a bell that rang out to call people to service. A white picket fence enclosed the lovely, large yard around the church, a few old fig trees provided shade and masses of brightly coloured flower beds surrounded the church.

Only the immediate family were invited to the wedding and Alice, Rose's youngest sister was her flower girl. They had rushed and made all the plans so that they could marry quickly before Rose's pregnancy started to show too much.

Rose looked lovely in her white calf length dress with cap sleeves and a modest neckline. It came in at the waist with a full skirt to help cover her expanding stomach. She wore a small pill box hat with a short veil at the front. Jimmy was dressed in a black suit, white shirt and black tie. Alice, who had just turned six, looked so cute in her little white satin dress, a garland of flowers on her head with her blond curls bouncing around her face. She carried a small basket with fresh roses in it as she walked slowly in front of Rose down the aisle.

Jimmy had so many thoughts running through his mind as he watched Rose approach him. It was his first time in a suit and his first time in a church, but he stood tall and wouldn't let on to anyone that he was feeling very, very nervous. Was he doing the right thing? He was only nineteen and hadn't really lived yet but what was the option if he didn't marry Rose?

He would have to leave the area, the shame of getting a girl pregnant and running away would be too much for his family to bear. He did love Rose and he would have to make this work for all their sakes. The ceremony was short and sweet, which Jimmy was grateful for.

Everyone gathered for photographs out on the church steps, afterwards the reception was held in the adjoining hall to the church. It was not a lavish affair and money was tight for this unexpected wedding, the family had all pitched in to help with the decorating and the food. Long tables were laid out and dressed with white linen tablecloths and vases of flowers from Loretta's garden, large pots of bolognaise, pastas, beef stroganoff, bread and steaming vegetables were added to provide the wedding feast. Tubs of ice filled with soft drink, beer and wine, tea urns and hot water for instant coffee were on a long table by the side of the hall. A single layer white wedding cake, made by Rose's mother, was decorated simply with flowers made of icing and an ornamental bride and groom.

Speeches were made, the cake cut and then it was time for their first dance. Jimmy led Rose to the dance floor and took her in his arms holding her close. Rose looked up at Jimmy, her eyes were so full of love and happiness it made him feel like a bum for ever doubting the marriage.

"Are you happy Rose?" he whispered in her ear as they glided around the floor.

"Oh Jimmy, yes this is the best day of my life. It's just perfect. I love you."

"I love you Rose."

Everyone enjoyed the simple celebration, dancing and laughing until it was time for them to leave. Everyone formed a circle to say goodbye at the end of the night wishing them well in their new life together.

Jimmy had a new job at the sawmill in South Kempsey and they had found a little farmhouse at Euroka to rent. Their family and friends had helped them by giving them furniture they no longer needed and luckily most of their wedding gifts were household items, crockery, cutlery, linen and saucepans. They had enough to set up their own little home. Loretta had given Rose the old cot she had used for each of Rose's siblings. Rose had sanded it back and given it a fresh coat of white paint.

There would be no honeymoon, Jimmy had started his new job at the sawmill the week before the wedding and had to be back at work on Monday. Rose had managed to find herself part- time work cleaning. She would work as long as she could before the baby was born. She knew it was going to be tough but she was determined to make it work. She loved Jimmy and she knew it would all come together now they were married and starting their life together as husband and wife. Soon they would have a baby to complete their little family.

KEMPSEY 15th JUNE 1961

Rose lay exhausted in the bed. She had been in labor for ten hours and finally at three forty five pm she had given birth to a healthy baby girl weighing six pounds fourteen ounces. Rose had been two weeks over her due date and started to wonder if this baby would ever be born. Her mother had told her about childbirth but the labor had been more painful and much harder than she had expected it to be, but once the beautiful baby girl was placed in her arms the pain was all but forgotten. Her mother had been by her side the whole time holding her hand and helping her through the labor and birth. Jimmy was still at work but he would be with them soon.

"Well Rose, you're a mother yourself now and I know you will be a great mother, you've had plenty of practice helping me with your brothers and sisters over the years. Loretta looked down at her first grand-child sleeping in her arms. "She is beautiful Rose."

Jimmy came rushing through the door. "Rose are you alright?" He stopped when he saw the baby in Loretta's arms. "Oh my! I'm a father!" Jimmy was all smiles, he was elated.

"Yes Jimmy we have a beautiful, healthy baby girl."

Loretta handed the tiny baby to him. He held her so gently, like a porcelain doll he was afraid of breaking. "She is beautiful, just like her mother." He gazed in wonder at the small, precious child in his arms. "Hello Ruby, welcome to our family." Rose had chosen the name Ruby because it was one of her mother's favourite gems and her favourite colour.

Loretta stood up, "I have to get home to the kids Rose. I'll be back tomorrow with Dad so he can see his granddaughter. Now get some rest" she kissed her daughters forehead. "I'm very proud of you darling. You're a strong girl, always remember that. I'll see you tomorrow."

After Loretta left, Jimmy handed Ruby carefully to Rose. "I'm going too, I'm meeting the boys at the pub to christen the baby's head. I'll come back tomorrow after work. Do you need anything?"

"No, I'm good. Mum bought everything for me when she came in this morning." Rose could not stop staring at this beautiful baby in her arms. She was a mother now. She promised herself she would love and nurture this child just like her mother had done for her. She knew things would be hard, now that she would no longer be working and they only had Jimmy's pay to live on, but she would make do with what they had. She must write a letter to Daniel and let him know that he was a grandfather.

Rose spent her days taking care of her beautiful baby girl, she was mesmerised by her, her cute little nose and tiny fingers, Ruby woke and demanded feeding every four hours, Rose enjoyed this time, sitting in the old arm chair breast feeding, bonding with this tiny life that was dependent on her for everything. Once she had finished and put Ruby down, she sat at the table to write to Daniel.

Dear Daniel

I received your letter and was very pleased to hear from you. It is lovely and sunny here now but it was pouring rain last Friday, it has been cold here too.

Mill work has been slack but is improving now, Jimmy has been working at night as well as during the day. We picked up a Volkswagen car last Monday and I am learning to drive it, and we also have a Morris truck. We went for a drive to Sawtell on Sunday, we were going to call in but I didn't know whether you would be home and it was twelve o'clock when we got there.

We will come up soon to see you. I am looking forward to seeing you again. Ruby is so cute now, she smiles and makes all sorts of noises when you talk to her. She is healthy and growing fast.

I'll have to finish off now as Ruby is crying. Lots of love Rose.

CHAPTER 3

Rose was very proud of herself, all the hard work had paid off and she had passed her driving test last week. Finally she had some independence and didn't need to rely on Jimmy so much. It was another hot day, the temperature gauge read ninety six degrees fahrenheit and there was no breeze anywhere. Ruby was so curious, crawling everywhere now and getting into whatever she could find. Rose was constantly moving things up higher so she could not get them, especially now that she could pull herself up onto her feet every chance she got. Ruby also had two top teeth coming through and had been grisly for the last two days.

Jimmy would be helping his father with some fencing this weekend and they had hoped to go to Sydney one weekend soon and have a few days looking around, maybe even going to the zoo. Last weekend Jimmy had gone out shooting and had hoped to bring home some rabbits but he only came home with a lot of mosquito bites and a bad mood. Rose had decided to change the furniture around in the house and had rearranged the lounge room and their bedroom, it was late when Jimmy came home and not wanting to wake Rose he fumbled in the dark towards the bed, flopping himself down but instead of landing in his comfy bed he landed on the hard wooden floor. There was a loud bang and thud waking Rose with a start.

"What the bloody hell?"

"Jimmy are you alright?" Rose sat up in bed. The room lit up with white light as he flicked the lights on.

"Bloody hell woman, I don't mind if you move the furniture around in the other rooms, but leave my bloody bed in the same place."

That was the one and only time Rose ever changed the furniture around in their bedroom.

EUROKA MAY 1962

Rose stood staring into the boiling copper, she moved the nappies around with a big stick until they were clean and ready to be wound through the wringer, wrung out and hung on the line. The last twelve months had been a real eye opener for her. Luckily she had helped her mother to care for her five younger siblings which had made it a bit easier for her to settle into motherhood. The farmhouse was old and draughty and they had to rely on water from the tank. The water had to be boiled on the wood stove or in the big old copper out the back. There was an old drop toilet outside in the small back yard, twenty yards from the house.

Her parents had moved to Kempsey a few months ago and now lived not far away from them. This was a blessing for Rose as they were close enough that she could walk to her parents' house pushing Ruby in the old cane pram her mother had given her. Jimmy worked six days a week and it was lonely at the farmhouse for Rose even though Ruby kept her busy all day, especially now she was walking and into everything. Jimmy had changed once the baby had been born, he'd become possessive and more and more jealous of the amount of time she spent with the baby. He was also jealous of the time she spent with her family. Rose was seeing a whole other side of her husband and she didn't like it.

Rose was still at her mother's one afternoon when Jimmy arrived home from work. When she walked in the door he glared at her!

"Where the hell have you been? Your place is here, I expect you to be home waiting for me when I get home from work. I'm your priority." He was yelling at her.

Rose burst into tears. "I'm sorry I just went to see my mum. I had to ask her a few questions about Ruby."

"Well just make sure you're home when I get home from work in future. I work hard you know, while you're here at home doing nothing."

From then on she'd keep an eye on the time and make sure she was home before Jimmy. Rose finished hanging the washing out and went inside to check on Ruby. She was still sleeping, it would be time for her to feed soon. She went to the kitchen to get the dinner on, roast chicken and vegetables with gravy. It would be ready when Jimmy walked in the door from work. He didn't like to be kept waiting. She had just finished mashing the potatoes when she heard him pull up outside.

"I've got great news Rose." He bounded in the door excitedly.

She turned from the sink to see him grinning so hard she thought his face would split. He grabbed her around the waist and pulled her close.

"I've got a job on a sheep and wheat station just outside of Spring Ridge, the moneys good and we have somewhere to stay as well. They run fifteen hundred sheep and there's a thousand acres of wheat. The station is eight thousand acres altogether. We will be packing up and leaving in two weeks."

Rose was dumbfounded, move, to a sheep station to god knows where? She was stunned. "But Jimmy

I don't want to leave my family and you haven't even discussed it with me."

He pulled back from her and held her at arm's length, she saw the colour change in his eyes and the vein on his neck start to throb. "I don't need to discuss it with you. I'm the one who goes to work each day to make the money that you spend, so you will go wherever I say we go."

"But what about my mum and dad? How often will I be able to see them if we move?" She felt deflated, she didn't want to move away from her family to some sheep station.

"Probably not often, but I'm your family now and that should be enough for you. I've already taken the job, like I said Rose the pay is good, we have somewhere to stay and it will be an adventure. There is nothing to discuss, we leave in two weeks so you'd better start packing. I'm going to wash, I suppose tea is ready?'

"Yes it will be on the table when you come back." Rose finished dishing out dinner, she was only seventeen with a year old baby and she didn't want to leave her mother, she relied on her help. She felt sick at the thought of leaving her family but she had no other choice, she must do what her husband wanted.

Over the next two weeks she packed up all their worldly goods. The furniture was sent by train, they packed the rest of their belongings into the back of, and on the roof of, their little Volkswagen beetle car. A small area behind the backseat was made into a bed for Ruby. It was a two hundred and forty mile drive from Kempsey to Spring Ridge so they were leaving early in the morning, around sunrise to get a good start on the day. Rose was filled with dread and nervous about moving away and worse still, she felt helpless. She had no choice but to do what her husband asked.

CHAPTER 4

The morning was crisp and there was still a frost on the grass as they bundled sleeping Ruby into the makeshift bed in the back of their old car. The sun was just starting to rise and the sky was turning blue, scattered with yellow and pink clouds as they drove out onto the road heading for their new home at Spring Ridge.

Rose could not help but feel trepidation at leaving the security of her family and home behind to go to a new life two hundred and forty miles away. It would take over twelve hours to get there along the winding roads over Walcha mountain on the Great Dividing Range with its steep cliffs, gorges and rivers that had fresh, sweet water flowing down from the mountains to the salty sea. As she looked out the car window watching the green fields and farms go past, she also felt a little excitement about her new adventure and new life out in the farmlands of Spring Ridge. As they started the drive up the mountain with its windy road and steep drops, Jimmy told her about the area they were moving to trying to get her mind off the car sickness she was feeling.

After World War II a lot of returned soldiers had moved to Spring Ridge to take up Soldier Settlement blocks being given away by the government. It was mostly farming and grazing land with rich agricultural soil. They grew crops of wheat and there were many sheep and cattle stations. Jimmy was going to work at one of the sheep stations as a general farm hand. Rose would be at home caring for Ruby, Jimmy and the house.

The road had become steep and as they went around corner after corner, climbing their way higher up the mountain Rose could feel the bile forming in her throat, her stomach was queasy and she knew she was going to be sick.

"Jimmy, I need you to pull over. I'm going to be sick."

"No you're not, it's all in your mind. Just look ahead at the road, you'll be fine."

"No Jimmy I'm going to vomit please pull over now."

Jimmy found the nearest small pullover area and brought the car to a stop. Rose jumped from the car and bent over as her breakfast came up and out onto the roadside.

"Okay we'll stop for a few minutes while your stomach settles. Here have some water." He passed her the bottle and she took long gulps to take the taste of vomit from her mouth.

"We don't have too much further to go on these winding bends then we will have fairly straight roads the rest of the way." He gave her a cuddle and stroked her hair. Thankfully Ruby was still fast asleep in her little makeshift bed in the back of the car.

They pulled into Walcha and Jimmy filled up the car with petrol while Rose went to the little cafe to get them a coffee and something to eat. They sat in the park and rested for a while so Rose could feed and change Ruby before heading off on the last leg of the journey. They drove through the country towns of Tamworth and Werris Creek finally arriving at Spring Ridge mid afternoon. They would stay here for the night at the Royal Hotel on Darby street, an old two storey brick building with an iron roof and a shaded apron at the front with a view across the plains. It was a typical country town with a sprawl of mostly timber and iron roofed houses with big wide verandahs.

There was a well kept church, a bank and a post office, a haberdashery store that stocked school uniforms, mosquito netting, fabric, ribbons and wool. The back of the butcher shop wall was lined in black and white tiles and a large poster of a massive bull dissected into cuts of meat, in the front display on crushed ice were trays of fresh meat. They sat in the little cafe and enjoyed cold milkshakes in metal cups and a homemade slice before making their way to the hotel to freshen up after their long journey. Their furniture was arriving on the train tomorrow.

It was early winter and the mornings were cold as they started to collect their furniture off the train carriage, Rose could see her breath creating little white clouds as she exhaled. The railway station consisted of a waiting room, parcel office, station masters office and a staff room. The railway transported goods and commodities produced on the land and the only train came in once a week. Jimmy's boss had arrived with the cattle truck to pick up their few possessions and they followed him out to the station which would now be their home, for how long, Rose didn't know.

The farm was a hive of activity, they had just started planting the wheat crop. The land was deep, heavy clay soil with a high natural fertility derived from basalt plains, the vertisols had long been treeless. There were denser forests of cypress pine and scattered eucalypts in the sandier soils on the ridges and slopes rising up from the plains. The plains natural vegetation was ideal for sheep grazing.

As they drove towards the main house Rose could finally see her new home, it was an old wooden cottage with an iron roof and a small yard with a fence made of three strand wire. How was she going to keep the inquisitive thirteen month old Ruby inside the yard and under control.

Dear Mum,

Just a few lines to let you know we arrived safely. The property here at Spring Ridge is a sheep and wheat station. There are fifteen hundred head of sheep and one thousand acres of wheat. There are eight thousand acres altogether. We are eleven miles from Gulgong and twenty eight miles from Mudgee.

If at any time you can come out for a visit I would love for you to stay with me as we can put two up. Three if you all would like to sleep in a double bed. It's a big house with three bedrooms. We had a small frost here this morning, it's no colder here than down there at home. We arrived last Saturday and the trip took us twelve and a half hours.

Everyone is busy at the moment planting the wheat crop. We are all well, Ruby is a handful now that she is walking and the fence around the yard is just wire so she keeps crawling under it, I have to watch her all the time she's always wanting to go outside and play in the water trough. I miss you and Dad very much and I hope you will be able to come for a visit. I hope you are well give my love to Dad and everyone.

Love from Rose.

SPRINGRIDGE

Every day was the same for Rose. Each day just like the one before. Routine. Jimmy would leave early each morning to mend fences, bring in the sheep for drenching or shearing and help around the farm doing whatever he was required to do. Rose would stay at the cottage trying to keep Ruby amused which was getting harder now. At fourteen months old she was always wanting to explore outside. Constantly heading out to the paddock next door where the large round water trough was, and trying to climb in to play in the water even though it was winter and the water was cold. Some days there was frost and ice on the ground until ten or eleven in the morning.

As she was serving dinner to Jimmy one evening she asked, "Jimmy what can I do about Ruby, I have to watch her every second, she keeps going over to the water trough, the water is deep for a little girl. The fence won't keep her in and she climbs under the wire."

"Just tie her up." He said between mouthfuls.

"She's not a dog Jimmy! I can't tie her up."

"No, I meant how about we get some rope, just long enough for her to play outside but not long enough that she can reach the water trough. We could tie it to the big old tree out the back and around her waist. At least then you could do other things without worrying about her."

Rose thought about this for a moment, she felt bad at the thought of tying her daughter up but at least that way she could get things done without watching Ruby all the time. "Okay I guess it can't hurt to give it a try. God knows what the boss will think if he sees our daughter tied up outside."

There were a few tantrums and tears on Ruby's part when she realised she couldn't get to the water but after a while she settled down and was quite happy to play in the yard tied up to the old tree by a long piece of rope.

Rose was bored sitting around the old house every day and Jimmy finally relented and took her and Ruby with him in the old ute out to the paddocks to feed the sheep. Ruby loved the animals on the farm and giggled every time the sheep would come up and nuzzle her hand for food. The boss's dog Snowy had given birth to five puppies a few weeks ago and they were going to take a look at them this afternoon after they had finished with the sheep.

Rose looked at the excited Ruby. "Do you want to see the puppies?"

Ruby's smile grew even bigger and she nodded and clapped her little hands and squealed "Puppies." They followed Jimmy up to the main house.

"Hi Jack, we've come to play with the pups if that's okay?"

"Hello Rose, they are over here. Look at that sweet little girl of yours." Jack picked Ruby up and tickled her under the chin. "Want to play with the puppies?"

This rugged old station owner melted every time he was around Ruby. He had five sons and no daughters, so he spoiled her whenever he saw her. Ruby sat and played with the border collie pups while they had a late afternoon tea with the boss and his wife Lynette. When it was time to leave Ruby cried every time they tried to take the pups away from her, she had taken a fancy to one pup in particular. He was a small ball of black and white fluff.

Jack smiled. "Oh let her keep it, she will have something to occupy her time and someone to play with."

"Are you sure Jack? Can we Jimmy? I'd love a pup." Rose was so excited she missed her dogs back at home.

"I suppose we could take him. Let's call him Spotty."

After another month Jimmy decided he wanted to move again a further three hundred miles west to a sheep and cattle station out past Brewarrina. So once again they packed up their belongings putting as much as they could in their old car and tied as much as they could to the roof. The bigger furniture was loaded on the train and would arrive in a few days. Rose did not want to move again and this move would take her further away from her family, but what could she do? She was already so far from home. She had made a vow to love and honour and obey her husband

and that meant following him to wherever he wanted to go, whether she liked it or not.

CHAPTER 5

BEEMERY STATION
SEPTEMBER 1962

Beemery Station was located halfway between Brewarrina and Bourke just off the Kamilaroi highway. Not far from the Barwon River with its coffee coloured water. The Barwon, Bogan and Culgoa
Rivers all combined near here to form the Darling
River. The station had cattle and sheep, lush green
pastures, a large homestead, staff quarters, cattle yards
and a shearing shed. Their house had a latticed verandah along the front and part of the sides. The lattice
and front verandah were in poor condition. There

were two rooms to each side of the corridor leading to the back of the house and the kitchen. One kitchen wall, the stove and chimney were made of the local brick baked at the Brick Kilns at Red Hill near Brewarrina. The bathroom and laundry joined onto the former back verandah.

Rose set about cleaning their new little home while Ruby played outside with Spotty in the fenced yard. They would be here for at least five months. Rose realised that Jimmy didn't like to settle in one place for too long and resigned herself to the fact that she better get used to a nomad life. It was okay for now but when Ruby was getting to school age she wanted her to have a settled life not this life of constant moving.

Dear Daniel,

I received your letter Tuesday and was pleased to hear from you. I'm sorry I didn't answer your last letter but the day after I received it I wrote several letters and posted them. I couldn't remember if I had answered yours or not.

We are all well, but nearly cooked. It was ninety four degrees fahrenheit here yesterday and it is ninety eight today. The photos you sent are very nice, I have them in getting printed. We hope to get down to Telegraph Point at Christmas but don't know whether we will get up your way to see you.

Jimmy shot a rabbit yesterday we just had it for lunch. It was lovely. There are a lot of wild pigs around and Jimmy has shot fifty seven. I have a blue bonnet parrot and a quarrien parrot as pets. We've caught only one fish since we came out here, a river Murray cod. That's all for now.

Love Rose

"Come on Ruby, let's go for a walk to the corn paddock and get some fresh mutti for dinner."

"What's mutti Mum?"

"It's what they call the young corn honey, come on let's go."

Rose took Ruby's hand and they headed out to the corn paddock. A flock of pink galahs were flying around overhead and landing in the nearby trees, squawking at each other in their loud screeching voices. They climbed through the fence and walked between the rows of corn. Rose picked six corn cobs and put them in the bag she was carrying with her. Rose loved the taste of fresh, young corn on the cob, hot off the stove and smothered in butter and salt. Ruby was bending down looking at the ants following each other in single file along the ground carrying seeds and food back to their nest.

Suddenly there was a loud crash and rustling behind them. Rose stopped still and listened, there it was again. She could hear something crashing through the corn coming towards them. She dropped the bag and picked up Ruby. The noise stopped, she stood still waiting. There it was again and it was getting closer. Rose started running back towards the house. Oh God she thought, there were wild pigs out here and the boars were huge with big sharp dirty tusks that could rip through a dog in one wild slash of its head.

She had to run faster, the breath was tearing in her throat and she was almost out of breath. It was no good screaming for help, all the men were too far away out in the paddocks with the sheep. The crashing noise was almost on her; she could hear it right behind her. The sound of the corn stalks being knocked down and trampled underneath was getting closer, she had to outrun it and get back through the fence to safety. Ruby was crying and screaming, her little arms wrapped around Rose's neck, clinging on to her tightly. Rose clambered through the fence and headed for the house. Once they were inside the safety of the fence she turned back to see Spotty jump through the fence behind them.

Rose collapsed on the ground laughing and crying with relief while Spotty licked her arm and jumped all around them. This was no wild pig chasing them, it was their excited dog, Spotty. Either way she would make sure she did not go out into the paddocks alone again.

"I'm going into town today to get the groceries. Do you need anything?" Rose asked.

Jimmy looked up from his breakfast. "No, and don't spend all day in there either."

"I won't, I'll do the shopping and take Ruby for a swim down at the river before we come back."

It took almost an hour to get into town. After she had finished her grocery shopping and packed the cold food into the cooler in the car she drove down to the Barwon river. The main aboriginal tribe here were the Burrabinja people, they used to camp on the river-bank. They had created fisheries which were a meeting place for several tribes in the area who camped where there was an abundance of water and plenty of fresh fish. The stone walls constructed in the river were built to trap the fish which made them easier to catch. Most of the stones had gone, either removed manually, or washed downstream in the floods. There was a small spot near the edge where the water was only about a foot deep, they splashed in the water for a little while to cool off. Rose felt very lonely, the only other woman on the station was the boss's wife who she didn't see very often.

"We'd best be getting home now. We don't want Daddy to get angry with us for being away too long, come on." She lifted Ruby up and dried her off. Placing her in the car and headed back to the station.

Even though it was lonely at the station, the days passed quickly. Jimmy started work at four am each morning so he could finish earlier and would not be working in the heat of the day. He was busy with the sheep, ear marking with the stations tag for identification and cutting tails off the lambs. Rose thought it cruel to cut off their tails but Jimmy explained that the wool tended to collect foreign matter rather easily, and the tail is particularly notorious. Not only is this unpleasant for all concerned, but a dirty tail attracts wool maggots and poses a serious risk of infection to the lamb. There had been a few major dust storms in the last few days and Rose was constantly sweeping and dusting to keep the house clean. Ruby was talking more each day and loved going with Jimmy in the old Land Rover.

Rose baked bread every second day and today was not a good day, everything seemed to be going wrong. No matter what she did she could not get the dough to rise. She didn't want Jimmy to know that she had failed so she took the uncooperative dough outside and buried it in the dirt in the backyard. The wood stove had now gone out and she could not get it to catch fire again, no matter what she did. Rose remembered she'd seen her father throw fuel on wood to get it going when the fire would not ignite. There was a small bottle of fuel out in the shed, she'd seen it there when she had put the ute away. Rose poured some fuel all over the wood in the stove, then threw in a lighted match. There was a loud bang and all the lids blew off the stove, up into the air landing on the kitchen floor with a bang, the force was enough to knock her to the ground. Jimmy was just coming through the back door.

"What the bloody hell?" he shouted at her. "What are you trying to do, blow us all up?"

"The fire would not catch so I put some fuel on it." Rose looked up at him. She had black soot all over her from the stove.

Jimmy picked up the bottle and started to laugh. "For god sake woman, this is aviation fuel, you're lucky you didn't blow the stove into orbit, and what's that big white mushroom thing in the backyard?"

"What mushroom? I didn't see a mushroom out there."

"Come out and I'll show you." He helped her up from the floor.

They went outside, in the spot she had buried the bread dough there was now a strange, large white mushroom. The sun and forty degree heat outside, along with the heat of the earth had acted like an oven, the dough Rose had buried had risen to form what looked like a dirty, white, bulging mushroom.

"Oh my, well that was meant to be today's bread." She could feel herself turning red. They looked at each other and broke into fits of laughter.

29th November 1962

Dear Mum

Just a few lines to let you know the news. We are all well and I hope you are the same. It is very hot here today. We had a big dust storm here yesterday. You couldn't see a thing and it has covered everything inside the house so I have spent ages trying to clean up. I have taken some photos and will show you at Christmas time when we come home.

Jimmy has been starting work at four am so he won't have to work in the heat of the day. He doesn't drive the tractor now he's working with the sheep. They are ear marking and cutting the tails off the lambs at present. There are a few black lambs and a couple of brown ones and one black and white one.

Well here it is, Sunday the second of December already and I still haven't finished this letter. I missed yesterday's mail so I'll have it ready for Tuesday. The mosquitoes are getting really bad here now. Ruby says more words each day and she likes going with Jimmy in the Land Rover. Her pup Spotty is starting to work and has grown a lot. Jimmy has shot about seventy wild pigs since we have been here and it's fairly hot again today but there is a breeze that blows now and then to make it a little better. We caught two perch out of the traps last week but they were full of bones and too small to eat so we threw them back in.

Well bye for now, I miss you all so much, give my love to everyone.

Love Rose.

BEEMERY STATION
January 1963

Jimmy had wanted to buy a new car so they had stopped at Gunnedah on their way back from visiting the family at Christmas, he had set his heart on buying a Holden and none of the car yards had anything suitable, or that he liked so they still had the little old Volkswagen. Rose had enjoyed her time at home at Christmas with the family, she was sad to leave them and return back to the station. It had rained lightly for a week since their return and the air was sticky, two of the trucks had gotten bogged in the wet ground driving across the paddocks and it had taken them most of the day to get them out of the mud. Then the wind started blowing strongly and things dried out quickly.

The fields greened up and the grass was lush and thick. It amazed her how things could change so quickly from being dry and brown to lush green in a couple of weeks after a little rain. It was always hot here with only an occasional slight breeze to help cool her down. Rose was finding it hard to sleep at night, the heat was suffocating. The mosquitos and sandflies appeared in what seemed to be thousands. Poor Ruby was being eaten alive, she had bites all over her, it was hard to stop her from scratching all the time even with calamine lotion dotted all over her skin. They had mosquito nets over their beds to try and stop them from biting in the night but one always seemed to find its way through the tiny holes of the netting. The constant, annoying sound of their drone as they flew around you, made it impossible to sleep. Rose was missing her family terribly, she felt so alone and isolated out here.

Jimmy had been suffering a sore chest for a week now, he'd had an X-ray last Monday in town and the doctor had told him it was just a pulled muscle, it had improved over the last week and he was ok again now. Jimmy started work early every morning mustering sheep, he was working a lot and always grumpy and tired when he came home late in the afternoon. He would complain about everything, the heat, the flies, the equipment, even the boss. He would tell her that the boss didn't know what he was doing and he could do a better job running the station. Rose knew it wouldn't be long and they would be on the move again. Jimmy had put a tender in to get the milk run at Telegraph Point and if they didn't get that, he had talked about renting a farm around there somewhere, or even going to South Australia to shoot rabbits, leaving in March. Rose hoped they would go back to the coast closer to her family, she missed being able to talk to her mother every day.

For the last two weeks Rose had been feeling ill in the mornings, she had gone to the doctor who had confirmed she was pregnant with her second child and due in early June. She had written and told her mother about her pregnancy and now more than ever she prayed that they would move back closer to her family, not go to South Australia, especially now, she wanted to be back near her mother when this child was born. Daniel was arriving soon for a visit. She must write and tell him the news.

Dear Daniel,

I received your letter last night, I am pleased you are coming out to visit. How are you travelling here and what time will you arrive? If you phone the main house and let me know I can come and pick you up. We are all well here at present and the last two days have been very very hot but it's a lot cooler today. You are going to be a Grandfather again, I am pregnant and due in June.Jimmy has been busy shearing now as well as mustering and drafting. He has another dog, a red kelpie called Red. Yes, not very original I know. We had a lot of storms and rain the other week and there's a lot of water around. Everywhere is green here just now. Jimmy has decided he has had enough so we will be on the move again next month, not sure yet if we will be back over there to live or going to South Australia for a while to shoot rabbits. I look forward to seeing you soon. That's all for now.

Love Rose

CHAPTER 6

HAWKER GATE – SOUTH AUSTRALIA
FEBRUARY 1963

Rose woke just as the car rumbled into Broken Hill. Yes, once again they were moving. Jimmy had decided he wanted to go rabbit shooting in South Australia. They had spent the last week taking most of their furniture and belongings from Beemery Station back to Wilson River to store at Jimmy's parents' house before making the nine hundred mile journey to Broken Hill. Rose was now five and a half months pregnant with their second child and she was feeling very uncomfortable squashed into the front seat of their old Holden ute with Ruby seated between them.

They were heading to Hawker Gate in South Australia. The rabbit plague was bad out there and Jimmy reckoned he could make good money shooting rabbits. There was a demand for their meat as well as the felt from their hides which were turned into hats and other things. They stopped at Broken Hill and stocked up on food and necessities before making the one hundred and eighty mile trip up into the deserts of South Australia. They drove through Silverton, then up to Wilangee, McDougall's Well and Border Downs. The dirt road became sandy and rough as they drove closer to Hawker Gate and the heat was becoming unbearable. The Hawker Gate Road was so named as it was the early route taken by miners and cameleers as they crossed the desert from South Australia to the goldfields.

They arrived at the dog fence and the gate on the New South Wales and South Australian border at Hawker Gate. The fence was six feet high wire netting topped with barbed wire; it had been built during the 1880's to keep dingos out of the relatively fertile southeast part of the continent and protect the sheep flocks of southern Queensland. The fence stretches nearly three thousand five hundred miles from Jimbour on the Darling Downs near Dalby in Queensland through thousands of miles of arid land, ending west of the Eyre Peninsula on the cliffs of The Nullarbor Plains above the great Australian Bight near Nundroo in South Australia. They crossed the New South Wales border into South Australia making sure the gate was closed behind them, and headed to Callabonna, the old farmhouse ruins in the middle of the sand hills where they would camp.

As Rose stared out of the window she was shocked, this was not what she had expected. They were in the Strzelecki desert now with its massive sand dunes and dry salt lakes glittering white with little to no vegetation. They crossed gravelled creeks draining from hills and lined with fat bellied river gums. Jimmy pulled the ute up beside the old farmhouse ruins situated on Callabonna Creek which runs into Lake Callabonna. They were seventy five miles south west of Camerons Corner, where the junction of South Australia, Queensland and New South Wales border met. You could be in the three states all at the same time.

"Oh Jimmy! How am I supposed to live here, it's so far from everything?" Rose was feeling anxious, this was not what she expected. It was a crumbling down old farmhouse that had been deserted since the late 1800's when the Ragless brothers gave up on their dream of having a sheep station out here in the sea of barren and desolate sand hills. It was nothing like Jimmy had described to her.

"It will be fine Rose. Don't worry we have plenty of food and there's a bore for water." Jimmy tried to reassure her.

"But Jimmy, I'm six months pregnant, what if something happens and I need to go to the hospital? It will take so long to get anywhere." Rose was becoming distraught now.

"Look if anything happens we just go to Tilcha Station, it's not far from here, they will radio for the Flying Doctors to come in. Stop complaining, it will be fine. Just give it a few days. We've only just arrived."

Rose knew it was no good arguing with him. She would try to make the best of the situation. She looked at Ruby who was sitting on her lap. How was she going to cope out here in the middle of nowhere with a twenty month old toddler?

Rose stood at the front of the farmhouse with Ruby on her hip, she could imagine it must have been a very grand home in its day with its walls made from the limestone carved out of the nearby outcrop, wide verandahs and large rooms, but now it was a very sad affair. They wandered through the house checking the rooms and deciding which ones they would use before carrying their belongings inside. They did not have a lot with them, only what they could fit into the back of the ute, the bare essentials. Rose would just have to try to make it as comfortable and homely as she could. There were no ceilings and the roof was missing in places. Some of the beams and roofing iron had fallen down inside, there were twigs and rocks on the floor and a couple of the sandstone walls were crumbling around them. Rose checked each room until she found one that seemed to be in the best condition and looked safe enough to live in, she swept and removed the debris from the room before making beds up on the floor using old hessian potato bags and blankets as their base. Jimmy cleaned out the fireplace and got some wood ready for a fire that night. They would be joined by another couple tomorrow and two brothers. At least she would not be alone out here.

Arthur and Carol arrived mid morning the next day in a white Ford ute with the back filled with their belongings and a large tarp holding it all in. Stan and Gilbert pulled up an hour later in an old beat up truck with a refrigerated back so they could keep the rabbit carcasses cold and fresh for market. The men spent the rest of the day collecting firewood and fixing up the farmhouse and camp area to make it as liveable as possible. The men would be going out at night rabbit shooting, leaving Rose, Carol and Ruby at the camp. Carol had a little dachshund dog called Poppy and Ruby loved playing with her, cuddling her and it followed her around wherever she went.

The men had just left for the evening, rabbit hunting and Carol boiled the billy for a cup of tea while Rose put Ruby down to sleep. They sat outside on fold up chairs watching the amazing burnt orange, deep yellow and vivid pink sunset. With no other lights around, the stars were incredibly bright, there seemed to be a million stars in the night sky and the pale, white glow of the milky way stretched across the horizon. The moon was a slim crescent in the night sky and the only noise came from the twigs, crackling and popping in the fire they had made outside to keep themselves warm during the cold nights. At least at night the onslaught of annoying flies eased off.

"I wish I could get Ruby to give up her dummy. She has a tantrum every time I try, and I end up giving in and giving it back to her." Rose sighed.

Carol laughed. "I have an idea, let's tell her that Poppy ate it and you won't have to worry anymore." Rose thought for a moment. "That could work and we can't just pop to the shop to get another one. I'll try that tomorrow."

They chatted a little longer before heading off to bed. The men would be out all night returning in the early hours of the morning with their catch. They would sleep for a while before gutting and cleaning the rabbits ready to be sent off and sold. They stored the rabbits in the old refrigerated truck that Stan and Gilbert had driven out to the property in.

Rose woke to Ruby shaking her awake crying "Mummy, Mummy where's my dummy?"

"Oh darling I'm sorry, but Poppy ate it last night. It's gone."

Ruby screamed "No, Mummy I want my dummy."

"I'm sorry Ruby but it's gone. Poppy ate it."

"No!" Ruby jumped up and ran to where Poppy was sitting outside. "Bad dog Poppy." She grabbed her ears and pulled them and started pounding her with her little fists. "Bad doggy, I want my dummy back." Ruby cried and sat beside Poppy, the little dog put its head in her lap and licked Ruby's legs. Ruby stopped crying and patted the dog wrapping her arms around its neck and squeezing, she stood up and dragged Poppy along with her. "Mummy, I'm hungry. But don't give Poppy any food, she ate my dummy."

Rose and Carol looked at each other and laughed.

"Ok, let's have some breakfast and then we will go for a walk. Let's see if we can find any fossils, I hear there are lots of dinosaur fossils out here." Rose looked at Ruby smiling hoping to take her mind off the missing dummy.

After cleaning up they walked along the stoney creek which drained into Lake Callabonna. Beautiful, gnarled, creamy gum trees threw patches of shade over the rocks. The red sand hills in the distance looked like red velvet and appeared comforting, conjuring images of lush vegetation and running streams, but up close they reared up with a raw strength that looked ancient and as eerie as old bones. The red dunes of siliceous sands, deep with semi-mobile crests and relatively stable slopes made way in some places for the dome shaped shrubs, sandhill wattle with its pretty yellow, orange flowers and needle bush tall shrubs. Across the plains of red earth, sparse shrub cover of bluebush and the thorny grey, rounded saltbush with its thick, soft, tooth edged leaves which almost appeared to be plastic grew as far as the eye could see. The spinifex grew in soft grey-green and yellow-grey clumps dotted on the sand. There was a small amount of water in the lake with low islands here and there.

A black swan glided gracefully on the lake and a wedge tailed eagle flew overhead. They had seen a few different birds as they walked, a black falcon and little quails with white bellies running through the grassy sand hills. A pair of black kites nested on two eggs near the ruins and wood swallows clustered on a branch and grass wren in the cane grass and blue bush.

Rose stood looking out across the vast expanse of the salt lake shimmering white in the sun. How the hell could she stay out here so far away from everything and everyone. She had been here for three weeks now and the days dragged on, she felt more and more uncomfortable every day with her expanding belly. The day was hot and still and the heat was unbearable. She had tolerated it so far but washing herself and Ruby in a bucket and walking out in the sand hills to use the toilet was just becoming too much, last night she had sat on the back step and cried. Enough was enough, she was nearly seven months pregnant. Jimmy would have to take her home, she could not stay out here in this desert a moment longer.

As they made their way back to camp out of nowhere came a "willy willy." The wind whipped up and the tall spiralling columns of air whirled just to the side of them kicking up sand, gathering the buck-brush, lifting it all up into the sky, the sand and debris becoming a cloud moving swiftly south east. Ruby was clinging to her mother's legs whimpering.

"That was close." Rose, was really hot and flustered now.

"Yes, let's hurry back before another one whips up." Carol picked up Ruby and they hurried back to camp. The men had risen and were cooking on the fire outside.

"Coffee is hot girls if you want some." Arthur had just poured himself a cup. He pointed in the direction they had just come from. "There's not much out there."

Rose took the steaming cup of hot coffee he offered her. "No, but it is very beautiful in its own way." She turned to Jimmy. "Jimmy, I want you to take me home. I can't stay here any longer." Her voice was shaking as she asked she thought he would refuse her.

"Okay, I'll take you back the day after tomorrow. You can stay with my parents while I come back here for another month or so."

"Thank you." Rose hugged him relieved. She had expected him to refuse to take her home.

They set out early heading for Milperinka. The sand in places was very soft and they got the car bogged several times. The only thing they had to dig themselves out with were the saucepans, it took ages each time to free the tyres. Finally they came up over a rise and in front of them was a shimmering lake and it appeared, no way around it.

"How are we supposed to get across all that water Jimmy? We will never make it and there doesn't seem to be any way around it."

Jimmy was stumped; he hadn't expected water here, strange he thought. There had been no rain recently and this was supposed to be a dry area. He squinted his eyes and looked further towards the horizon to the east.

"Hang on, that's a car coming across there and it looks like it's got dust behind it."

They waited and watched as the car got closer and seemed to be driving through the water. It was a dry salt pan, with the sun glaring down on the sand, it gave the illusion of water, it looked so real, but it was a mirage. They continued on to Milperinka then Wanaaring, camping on the side of the road under the stars. They started out early the next morning as the sun was rising. There were hundreds of kangaroos in front of them, they were everywhere, jumping across the road and feeding on the fresh green grass shoots by the side of the road. The Roos would not move as the car approached even when Jimmy beeped the horn, they simply looked up then went back to munching on the grass.

Jimmy pulled the car up. "You're gonna have to drive. I'll hang out the window and shoot them."

"What?" Rose looked at him startled.

"Come on, get in the driver's seat. They aren't gonna budge and we need to keep moving. They are starving, this is the only place there is green grass for them and they are bloody pests. They destroy the food for the cattle and sheep."

Rose drove towards the mass of roos, Jimmy leaned out of the car window and let off a few rounds hitting and killing roos with each shot, Jimmy was a good shot. The rest of them scattered as they drove through. Finally they reached Bourke that afternoon. Just two more days driving and she would be back in a proper house and a comfortable bed, Rose couldn't wait. All she could think of was having a nice long soak in the bathtub to wash off all the sand and red dirt that seemed to be ingrained in her skin and in her clothes.

CHAPTER 7

WILSON RIVER

APRIL 1963

Jimmy was still over in South Australia rabbit shooting, but he had promised Rose that he would be back before the baby was due in June. He'd been away now for twenty seven days. Low, dark, ominous black clouds had rolled in from the northeast, the sky became heavy and the wind picked up, howling through the trees. The first crack of lightning lit up the sky and within seconds the rolling boom of thunder reverberated overhead. The old red dog cowered under the seat on the verandah. The rain fell slowly at first then heavy and hard as if poured from buckets, cascading steadily like a waterfall, falling so thick and fast that you could not see even a few yards outside of the house. Inside the house the howl of the wind and beating of the rain was louder than the conversation, Jimmy's parents and Rose had to shout to hear each other above the rain crashing on the tin roof. It was as if someone was on the roof beating it with a sledgehammer.

The lightning forked its way to the ground, unveiling a brilliant shock of white against the dark sky. The rain fell for days, the river had been rising steadily, turning it into a swollen torrent, the turbulent brown flow eddied its way downstream bringing sticks and other vegetation, it was so thick, it was like gravy. The angry water tugged at the river banks eroding the soft mud, finally bursting its banks. The water flowed swiftly and strongly over the road, the paddock in front of the house was now completely under water. They had woken to water seeping into the house even though it was built up on the higher part of the paddock and had been built a foot higher than the 1949 flood, this flood was looking even worse. Rose was scared but got busy doing her part.

While they waited for the milk boat to come and evacuate them to higher ground, everyone pitched in to put the furniture and belongings up on the tables and benches, trying to save as much as they could from the rising water. Jimmy's parents Betty and William had taken great care of Rose and Ruby while Jimmy was away but they were worried about the rising water and with Rose only a month away from giving birth, they knew they had to evacuate and get her and Ruby to safer ground. The milk boat would soon be here to collect them. The small wooden row boat that was normally kept moored down at the milk wharf on the river, was now tied up to the fence outside the house and was floating level with the front door. Rose was helped into the little boat first then Ruby was passed into her. William rowed them across the paddocks to the cattle yards which were still above the water, then across to the wharf were the milk boat was waiting to take them across the swollen river to the butter factory's wharf where the truck would be able to access them and take them to safety out of the fast flowing water filled with debris.

They waited here while William went back for Betty and their bags.

The truck came slowly around the corner towing a flatbed trailer with families from further down the river already on the back, huddling under tarps trying to keep warm. Heavily pregnant Rose was helped into the front seat with Ruby to make the two mile trip to the Telegraph Point primary school where everyone would bunk in together until the flood waters receded and they could return home.

They spent the next few days at the school with other families contemplating what might be left at their homes and farms after the flood waters receded. As quickly as it had begun, it ended. The sky was clearing and although the rains had stopped the air still felt damp and heavy. A lot of debris had washed down from further upstream, the river had become a swollen, dirty mass pushing branches, trees, dead animals and all kinds of debris and rubbish downstream as it surged towards the ocean. They hoped that there would not be too much damage when they could finally go home but they knew there would be a lot to clean up, regardless.

On returning to the farm a week later they found the water had subsided leaving a watermark just over two feet high up the walls and the floors of the house were covered with two inches of thick smelly mud. They set about the task of washing and sweeping the mud from the house. The damp smell and pungent odour from the mud made Rose feel sick. Luckily the water had not risen any higher and the belongings they had placed up onto tables and cupboards were still dry. Rose moved a box that was sitting on the sink and curled up in the sink was a black snake, she screamed and the snake slithered out down the cupboard and out the back door. She had lost all the photos from her trip out to South Australia with Jimmy, the camera had been in the glove box of the car which was submerged in the water.

Over the next week they did a lot of clearing around the farm, removing the logs and the trees that had been washed up by the floods. They dragged all the wood into a pile in the middle of the paddock. Giving it time to dry out they would then have a big bonfire. Luckily the dairy was on higher ground and had only just escaped the flood waters. It was now hot and sunny and the heat from the sun and the wind had dried the mud, and grass shoots started to break through, turning the paddocks into lush green pastures once again. The soil was rich and fertile which made it ideal for farming. The cows were now able to be brought down from higher paddocks at the back of the farm.

14th May 1963

Dear Daniel,

I'm sorry I haven't written before but with all the floods and then the clean up, I just haven't gotten around to it. We have had two floods and the first one was really big, it came thirteen inches deep inside Jimmy's dad's house, water has never been inside before in the thirty six years they have lived there. He lost eight head of cattle. We were flooded out for a week and between shifting things up high and cleaning up when the water went down it's been very busy, the second flood only just covered the bottom step.

I'm staying with Jimmy's mother and father again now but I've been in Kempsey for the last week because of the floods. Jimmy is over in South Australia shooting rabbits, he has a caravan over there to live in. I hope you are much better now. Ruby and I are well and Ruby is getting fat. That's all for now love from Rose.

Jimmy was due back in the next two weeks and Rose couldn't wait to see him. She hoped that she wouldn't go into labor before he arrived home. She wanted him there with her. Hopefully he would want to stay home now and settle down. Rose didn't like moving all the time, she wanted to settle and be close to her family.

Fred was born on the 17th of June 1963, two weeks over her due date, he was a big baby with a strong set of lungs. Jimmy had only been home a few days before she went into labor.

26th June 1963
Dear Daniel,
Just a short note to let you know the news. I had a baby boy on the 17th June. We called him Fred. He was a big

baby, seven pounds eight ounces. We are well and I hope you are the same.

It's cold here and we had a big frost yesterday. We have the phone on now, the number is Telegraph Point, thirty four. Jimmy's mother and father are on holidays and they will be back any day now. Jimmy is going to Sydney on Monday, he applied for the Commonwealth Police Force, he received a letter from them, they want to interview him. Betty is going to help me with the children and the milking while he is away. I'll have to go now it's milking time.

Love from Rose

They stayed with Jimmy's parents only another month after Fred's birth before moving to a house beside the mill in Telegraph Point. Jimmy now had a job in the mill so he could stay closer to the family. Rose stayed home caring for two year old Ruby and one month old baby Fred. The house was right beside the mill, with the highway on the other side and the railway line out the back of the house making it very noisy and almost impossible sometimes to get the children to sleep with the constant train whistles and clatter on the tracks. At least Jimmy was happy for the moment and hopefully they would stay here for awhile.

It had been cold at night lately but the days were lovely and sunny, with a few days of bad wind and big frosts in the morning. Jimmy was working, splitting posts out in the forestry for a bloke in Port Macquarie. They had been to see about a share farm at Glenrock the other night and hoped they would get it, Glenrock was halfway between Kempsey and Fredrickton.

Fred was doing really well and Ruby thought her little brother was just great, she wanted to nurse and hug him all the time. Ruby was growing up so fast and talking all the time, they had all been sick with a cold the last week. Rose felt miserable today, her nose was running, it felt like she had a frog in her throat and she could hardly talk. Last week she had been to visit Daniel in Bellingen and had come back on the train. She had managed okay on the train by herself with the two small children, one of the railway men put the suitcases on the carriage and the conductor took them off for her.

It seemed like the foxes had been having Christmas, in the last month they had come in through the night and taken the Sussex rooster and a pullet out of the chicken coup and then a week later one had dug into the back pen and taken two bantams, three chickens and a hen. The foxes had taken them out under the mulberry tree and eaten them, leaving feathers and bones strewn across the ground.

Jimmy didn't pass the spelling test for the Police Force and they had told him to come back in six months time, he had been in a bad mood ever since receiving the letter and then his tonsils flared up and he went to the doctor who gave him a needle which helped, he was feeling better but his throat was still sore and he was a grump. Jimmy had argued with the owner of the mill where he worked and they had been asked to leave now and find somewhere to live, luckily Jimmy had been asked to work on a farm two and a half miles away and they would be moving there but they had no house to live in and all four of them would be living in a borrowed caravan for the time being.

Daniel was coming for a visit next month, where he was going to sleep. She wasn't sure, it was cramped as it was in the caravan, she would ask Jimmy's Mother if it would be okay for him to stay there.

Dear Daniel

I hope this letter finds you well. Everyone here is good. Jimmy has been busy working on the Holden. He had taken the engine right out of it and has put new parts in the gearbox and had the crankshaft ground. He is putting new bearings in too. We are living in a caravan now where Jimmy is working about two and a half miles from Telegraph Point on the road to Kempsey. We got the farm at Glenrock but we don't start there until the first of October. It is a share farm.

It's been cold here lately and we have had a couple of good frost's out here where we are but Jimmy's father says they've only had just a bit of a frost there. Fred is growing and he is eleven pounds five ounces now. He grins and makes noises and looks around when we talk to him. Ruby thinks it's great when he grins for her.

When you come down will you bring the photos you took at Spring Ridge and at Bourke please and bring your camera as I would like you to take some photos of Ruby and Fred. Jimmy will probably be going over to the share farm on Sunday, he is going to put feed in for when we take over, there are no cows milking yet as the flood put them back. There is a tractor, milking machines and everything there so we don't have to get anything. I had a letter from Lynette the other day and she and Alan are getting engaged on Sunday. That's all for now. Love Rose

SEPTEMBER 1963

With two small children to care for as well as helping on the farm, the months seemed to fly past so quickly. August had been lovely and warm and they had only had a few good frosts. Jimmy's mother had welcomed Daniel into her home so that he could visit with them. Rose had picked Daniel up from the train station in the old Holden car, it still jumped out of gear and was hard to start, Rose didn't like driving it and she did not feel safe driving it too far.

Daniel had stayed for a week, they had spent time in the garden planting flowers and he loved playing with his grandchildren. Rose still could not call him Dad, it just didn't feel right. Daniel was caring but somewhat reserved at times, she knew he could feel her hesitation. Jimmy had been over at the share farm for a few days, he was planting feed in ready for when they took over. Fred was growing so fast, he laughed out loud and was such a happy baby, Rose was busy organising his christening and Ruby wanted to go to work with Jimmy every morning, she liked going on the tractor, sitting on her father's lap.

Two of the roosters kept fighting each other and one had to be killed, only two hens were laying but it still gave them enough fresh eggs for each day. Spring had arrived, the "pig face" had come out with their vibrant red flowers and Rose had planted carnations and larkspurs, if she could keep the kids out of the garden they too would flower soon. They had planted two bags of potatoes, watermelons, rockmelons and cucumbers. Jimmy also planted grammars and pumpkins in with the corn. The rain had come and everywhere had started to green up.

Rose did not like guns and was not happy that Jimmy had bought another rifle, it had a peep sight on it, he had paid fourteen pounds for it. They wouldn't be going over to the share farm now until the end of October, as the feed hadn't come through as well as Jimmy had expected it to.

NOVEMBER 1963

Jimmy was busy mowing, there was a lot of smart weed and thistles in the paddock and they had to be cleared, they were now milking twenty three cows. Fred could sit up on his own now for a couple of minutes and Ruby wanted to go everywhere with Jimmy, she would beg and plead with him until he relented and would take her on the horse with him to bring the cows in for milking.

"Go faster Daddy, make the horse go faster."

"Okay but you have to make sure you hang on tight to the saddle. Are you ready?" He looked down at his little girl, he felt so full of pride for his children.

Ruby squealed with delight as Jimmy put the horse into a canter and they rounded up the cows and headed for the dairy. Jimmy showed Ruby how to milk the cow, holding her little hands around the base of the teat, then slowly squeezing the teat, bringing in each other finger one at a time in a smooth rolling action, forcing the milk out of the teat and into the milk jug placed underneath the cow. Her hands weren't big enough but with his help they managed to fill up the milk jug.

"Now you take that home to Mum while I finish the milking." He kissed her head and she walked slowly back to the house with her milk jug.

"Look Mummy, I helped Daddy milk the cow!" Ruby was so excited and pleased with herself. Rose loved bringing children up on a farm, they learnt so much, she had loved her time as a child on the farm her parents took care of, it may have been hard work but the lessons it taught her and the fun she had had with her siblings, she wouldn't trade for anything.

Rose stood by the cattle yards with Fred on her hip and Ruby beside her looking through the fence rails as Jimmy de horned four of the cows. The horns were removed because they could pose a risk to humans, other animals and to the cows themselves, sometimes getting caught in fences or preventing them from feeding.

"Poor cows, Daddy is cutting their ears off." Ruby was beside herself.

Rose laughed "No darling it's not their ears, it's their horns, it's better for them so they don't hurt each other or us and this way they won't get their horns caught in the fence. It's okay, it doesn't hurt them." She took Ruby's hand and they headed back to the house. "Come on, you can help me plant some bean seeds in the garden and feed the parrot."

Jimmy had the engine out of the old Holden again, the head was warped and he had to get it shaved, once that was done he had to put it all back together again, hopefully this time it would be fixed.

CHAPTER 8

26th APRIL 1964

Dear Daniel,

I received your letter on Friday I'm glad you are well, we are all well too. I am pregnant again and due in October, I only had morning sickness for a few weeks this time and I'm feeling much better now. It poured rain here Tuesday and Wednesday and made everything wet and sloppy again. It was nice and dry. Jimmy had a boil on his arm last week and the pain was so bad he went to the doctor on Tuesday afternoon and the doctor cut it open, it's still very sore.

We picked up twenty one chickens last Monday, black and reds. None have died yet they are three and two weeks old. Jimmy went over to John's yesterday to fix a fence for him. John is in hospital, this is about the third time he's been in since Easter, he has bad nerves. We have some of the corn pulled, but the rain has put us behind. The paddock was too boggy so Jimmy is going to pull again tomorrow. The choko vine here only has a few on it, if you could bring some of yours down it would be okay, I like them. We have the potatoes up. The row Jimmy put in when you were here are so high they are falling over. I'll have to go now, it's past bedtime. Love Rose.

31st July 1964
Dear Daniel,
Just a few lines to let you know the news. We are all well and I hope you are the same. I had a cough for a couple of weeks after I had the flu but I am over it now. Ruby and Fred never got it bad, I took them to the doctor before they got too sick and got some medicine for them.

It hasn't been really cold here for the last few days, but we had some big frosts before that. We are just about settled in here now, Jimmy started work on Monday and he likes the job.

The baby has been very active kicking me, and sometimes it feels like it is doing cartwheels, it becomes quite uncomfortable. Fred has two double teeth and is getting two more and two others in the front, he has been cranky the last few days. We sent the pigs to sale before we left the farm but they only sold for eight pounds each. The house here is nice, it's not very big. When are you coming down again? I'll have to go now as Jimmy will be home soon for dinner. Love Rose

Rose continued to write to her father Daniel and he had just been to visit them. They'd spent time in the garden planting carnations and "pig face" plants. Daniel enjoyed this time with his family and took lots of photos of the children. As hard as she tried, Rose still felt uncomfortable with him, there was just something she couldn't put her finger on, something missing. She had to keep trying, after all he was her father. Why don't I feel a bond with him? she thought. Maybe it was because she had not grown up with him?

On the 28th October 1964 Rose gave birth to another beautiful baby girl with a mass of dark hair. She was small, only six pounds one ounce, but she was feisty.

"Another girl, looks like this one will be a handful," Jimmy said as he held the small child in his arms, she squirmed and wriggled. "Let's call her Lilly-Anne, she looks like a flower, we could call her Lilly for short."

Rose looked at him and smiled. "Yes, I like that name, I think it suits her." Rose could see there was something more on his mind. "What is it Jimmy?"

"Umm, well I know you want to stay here but I've been offered work in Rockvale near Armidale on a sheep station. So once you're ready to go, we will be moving, we need to move up there next month."

Rose knew it would do her no good to argue or question his decision. Once Jimmy made up his mind, that was it. So once again they'd be packing up their belongings and moving to another new home. There was so much more to pack up now with three children, one a newborn baby. Rose wished he could settle.

31st October 1964

Dear Daniel,

Just a few lines to let you know the news. We have another daughter, she was born on Wednesday the twenty-eighth we called her Lilly-Anne, she is only six pounds one ounce but is doing well and looks a lot like Ruby. I am well as is Jimmy, Ruby and Fred. The car has been breaking down again and we had two punctures in about a week. We went to Rollands Plains rodeo a fortnight ago, it was a good show. Jimmy went to the Kempsey rodeo today, he said it wasn't very good. We have had a few light showers in the last few days but it hasn't been hot. I am going home from the hospital on Wednesday. I have been here since Tuesday night. Ruby says the baby is hers, and she wants to nurse Lilly all the time.

We will be moving again in a month, Jimmy wants to go out to Armidale to work on a sheep station. Once we get settled there I will write to you with our new address.

That's all for now, Love Rose.

CHAPTER 9

ROCKVALE - ARMIDALE
NOVEMBER 1964

Rose got car sick every time they drove over this dreaded Walcha mountain. It never got easier to travel on this narrow, winding mountain road. If she was driving, she was fine but as a passenger she always got motion sick. She wanted to drive now but Jimmy refused, he always had to drive. Now they had three small children in tow, it took longer to go anywhere. The sheep station they were going to be living on was only a short distance outside of Armidale, in the New England high country which is renowned for growing some of the finest wool in the world. The green pastures and undulating hills as far as the eye could see had sheep dotted all over them, looking like cotton wool balls on a blanket of green. The area was a natural beauty with its meandering rivers and unique landscape of deep gorges and dramatic waterfalls. At this time of the year, the heat and humidity would bring on increased rainfalls and thunderstorms.

Gold had been discovered here in the 1850's which had brought a boom to the town and the heritage architecture reflected the grand ambitions of the 19th century settlers. As they drove through town Rose admired the beautiful old buildings. They pulled up at Central Park so the kids could go to the toilet. Ruby had been complaining for the past hour she needed to go but Jimmy would not stop, finally relenting he pulled up beside the band rotunda which was a memorial to those who had served in the Boer War, the memorial fountain was dedicated to those who served in World War I. It was a lovely shady area with picnic tables and toilet facilities.

"Hurry up you lot. Don't take all day." Jimmy yelled impatiently.

"Oh Jimmy, just give me a minute. I'll give the kids a quick wipe over to get the grime of the trip off them. You want your kids to look respectable when we get there don't you?"

Jimmy shrugged and waved at her to hurry. Rose wiped Ruby and Fred's face with a damp cloth then washed their hands and tidied their hair. Lilly was still asleep in the car. On the other side of the street were dominant buildings of stone and brickwork with two cathedrals. St Mary's and St Joseph's Church with its tower turrets and needle spire. It was impressive. The town was truly pretty and clean, people were going about their daily business. As they drove past the two storey brick Imperial Hotel with its cast-iron frieze work on the verandah and bullnose awnings.

Jimmy turned to her. "Nice old pub that one, I had a beer there when I came up to see the boss about the job. It's very grand inside. Maybe we could come in for dinner one night just the two of us, that's if we could get someone to mind the kids for us."

Rose smiled. "That would be lovely Jimmy."

They hadn't really had any dates or time alone since they were married. They always seemed to be on the move to the next job. Finally they pulled up outside their new house. They had been given one of the married quarters on the farm. Jimmy would be doing all sorts of jobs on the farm from fencing, fixing the windmill and troughs, bringing in the sheep and general rouse-about.

The old shearing shed was further down the road with its high peaked, rusting corrugated iron roof and giant grey walls of rough timber. The main house was set up on the hill about two hundred yards from the workers quarters. As they pulled up toutside a man and woman emerged from inside the house.

"Hello, you're finally here." The woman had dark brown hair to her shoulders, wore a floral dress with a black apron over it. The man was tall and thin, had short dark hair and a big grin. "I'm Jenny and this is my husband Steven. I've opened up the house for you to let some fresh air in, it was a bit stuffy in there."

"Thank you, that's very thoughtful of you." Rose liked her instantly; she had a friendly, cheerful attitude.

"Oh look at these beautiful kids. Let me help you get them inside. We have two kids as well, a boy and a girl about the same age, they will be able to keep each other occupied." Jenny picked up the sleeping Lilly and grabbed Ruby's hand. "Come on, let's see your new home shall we?"

The day was drawing to a close, a lingering pale pink, mauve light hovered above the rolling hills, giving way to the night sky. Jenny had made tea for them all. They had shepherd's pie, pumpkin, peas and carrots with gravy with thick slices of bread and butter and for dessert freshly baked apple pie with cream. The men sat outside on the verandah while the kids played in the lounge room and Jenny and Rose cleared the table and took the plates to the sink to wash up. Jenny washed the dishes as Rose wiped them and they chatted easily, like old friends. This time at least she would have someone close by that she could talk to, and the kids would have friends to play with.

The weeks turned to months and they settled into a steady routine of work on the farm. Rose and Jenny would often take the children down to the creek for picnics while the men worked. They would pack picnics and sit on the lush green grass under the weeping willows and the casuarina trees that lined the banks.

Rose loved the delicate mauve clusters of flowers on the jacaranda trees, they bought her a sense of calm. It was so relaxing enjoying a cup of tea and fruitcake with Jenny, while the children played happily in the shallows of the creek laughing and squealing as they splashed at each other. Lilly lay on her back on the blanket kicking her little arms and legs in the patchy sunlight filtering through the trees, giggling to herself.

"We thought we might go for a drive to Wollomombi this weekend to have a look at the falls and maybe do some fishing. Why don't you, Jimmy and the kids come along?"

"That sounds like fun Jenny. We could pack a picnic lunch and hopefully the boys could catch us some fish for dinner." She nudged her friend and laughed.

They set out early on the June morning with a sparkle of frost still on the ground. The falls were twenty five miles east of Armidale on the Waterfall Way. There had been some rain a few days earlier so the water plummeted over the six hundred and fifty feet cliff to the gorge below. The sound of the water crashing on the rocks below was healing and the spray of water bounced off the rock's back up the gorge in a fine mist creating a faint rainbow in the sunlight. They stood and marvelled at the sheer power of the cascading water before heading further down the road to find a spot where they could go fishing.

They chose a nice open area with a rock pool for the kids to swim in at the base of some small rapids. The women set up the rugs and food and watched the children, while the men headed further up the river to try their luck fishing.

Jenny poured Rose a cup of coffee. "Does Jimmy treat you alright Rose?" She was looking at her with concern.

"Um yes. Why do you ask?"

"Oh it's just the way he speaks to you sometimes, I think it's quite mean and degrading." Jenny kept her eyes locked on Rose.

Rose fidgeted and looked away, she felt uncomfortable with this conversation and embarrassed that someone else had picked up on the way he spoke to her.

"You don't need to be embarrassed Rose. You're not doing anything wrong. He's the one who is in the wrong. No one should be spoken to the way he talks to you."

"Oh I know" said Rose quietly "but he has a lot on his plate with a wife and three young kids to feed. He does work hard and he gets tired. Jimmy does expect everything to be perfect and for me to be there waiting for him when he gets home from work each day. It will get better soon I'm sure." Rose wasn't sure who she was trying to convince her friend or herself.

Jenny decided to let it go for now, she knew it was no good trying to convince her friend that her husband wasn't treating her right. Besides from what she had observed it wouldn't do any good to say anything to him anyway. Jenny had heard the way he yelled at her and the kids, beating down her self confidence, degrading her. What could she do? Nothing except be there for her friend if she needed her.

Their talk turned to the weather, it was early winter and the nights were becoming colder and most mornings they awoke to a thick fog blanketing the valley which cleared to bring forth a bright sunny mild day. There was frost covering the ground most mornings now.

"The rain will start again soon, it gets cold out here in the middle of winter, we usually have westerly winds and showers of rain and very occasionally if it's cold enough we get snow."

"Snow?" Rose was shocked she had never seen snow. "Oh I'd love to see snow but I don't like the cold."

"Well you can't have one without the other I'm afraid." Jenny chuckled. "Oh here come the men, looks like we have fish for dinner."

Jimmy and Steve had appeared around the bend in the river carrying two large rainbow trout each.

22nd May 1965

Dear Daniel,

I received your letter today and was pleased to hear you are well. We all have colds here. Betty has chicken pox and has to go to bed for a week. We got word from the doctor today and Fred has to have splints on his legs at night to try and correct them, his legs bow in and the doctor thinks it's because he started walking so soon and he is a little bit podgy. We are taking him over this afternoon to get his legs measured so the doctor can order them.

We sold the ute last week and got a car. It is a 1959 Holden Special, it goes well. The ute was getting too crowded. Niangala is twenty eight miles out of Walcha and we didn't get any pigs there. I don't think you've been there. It was hot here too on Monday the eleventh. Jimmy was out at Gibbons and it was one hundred and six degrees out there in the shade. We haven't had any good rain here so its brown everywhere now.

Lilly is growing, she grins and makes noises now and can nearly roll over. When are you coming down again? Jimmy said to ask you if there are any pigeons yet? I have to go now.

Love Rose.

CHAPTER 10

JUNE 1965

A string of harsh coughs shook Lilly's pale, fragile little body. She was struggling to breathe; her breathing was fast and shallow. She had become listless and her chest heaved and rattled with each strained breath. Rose sat holding her eight month old baby girl tightly in the Armidale hospital corridor waiting to see a doctor. The corridor was stuffy and the air smelt of bleach. There were marks and scrapes on the corridor walls from hundreds of trolleys that had bumped into them over the years. The floor was slate grey lino and was highly polished. The ceiling polystyrene squares had been laid in a grid, like a fashion statement. Near the door there were dispensers for rubber gloves, hand sanitiser and soap. Patients where wheeled past on trollies, doctors hurried around from room to room until finally a nurse called her to come into the examination cubicle.

"I'm sorry for the wait but we are just snowed under at the moment. The doctor will be with you shortly." She pulled the curtain around the bed and left Rose there with Lilly who was still coughing harshly, each racking cough shaking her little body as she struggled to breathe. Rose was beside herself, she felt so helpless. This waiting was the worst, her baby girl was so sick and she could do nothing but hold her close and tell her everything would be ok.

The doctor finally arrived to examine Lilly, moving the stethoscope over her back, he listened to her chest, there were pronounced crackles in her lungs, the doctor ordered lung and chest X-rays as well as blood tests.

"Well I'm afraid she has pneumonia. We will need to put her into an oxygen tent, it will help her breathing. She will need to stay in hospital for a few days and we will administer an antibiotic to help clear the infection." The doctor smiled at her and patted Rose's hand. "It will be fine dear, we will take good care of her."

Rose nodded and she could feel her bottom lip start to quiver and tried hard to hold back the tears she could feel prickling at the back of her eyes. Her baby girl had to stay in hospital and she couldn't help her. They placed Lilly into a crib with a frame over the top and clear plastic cover. The plastic was stretched tightly around the crib and tucked under the mattress, then the oxygen was blown through the pipe into the tent. After twenty minutes Lilly's breathing became easier. The nurse came back with a medical tray with a needle on it.

"This will help beat the infection. It's penicillin." After injecting Lilly the nurse turned to Rose. "Would you like a cup of tea or coffee?"

"That would be great but I don't want to leave her." She turned to look at her child laying in the strange tent contraption.

"That's okay I'll bring it back for you in a minute." She turned and left Rose alone in the room with Lilly. Rose sat staring at her small helpless child, struggling to breath. Suddenly Lilly let out an ear piercing scream, she gasped for breath, she was choking. Lilly's face was turning blue and her eyes were wide open and bulging.

"My god what's happening?" Rose screamed out for a nurse. "Someone help she is going blue, she can't breathe! Help me!"

The nurse came running back to the room followed by the doctor. Lilly's little arms were flailing around and she had broken out in hives. Her throat and tongue were swelling.

"She's having an allergic reaction to the penicillin, quick nurse give me the Epinephrine needle we need to calm her down. Grab her tongue and don't let her swallow it."

Rose was beside herself; she could not believe this was happening; she could do nothing but watch the doctor and nurse trying to save her daughter's life. The doctor injected clear fluid into Lilly's tiny bottom and within minutes her breathing slowed and the swelling began to subside.

"It seems your daughter is allergic to penicillin. We will try another medication to help with the infection." He patted Rose's arm. "Don't worry, she is going to be fine, she's a fighter. We will make a note on her charts not to administer penicillin again." Lilly spent the next few days in hospital in the oxygen tent, Rose stayed with her and Jenny took care of Ruby and Fred. Finally Lilly was well enough to be taken home. It was cold and wet, the chill in the air felt like the air was blowing straight off snow.

Jimmy had the fire burning in the lounge room when she returned to the house, it was lovely and warm inside. He sat down holding little Lilly on the lounge, looking down into her little face her cheeks were red from the cold outside.

"I think we will return home to Telegraph Point. I've been talking to Dad. He needs my help on the farm, he's getting too old to manage it by himself now, we could settle down there and stay in one place. I know you don't like all the moving around and it will be good for the kids to have all their cousins close by to grow up with." He looked up from the sleeping baby to Rose.

"Really Jimmy? Could we? I miss my family and I don't like this cold weather at all. It seems to always be raining lately."

"Yes, let's pack up and head home."

17th January 1966

Dear Daniel,

Just a few lines to let you know the news. We are all well and I hope this finds you are the same. It is hot here today but there is a cool breeze blowing every now and again. It's dry again and we need rain badly. Janice and Connie came down last week and had a couple of days with us. We went fishing at Blackmans Point one night but all we got were mosquito bites.

Jimmy went out to Gibbons Saturday, Sunday and today, he is getting cattle in for them. Lilly has been grizzly lately. She is getting double teeth, she climbs like a monkey now. My dahlias are in full bloom and I've got six different colours out of the six plants I bought. It's getting too dry for anything to grow. The dog Rusty got into the garden one night and scratched out nearly all the phlox from the garden bed. I was not happy with him.

The cows are still milking well but they will start to drop if we don't get rain soon. Jimmy sold the old cow and got thirty three pounds for her. His father sold the two biggest calves that we were feeding on the bucket and got eighteen pounds each for them. Your house should be nice when it is finished, I'll bet it's been keeping you busy.

Jimmy bought a Studebaker truck he is going to start up a wood run. I got a new steam and dry iron a fortnight ago. The other one went bung and they gave me a four pound trade in on the new one. The black pig had eleven little ones last week but one died and the white pig had six piglets a few days later. Jimmy's grandfather died yesterday morning he had cancer in the mouth and neck, his funeral is in Armidale tomorrow. Jimmy is going up but I'm not going. I will help with the milking while he is away as well as watch the kids, they keep me on my toes. I'll say bye for now.

Love Rose

CHAPTER 11

WILSON RIVER

NOVEMBER 1967

Rose loved being back home closer to her parents and brothers and sisters. They had moved into the old three bedroom house on the riverbank across the paddock from Jimmy's parents' house. It was an old wooden house with a red tin roof, there was no inside bathroom and the toilet was a small tin shed with a drop toilet out the back in the orchard. The house was built on a small part of land and was perched right on the river bank with the back of the house looking over the river and the front of the house facing the dirt road that led down to the ferry. The house had been built by Jimmy's father when he had first moved to the farm with his young family many years before. Jimmy's parents were now in a bigger house his father had built, higher up in the front paddock looking out across the front paddock to the river.

For the last few years Jimmy had helped his father out on the farm, as well as driving and operating earthmoving trucks and backhoe's part time to help with the running costs of the farm. It was a hard life running a dairy farm now, things were becoming more motorised and the health department had introduced so many new rules and regulations which all dairy farmers had to abide by. The big companies were making it hard for the little dairy farms to make a living. The cost to convert the dairy over to all the modern machinery to keep it running was not viable, so they had decided to stop selling milk and only milked what they needed for the family now. They grew corn and turnips on the farm as well as raising cattle for sale.

Jimmy's moods were hard to handle at times, one minute he was a loving husband and father and the next he was yelling and screaming abuse at her telling her she was useless and ugly. He even took the power cord to the radio to work with him so she couldn't listen to the radio. Jimmy said she wasted too much time listening to music instead of doing her work. What he didn't realise was that the cord for the frypan also fitted the radio, Rose just had to remember each day to unplug it before he arrived home from work. He had even hit her a few times but was always very sorry afterwards, promising her that it would never happen again. Rose put it down to the stress of trying to run the farm as well as working another job. His boss, according to Jimmy was a bloody idiot and had no idea how to run a business, and he didn't like being told what Jimmy thought he was doing wrong. "That man just can't take good advice" he'd say.

Jimmy's eldest sister Kathy had passed away suddenly at the age of twenty nine from a cerebral haemorrhage leaving five children for her husband Tony to care for, he was not coping with the loss of his wife and trying to care for young children so the children were separated and sent out to other family members to help care for them. Mitchell was fifteen and was now sharing a room with four and a half year old Fred, Jimmy had him helping on the farm as well as going to work with him some days in the truck. Mitchell was a quiet, polite young man and would always lend a helping hand with the younger children. Lilly adored Mitchell; she thought he was her big brother too, she followed him everywhere. Today once again they had to repair the chicken pen where the foxes had dug underneath the wire during the night and pulled out a hen, two of the bantams and three chickens, they killed and ate them under the mulberry tree across the road from the house, leaving feathers everywhere. Before beginning the repairs, they were going to the corn paddock to pick some pumpkins and gramma's that were growing between the corn rows.

With little Lilly holding Mitchell's hand the three of them set off across the paddock, to the little wooden bridge made of old sleeper rails that crossed over the drain into the cornfield. The corn was almost ready for harvesting, the tall yellow, husky stalks reaching towards the sky, they were thick and had to be pushed aside as they made their way through the rows. There was always the chance of coming across snakes in here too, so you had to be careful where you walked.

"You sit here Lilly while we pick some pumpkins." Rose laid down a blanket on the grass for Lilly to sit on with her toy teddy. "Don't go anywhere, stay here where I can see you." She turned to the red kelpie dog. "Stay here Mini and watch her." The old red dog sat down obediently beside Lilly, it seemed she understood every word that was said to her. Lilly sat beside the dog and played with her teddy.

"I'll start up this row on the pumpkins." Mitchell grabbed his hessian bag and disappeared between the corn stalks.

Rose picked up her hessian bag with a quick glance at Lilly to make sure she was settled and started to pick the gramma's they only needed to fill three hessian bags each, that would be enough to sell at this week's markets. She called out to Lilly several times to make sure she was still sitting on the blanket. Rose was almost finished when Lilly did not reply.

"Lilly, Lilly!" Rose stumbled back through the corn stalks Lilly was not on the blanket and the dog was gone too. "Lilly, where are you? Lilly! Answer me now, this is not a game. Lilly!!!!" Rose was becoming frantic. The river was so close and there were creeks and water wells nearby, "Lilly answer Mummy" she screamed.

Mitchell could hear the commotion he knew by Rose's scream something was wrong, he dropped his bag of pumpkins and ran back through the corn rows.

"What's happened?"

"Lilly is gone, oh god I hope she hasn't fallen in the creek! Look, there's her teddy by the bridge. Lilly! Lilly! Answer Mummy where are you? Mini here girl" Rose whistled for the dog as she ran towards the creek.

Mitchell jumped into the water; it was only a few feet deep but murky, stagnant water, he thrashed around to see if he could find her.

"I won't be able to forgive myself if anything happens to her, Lilly! Lilly, where are you?" Rose whistled for the dog again, the old red dog came running back across the paddock from Jimmy's parents' house.

"There's the dog, maybe she's gone over to see her Pa?" Mitchell looked at Rose. "You go see if she's there I'll keep looking here."

Rose ran as fast as she could across the paddock through the wire fence to the house arriving at the gate she flung it open, gasping for breath. "Lilly?"

"She's here love, having a cuppa with me." William sounded surprised at the state of Rose. "What's wrong?"

Lilly was sitting up on the old church pew on the front verandah beside her grandfather "Pa" drinking a cup of tea, totally unaware of all the drama and distress she had caused her mother.

"Me have tea and cake with Pa." Lilly grinned at her mother, cake crumbs falling from her mouth.

"Lilly you scared the hell out of me, I thought you'd fallen in the drain. I told you not to move." Rose scooped the wide eyed child up in her arms hugging her tightly.William looked adoringly at his grand-daughter.

"Love, you can just leave her with me when you need to do anything. I love having "Chicken" with me, you know that and she does love a cuppa with her old Pa." He had given her the nickname of "Chicken", because she was always scratching around and into something like a little chicken.

Mitchell arrived soaking wet, mud up to his waist, the red dog Mini right behind him, he smiled when he saw Lilly. "I should have known she would have headed to her Pa for a cuppa. Actually I wouldn't mind one myself, any left in the pot, Pa?"

Rose realised she couldn't get mad at her baby girl, she was too young to understand, in future she would leave her with her grand-parents for safekeeping, Lilly was such an inquisitive child and climbed like a monkey, into everything and wanting to explore all the time, she was a handful that was for sure.

"I could do with a cuppa myself after all that excitement," said Rose. "Sit down Mitchell I'll grab us a cup and see if there's some cake left if Lilly hasn't eaten it all."

CHAPTER 12

9th DECEMBER 1968

They had saved up enough money to buy a black and white TV, the children loved it and they were now sitting in front of the TV watching the Mickey Mouse Club. Ruby always the performer was up and dancing and singing along to all the songs, putting on a show for Fred and Lilly who would sit and giggle at her. Rose was in the kitchen peeling the potatoes and preparing dinner when the phone rang. It was her mother, she was crying and not making much sense.

"Hi Mum, Mum slow down what's happened?"

"It's Alice, she's been in a terrible accident, the North Coast Daylight Express Train collided with the school bus at the Middleton Street level crossing." Loretta was distraught.

"Oh my god Mum, is she okay? Was anyone else hurt?" Rose was trying to control her voice from breaking so as not to upset her mother any more than she already was.

"She's in a coma, she's critical but stable. They are not sure if she will make it. Four schoolgirls were killed instantly, two are critical and there are about seventeen others injured."

"I'll come straight over Mum, I'll have to wait for Jimmy to get home to watch the kids."

"No it's okay love, there is nothing you can do right now. Wait until tomorrow. We will know more then." Loretta sobbed.

"Are you sure Mum?" Rose wanted to be there for her mother; she knew she would be beside herself worrying about her youngest child.

"Yes, it's alright your father is with the other children at home. They are all upset and worried as you can imagine. I have to keep myself together for them.

I just needed to let you know and I didn't want you to see it on the news before I got a chance to speak with you." Loretta tried to stifle the lump in her throat.

"Oh Mum I feel so helpless, I'll be over tomorrow, as soon as I get the kids off to school. Stay strong Mum, everything will be okay, Alice is a stubborn little thing, she will get through this. I love you Mum."

"I love you too darling, I must go, the doctor has just come out of the operating theatre, I need to speak to him. Just go to the house tomorrow, they aren't allowing anyone to visit at the hospital except your father and me, I'll see you tomorrow."

The phone clicked dead, Rose stood with the receiver in her hand, with the phone line making that annoying, beeping, engaged signal. Her darling little sister, only thirteen years old and in a coma, the uncertainty, not knowing if she would live or die was ripping Rose's heart apart. She had a sleepless night with her sister and mother on her mind.

The next day when Rose pulled up outside her parents' house, there were already people coming and going, offering to help the family in any way they could. Martin stood at the door his face was ashen and his eyes red, he looked like he had not slept. Rose threw her arms around her father's neck and cried.

"Oh Dad, is there any word yet on Alice?"

"Nothing new love, she's still in a coma and critical, they say she may not wake up for weeks, that's if she does at all." His voice choked. "She's had a massive knock to her head and was found unconscious twenty feet from the bus hanging over a wire fence. Come on inside, I'll make us a cuppa."

Martin told her what had happened. The school bus was on its usual afternoon home run, on its way to drop all the kids home from school, the crossing gates were open as the bus approached the train line, the bus driver continued through thinking it was safe to cross the tracks as the gatekeeper always put the gates down when a train was about to come. Well it wasn't safe, for some reason the railway gatekeeper had not closed the boom gates. Why, at this stage they were unsure, as he was in shock and sedated at the hospital. The train driver had not seen the bus on approach as his view was obscured by the embankment and by the time his fireman had spotted the bus crossing the line, it was too late. The driver applied the emergency brakes and the fireman sounded the siren but there was nothing they could do. The train was only ten feet from the crossing and the bus was halfway across, the train hit the rear of the bus ripping it open and spinning it around and off the tracks onto the embankment beside the line. Neighbours hearing the crash and the screaming came running to find children scattered everywhere, bleeding and crying, they stayed with them, attending to the injured children as best they could with umbrellas shielding them from the rain, blankets and pillows. They waited with the children as the rain continued to fall, trying to comfort and care for them until the doctors and ambulances arrived. The scene was like a war zone, children were hurled from the bus and were laying all over the track, road and fences, some of the bus seats were flung a distance of fifty feet. The back of the bus was ripped open and a mangled mess from where the train had impacted and the front was smashed in where it had ploughed into the embankment. Four schoolgirls were killed instantly and there were seventeen people injured, two of them critical. One of those critical girls had passed away during the night, the other was being flown to Sydney for emergency surgery. Alice was found unconscious, hanging over a fence near the tracks, her dress was ripped and her shoes had flung off in the impact, blood was oozing from a gaping wound in her head. Someone had pulled her from the fence and wrapped her head to try to stop the bleeding until help arrived. Now she lay in a coma, her injuries were so bad, they did not know if she would recover and if she did, whether there would be any permanent brain damage. Loretta had been in town shopping at the time and had intended catching that same bus home but luckily she had been late to the bus stop and had missed it by only a few minutes, or she too would have been on the bus and involved in that horrific collision and possibly laying beside her daughter in hospital or worse.

Parents were angry, demanding answers. They had been petitioning for a railway bridge overpass for years, but the council had felt it wasn't necessary. There had been a few near misses at this crossing before and it was only a matter of time before something like this was bound to happen. What made it worse was that it was a bus load of school children that had now paid the price for the council's lack of foresight.

Rose sat in stunned silence listening to her father as he told her about the accident. The mental picture of her little sister hanging over the fence bleeding made goosebumps rise on her arms. What if she died? What if she never awoke from the coma? After having children of her own she could imagine what her mother must be going through. Her poor mother, she must be beside herself.

"When can we see her Dad?"

"Not for a few days darling," Martin placed his arm around Rose. "They are only letting one person at a time in and only the parents at this stage. Don't worry, I'm sure she'll be fine."

Rose could tell that her father was very worried and trying to stay positive for everyone, keeping his own grief and sorrow hidden. That's the sort of man he was, she loved him so much and wished she could do more to help. Loretta had stayed at the hospital not leaving Alice's side all night. Rose helped her father around the house until she had to return home to her own children.

"Tell Mum to call me if she needs anything Dad, I'll get here as quickly as I can." Rose kissed her father and held him in an extra tight hug before leaving.

Loretta stayed by Alice's bedside praying her daughter would wake, she had been in a coma for eight days before finally opening her eyes much to everyone's relief, but would not, or could not speak. The doctors had told her parents it was probably shock from the accident and to be patient and give her time to recover.

Loretta and Martin stood in the hospital corridor outside Alice's room. It was Christmas day, sixteen days since the accident, they had bought Alice's Christmas presents with them as well as her brothers and sisters, hoping to cheer her up. It was going to be a long recovery and a few more weeks in hospital before she would be allowed home with constant care.

"Now remember kids, Alice has been through a terrible ordeal so don't be upset when you see her. She still hasn't spoken yet, we need to be patient with her." Martin looked down at his children hoping they wouldn't be too shocked to see Alice with a bandage around her head and attached to a drip. They filed quietly into the room Alice was sitting up in the bed, propped up with pillows, dressed in a pink nightgown, her bandages had been reapplied that morning by the nurses, she smiled as she saw her siblings who came running to the bed, all trying to give her a hug at the same time.

"Come on now kids give her some space, be careful." Loretta tried to calm the children, she knew they were relieved to see their sister and excited.

Alice was so pleased to see her brothers and sisters, it had been hard for her the last few weeks trying to come to terms with what had happened to her. She had been having nightmares about the accident and mourning the loss of her friends. Alice knew she had been lucky to survive, if she had been sitting just one seat back in the bus, she would have died like her friend Michelle, who she had only been joking and laughing with seconds before the train hit. She would be thankful everyday of her life for being spared.

Alice smiled, "Merry Christmas." These were the first words she had spoken since the accident.

The room was silent for a moment then everyone cried and hugged. Martin put his arm around Loretta watching his children, a tear running down his cheek, everything was going to be okay. Alice was going to pull through this, she would be okay.

CHAPTER 13

KEMPSEY

JULY 1970

Rose had been feeling unwell for the last few days and had been having cramps and spotting. She was six months pregnant with her fourth child and thought it best to go to her mother's for a few days. She was going to see her doctor tomorrow, the children were on school holidays and she felt too unwell to care for them.

"Just put your feet up on the chair and rest Rose, I'll make us a cuppa. Go on you kids, outside and play with your cousins. Better still go down to the bee shed and see if your Grandfather wants a cup of tea." Loretta shooed the kids outside, she loved having all her grandchildren around, the house was full of laughter and chatter. Martin was a beekeeper and had the back shed set up to extract honey from the hives, the children loved hanging out with him and his honey, chewing on fresh honeycomb. She needed to talk to Rose alone, she had a feeling that Jimmy might be abusing her daughter and she did not want history repeating itself.

"Thanks Mum." Rose took the cup of tea gratefully. It was nice to have someone take care of her for a change.

"I'll get right to the point Rose, is Jimmy hitting you?" Loretta looked straight into her daughter's eyes challenging her to the truth.

"Mum, well um." She swallowed hard and fought back the tears. She didn't want to lie to her mother, but she was too embarrassed to tell her the truth.

"Don't make excuses to me girl I know when." Loretta paused. She had never told Rose of the abuse she had suffered at the hands of Daniel. "I know when something's not right."

Tears welled up in Rose's eyes she knew she could not hide it from her mother, she still had a bruise on the inside of her arm where Jimmy had grabbed her a few days ago when she had dared to speak back to him. "It's not too bad Mum, he's under a lot of pressure with work and trying to make ends meet and me having another child hasn't helped, because now I can't work as much."

"Don't make excuses for him Rose, there is no excuse good enough for a man to lay a hand on a woman. A real man doesn't hit a woman."

Rose knew she could not argue with her mother, but what could she do? She had three children and one on the way, how would she possibly cope on her own if she left him? Rose felt a gush of warmth between her legs and looked down, she could see bright red blood seeping through her skirt just as a pain gripped her stomach.

"Mum! Something is wrong, call an ambulance quickly, something is wrong with the baby." Rose grabbed her stomach in agony as a sharp pain gripped her.

As they loaded her onto the stretcher and into the ambulance Rose could see her frightened children holding onto her mother, crying, Lilly was screaming for them not to take her mother away.

"I'll call Jimmy and get him over here, don't worry about the kids, they will be fine." Loretta knew this was not going to be good, Rose was only twenty six weeks pregnant, it was too soon for the baby to come.

Violet was born at two am the following morning. She weighed only two pounds and was so very thin and tiny, her skin was wrinkled and a reddish-purple colour and was so thin you could see the blood vessels underneath. Her face and body were covered in soft hair, she had no muscle tone, no eyelashes and had not yet opened her eyes. She was too immature to suck, swallow, and breathe at the same time and was being fed intravenously as she struggled to breathe on her own. Rose had lost a lot of blood and had to have a blood transfusion. The doctor came into the room to see Rose and Jimmy and explain what was going to happen next.

"It's not good news, I'm sorry. Rose you had what's called placenta previa, as you know the placenta provides the growing baby with oxygen and nutrients from the mother's bloodstream and the placenta is normally above the baby, in your case the placenta has implanted at the bottom of the uterus, covering the cervix. Your placenta erupted and that's why you went into labor early, you are going to be fine." The doctor paused, he hated giving bad news to parents but that was all part of his job. "I'm sorry but your baby is not likely to make it through the night. At twenty six weeks there is also the high possibility of medical complications and serious, lasting disabilities if she does survive. You need to prepare yourself, spend some time with her and hold her, let her know she's loved with the time she has left here on this planet." He patted Rose's hand and left them alone with their tiny baby girl.

Rose sat and cradled little Violet close to her chest, cuddling and kissing her for the next five hours hoping that her beautiful little baby girl could feel the love she had for her, as Violet took her last breath and passed away in her arms, Rose felt a part of her die inside, creating a void that would never be filled. Rose never got the chance to see into her baby's eyes or hear her cry. The nurses came and took her baby away and gave her something to help her sleep. As she drifted off into the darkness, the tears fell from her eyes for the child who would never get to grow old.

4th January 1971

   Dear Daniel,

   Just a few lines to let you know the news. I don't seem to get much time to write lately. I am milking fourteen cows twice a day and feeding fifteen calves. I'm going into Kempsey today to see if I can buy more calves. Jimmy had all the corn planted by New Years Day and then we went up to the creek for a swim. He cemented the water tank on the high stand yesterday. Robert came down and helped him.

   The new black and white cat Skippy has had four kittens and one is pure white. Trixie has six pups under the house and old puss had kittens last week. Lilly had to be rushed to hospital two weeks ago, she had appendicitis and had emergency surgery to have them removed they said she was very lucky they didn't burst. Of course Lilly wanted to keep them and has them in a solution in a bottle, which she proudly shows everyone. She sits them up on the cupboard with all Jimmy's dead snakes he has in the bottles and waits for someone to ask what sort of snake it is. Yesterday she went to the toilet and her side split open where the scar was healing and I had to rush her back to the doctor.

We dug up half the spuds yesterday afternoon, they are lovely big ones. Saturday we took a few heifers over to Kempsey and put a couple of new wires on the fence, to keep them in. We went into Marbuk Park Saturday night to a rodeo. It was a good show but we had to stand up all night and gee, it made me tired. One bucking horse ran head first into the fence nearly killing itself. I had five fowls die. The vet said it was a liver virus and I lost two calves with scours.

Must go and get ready or I'll be late for the sales.

Love Rose

CHAPTER 14

KEMPSEY

MAY 1972

Rose was digging around in the dirt of the old New South Wales bank in Kempsey, she had unearthed a few old bottles as well as some old coins, she was helping Jimmy at work today. When he had come home and told her he was going to knock a hole in the bank wall at Kempsey, she thought he was joking. Jimmy had the job of digging up the old footings at the bank so they could build a new extension. The last two years had been hard since losing Violet, then with Lilly being in and out of hospital so many times with croup or pneumonia the doctors finally decided to take her tonsils out, then six weeks after that operation her appendix almost exploded and she had to be rushed to emergency surgery to have them removed. Just after having her stitches out her scar burst open and it was another rush to the hospital. Lilly would be the death of her, she was a real little tomboy, she loved riding the horses and climbing trees and didn't mind getting dirty.

Jimmy had decided to start a business for himself and had bought a backhoe and an old Bedford tip truck. He had taught Rose to drive the truck and she had passed her heavy rigid test a year ago, and now she would go on jobs with him driving the tip truck. Rose was amused at the looks on the faces of people, especially men when she climbed down out of the driver's seat, she stood only five foot one inch tall and was driving large tip trucks.

While she waited for the truck to be loaded she would knit to fill in the time, at the moment she was knitting Fred a jumper for the coming winter. Rose hated the fact that she had to leave so early in the morning at five am while the children were still asleep. Ruby who was now eleven and a great help, she would get her brother and sister up and ready to catch the bus to school. Rose would leave biscuits or cake and a piece of fruit for their recess snack and money for lunch on the bench before she left each day. It was always late when they returned home each day and Ruby and Lilly would help prepare the vegetables for dinner and set the table while Fred did his chores around the farm.

Rose was grateful for her three children; they were so happy and helpful. Jimmy on the other hand was never happy or satisfied, he expected too much from the children expecting them to work hard and do things that were sometimes above their capabilities.

Last night while they were eating dinner Lilly had finished before everyone else and wanted to go outside to play before it got too dark. She rose from the table while everyone else was still eating and Jimmy had slapped her on the back of the head and yelled at her to sit down and wait for everyone to finish. Rose had jumped to her defence and had copped a slap across the face from Jimmy and told to shut up. She reached up and touched her face, it was a bit swollen, red and tender from where his hand had hit her. Poor little Lilly was beside herself so upset that she had caused her father to hit her mother. The children had seen and heard way too much abuse for their tender ages and it was getting worse, Jimmy had started drinking and sometimes quite heavily. They all knew to keep out of his way because he became even more abusive not only with his words but with his fists as well.

Why did she stay with such an abusive man? It wasn't just the physical abuse but the verbal and mental abuse as well. Jimmy's words were hurtful and demoralising, not just to her but to their children. She wished she had the courage to leave, but how would she cope on her own with three children to support? Once when they were fighting, she had told him she would leave him, he grabbed her by the throat and pushed her hard up against the wall and told her that if she ever left him, he would hunt her down and kill her and the children. Rose believed he would, she could not risk that happening, she just had to hope that she could manage him, and that one day he would change.

Finally she was on her way with the last load of the day, at least she would be home early today, she would write to Daniel after dinner tonight. The children were at the dairy with the cow called Honey, Fred was milking her and they were filling up the milk bottles to take to their grandparents. Lilly would stand there with her mouth open while Fred tried to squirt the milk in her mouth, most of it would go all over her and not much in her mouth, they loved playing this game and giggled as the milk squirted everywhere. The kids loved the old Hereford bull called "Ice-cream" whom they had reared from a calf and they would ride him around like a horse until Ice-cream got tired of it and would shake himself and roll over until they all fell off in fits of laughter.

A farm was a great place to raise children, they could see how their food was grown and harvested and how to look after animals. Even helping when an animal had to be slaughtered for food, learning that life was not always easy. They had pet pigs and lambs, they would help feed the calves and husk the corn at harvest time, they could all ride horses and Fred, who seemed much older than his nine years would drive the tractor and do his chores with no complaints. There was always family around with plenty of cousins to play with and get into mischief with.

The children hated the old drop toilet out the back in the orchard and at night if they had to go, Rose would have to go out with them standing guard to make sure no monsters came out of the river to get them. It was eerie standing out there at night, no street lights, no traffic, the only sounds were trees rustling, the night noises of birds, an occasional splash from the river and creatures settling down for the night, it was no wonder the children were sacred. The children were growing up so quickly, and washing in a large dish on the back porch was not going to work for them for much longer. Ruby was already starting to grow into a young woman and needed her privacy. Rose had been begging Jimmy to build a proper bathroom with an inside toilet onto the back of the house. Jimmy finally agreed but only after the wall in the girls' bedroom had fallen in one morning and left the girls staring at the back yard and river. He had started work on the bathroom extension, soon they would have a shower and a modern, flush toilet. Rose couldn't wait for an actual, real bathroom.

The roof leaked in the bedroom the girls shared and whenever it rained they would be running around with buckets and saucepans trying to catch the water leaking from the roof.

Whenever Lilly went missing Rose knew where to find her. Lilly loved going over to her Pa's every day to have a cup of tea, they would sit, side by side on the old church pew on the front verandah overlooking the farm discussing what she had done that day or just sitting, not talking, sipping tea and eating Ma's homemade biscuits. William loved his time with Lilly, his little chicken as he called her, and when Betty would come out and yell at him for whatever he was supposed to have done wrong, he would just nod and say "yes dear" and turn to Lilly with a smile and wink.

19th May 1972
Dear Daniel,

Here at last, to drop you a note, we are all well and hope you are the same. It has been lovely here during the day but the nights are cool. There has been a frost nearly every morning. We have been flat out, working every day to try and catch up. Peg, John and I pulled the corn on Sunday and Monday so we don't have to worry about it now.

I have been driving the truck for Jimmy and we worked four days in Kempsey digging up the old footings of the NSW Bank. I found six different old bottles buried in the dirt. When Jimmy said he had to go to Kempsey to knock a hole in the bank I thought he was joking. We should have our new automatic phone in about three weeks now. One cow was sick the other day. It seemed like "three day sickness". I hope the rest don't get it.

The kids ride their bikes nearly every day after school and usually don't come in until dark. They are going to Beechwood this Friday for a school sports competition. I'm going in amongst the hens with the axe while they are away. I haven't had any eggs for weeks. Well I best go and get the washing in before it gets damp. Bye for now.

Love Rose.

WILSON RIVER
JUNE 1972

The children were excited, tonight they were having a big family get together at the farm with all of their cousins. They had gathered a stack of wood in the front paddock to have a bonfire and after dinner they would be letting firecrackers off. Jimmy had a large family, with all his brothers and sisters and their partners and children there would be at least fifty people there. Betty had been busy cooking for days and everyone brought a plate, they had slaughtered a cow to cook on the barbecue. They brought out saw horses and old doors to place on top to make tables, tablecloths covered the old doors and the food was arranged for everyone to help themselves.

It was a lovely warm evening and everyone was in good spirits. It was fun to catch up with all the family, and at least Jimmy was on his best behaviour in front of his family. Rose was sure they knew what went on behind closed doors, but no one ever questioned her or asked her if she was okay, it was easier for them to pretend that everything was fine.

William called out "Ruby and Lilly come over here and sing a song for your Pa." He smiled and beckoned them to him. Ruby was outgoing and she loved to sing and perform, whereas Lilly was shy.

"Come on Lilly, let's sing "The Banks of The Ohio" just like we practised." Ruby encouraged her.

"But that's different, it's just us in our bedroom." Lilly glanced around nervously. "Everyone is looking at us, I can't." Lilly hid behind her mother.

"Come hold my hand Lilly, look at me and pretend we are in our bedroom." Ruby took her hand and faced her little sister and started to sing, her voice was pure and sweet.

"I asked my love to take a walk, to take a walk, just a little walk, down beside where the waters flow, down by the banks of the Ohio."

Ruby smiled and squeezed Lilly's hand. Lilly adored her big sister and wanted to be just like her, she didn't want to let her down, so she joined in for the chorus just like they had practised.

"And only say that you'll be mine, in no others arms entwined, down beside where the waters flow, down by the banks of the Ohio."

Rose watched her daughters sing with such pride, they were so beautiful and talented, she hoped that they would have a good life and she would make sure they would not end up in an abusive marriage like hers. The song had come to an end and everyone clapped and cheered. The girls did a little bow and hugged each other.

"See Lilly it wasn't that bad really was it? You just have to believe in yourself. I'm very proud of you." She hugged her little sister again, then ran off to join her cousins.

The bonfire was crackling high up into the sky, with embers floating away on the light breeze. The children ran around playing hide and seek in the dark, their laughter filled the air and the excitement was building for the anticipated fireworks to come. Every now and then one of the boys would let off tom thumbs. They were small, red and green sticks all joined together with a wick at one end which they would light and they would all bang and crackle, exploding to the delighted screams of the kids.

Jimmy had attached two Catherine wheels to the fence with nails and set up fireworks all in a line ready to be let off, one after the other. "Okay stand back everyone I'm going to light the fireworks."

Everyone moved back a safe distance, awaiting the first fireworks to be sent off high in the air. First was the skyrockets to go, they hissed and a spray of golden sparkles erupted, then bang, they shot straight up into the air before exploding into a spray of a red stars, the long trailing embers lingered before falling slowly to the ground, the roman candles sent up a stream of silver sparks tumbling like a waterfall in a glittering silver shower, sprays of crimson lava spewed from the fountain firework like a mini volcanic eruption. The sky was dancing with bright sparks of colour, the night was filled with loud and colourful explosions. Last to be set alight were the Catherine wheels, they took off whirling around in a spiral, spinning faster and faster with a glittering trail of yellow flying out, suddenly one flew off the fence flying horizontally across the field just like a frisbee, scattering the crowd with screams and laughter, it headed straight for William hitting the ground and bouncing over his head before chasing Fred across the paddock, his screams of fear and delight filled the air as it flew passed him, just missing him. Everyone burst into laughter at the narrow miss. The smoke from the fireworks hung in the air drifting away on the breeze, the smell of gunpowder was strong.

"Well, that was a close call." William laughed. "Bloody thing nearly took off my head!"

Rose loved William, he was the matriarch of the family and a gentle, caring, loving man. He never raised his voice or his hand to anyone. Why couldn't Jimmy be more like his Dad, he was more like his mother. Betty was a strong woman and she ruled the house with a firm hand. Jimmy had mentioned a few times of the floggings he had received from her. Rose was sure Betty knew how cruel her son could be, she had seen the bruises on Rose's arms but never asked her about them and by the look she gave Rose, she knew not to mention anything. The one time she had tried to bring up the subject and talk to Betty she was told *"He is your husband and you must obey him, remember your vows Rose, for better or worse."* Rose never mentioned it again. Her ribs were still aching from the bashing he had given her two days ago. Her mind wandered back as she sat alone staring into the flames of the fire.

"Rose, come down to the shed now!" Jimmy yelled at her from the back yard. The children were doing their homework at the kitchen table when she heard him calling her, she knew what that meant and she felt a shiver go through her body. He would call her to the shed so he could bash and humiliate her, where no one could see his low act. Rose's stomach turned into a hard knot, if she didn't go he would come and hit her in front of the children and they had seen enough already. Fred looked up at his mother with pleading eyes.

"Don't go Mum."

She could see the sadness and despair in his eyes, he knew what his father was about to do to her and he couldn't do anything to help her. He was still young, only eleven, but he was starting to fill out into a big, strong, stocky boy and one day he would stop his father from hurting his mother. He promised himself that.

"I have to go Fred, you kids stay here, I'll be back in a minute." She touched him gently on the shoulder and smiled before going out the back door to the shed where she knew she would receive a flogging for something she had obviously done to upset Jimmy.

"Rose, get in here now!" She could tell by his voice that he was getting angrier by the minute. As she came through the door he threw a half empty bottle of beer at her head just missing her as it crashed and shattered up the wall. On the bench beside him were a dozen empty bottles. He had been drinking again, it was always worse when he was drunk, he always blew everything out of proportion. He grabbed her hair and pushed her up the wall, with his other hand around her throat squeezing tight, he forced her head up and back so that she was looking into his face, his jaw was clenched tightly his face was only inches from hers and she could smell the beer on his breath, his eyes were red and glassy, his voice was like an animal snarl, vibrating with fury.

"I thought I told you to never speak back to me in front of anyone, how dare you undermine me in front of the guys on the job site today. You think you're so good don't you? Just because you can drive a truck." He was spitting on her as he spoke, she knew not to say anything, it would only get worse if she tried to defend herself, it was better to shut up and take the inevitable bashing she was about to receive, she hoped it would be quick and brief.

"What? Nothing to say now you fucking, smart mouthed bitch, you had plenty to say today."

"I'm sorry Jimmy, I won't do it again."

"You're right you won't and here's something to remind you not to." With his free hand he hit her hard in the stomach as she fell to the ground winded, he kicked her three times in the side. A hot burning fire went through her rib cage, it felt like he had broken her ribs. He turned away and picked up another beer.

"You're a fucking slut like your mother, having that wog visit you when you were born. Now get inside and get my dinner on the table and make sure those bloody kids help too."

Rose picked herself up and scrambled out the door before he changed his mind and hit her again, at least this time it was quick not like other times where he'd continually bash her on and off for hours. He always made sure that he hit her where no one could see the bruises and she would always cover them up, she didn't want anyone to know her shame or embarrassment and besides he made it clear it was always her fault. What did he mean by his comment about her mother and the wog? Did he mean the Italian who had been on the farm in wartime?

"Are you alright love?" William was standing in front of her chair looking at her. "You looked so far away and you seemed so sad, is everything okay?"

"Yeah Dad, I'm okay, I think I need a cup of tea and some of Betty's yummy slice." Rose kissed his cheek and walked away.

William knew things were hard for her and he was sure his son was hitting her but he could do nothing to help her except be there if she needed him. He had tried to talk to Jimmy and told him to treat her right otherwise she would leave and take the children. Jimmy had told him to mind his own business, she was his wife and would do as she was told. William would need to keep an eye on Rose, he loved her like his own daughters he had to be careful with what he said, he didn't want to be the cause of anymore pain for Rose.

CHAPTER 15

APRIL 1973

Rose was sitting at the kitchen table writing a letter to Daniel, it seemed like there were never enough hours in the day anymore. All she seemed to do was work, clean and take care of everyone. The years were going by so fast and the children were growing so quickly. She had better hurry up and get this letter written before the kids got home from school.

30th April 1973

Dear Daniel,

Just a short note to let you know the news, hope you are well. Ruby had four days in hospital and she had complications with the mumps. She is okay now and back at school. Lilly also had the mumps and now Fred has them too, the swelling came up last night. It's been hot here lately, even at night. The new metal crusher should be working on Wednesday.

We worked all over Easter and only had Good Friday off. I took the kids to Port Macquarie on Easter Sunday to see the procession. The axle broke in the Commer truck last week, the tractor driver broke the top off the ram and Jimmy ran over his tool box, so it's been a bad week. Now the TV has gone on the blink, so I'm just off to town to try to get it fixed. Best go bye for now.

Love Rose

The school bus pulled up outside just as she had finished and sealed the envelope and Lilly came running through the door crying, dropping her school bag on the floor she flung herself at her mother.

"Oh darling what's wrong?" she held her in her arms while Lilly cried. "Tell me what's wrong?"

Lilly tried to tell her mother through her sobs "The kids are picking on me and calling me "hairy- anne" because my arms are so hairy. Mum, can I shave my arms please? They say I'm like a monkey." She burst into tears again.

How could children be so hurtful? Lilly was only nine and a pretty little girl, sure she was a bit of a tomboy, but that was no excuse for nasty things to be said.

"Listen to me honey, the only reason they tease you about your hairy arms is because you are so beautiful and talented and some people envy that, so they find something, anything they can to criticise and tease you about to make you feel bad and themselves feel better."

"I don't care, I want you to shave my arms Mum please." Lilly was begging her mother she hated the way that the kids teased her.

"No, I won't shave your arms. The hair will only grow back thicker and darker but what I will do is we'll get some bleach and lighten the hairs. Okay?"

Lilly thought for a moment and nodded.

"Did you know that they say that hairy arms are a sign of strength? They are jealous of you, I know it's hard but just ignore them if you can." Rose hugged her baby girl closer, a tear ran down her face. It hurt her to see her beautiful child so upset. "Now go and get changed, I'll finish writing this letter and we will go across and see Pa for a cup of tea."

Lilly hugged her mother and went to her room. Okay she thought if it meant strength the next time they picked on her she would show them how much strength she had in her little hairy monkey arms.

CHAPTER 16

Rose loved being able to give her children gifts at Christmas, she wished that they had more money so she could spoil them but she always made sure she gave them something they wished for. Ruby was so excited when she opened her recent Christmas gift - a guitar. Rose has been keeping it a secret for weeks and knowing how much Ruby loved to sing and perform she knew she would love to learn guitar. Ruby had asked to take ballet lessons in town but Jimmy had said no, it's too expensive and we don't have time to take you in and out of town to lessons. Ruby had been teaching herself to play guitar using a book and Jimmy had helped a little as he had played guitar when he was a kid.

Ruby preferred to help her mother around the house rather than work on the farm, she liked to keep things neat and tidy and hated the feeling of dirt on her hands but today Jimmy insisted she help him.

"But it's Saturday Dad, do I have to?"

"Yes you do, we all have to do farm chores Ruby, there are no days off on a farm girl, so come on." Jimmy put his old work boots on and headed for the tractor.

Well of course there was no choice, so Ruby went out to help Jimmy. Her job was to walk behind the hay mower which Jimmy pulled behind the tractor, each time the blades clogged she had to reach in and clear the built up grass. When she had taken her hands away from the blades Jimmy would be watching, he'd nod, turn back to the front of the tractor and start the blades. Ruby hated this job but like anything, if she was going to do it she would do it well. She had just pulled her hands out from the blades after clearing the grass, Jimmy turned back and started the mower at the exact moment Ruby noticed more grass clogging a blade and had reached in to clear it. She screamed an ear piercing scream, as the blade cut through three fingers on her left hand. Jimmy shut the engine off and jumped down.

"Oh my god, what have you done? Let's get you to your mother and to the hospital." Jimmy told Ruby to hold her hand up in the air while he drove them back to the house as quickly as the tractor would go, the blood was pouring down her arm, running all over her. Ruby was crying and scared, there was so much blood, did she still have her fingers?

Rose was beside herself with worry for her eldest, Ruby was pale, crying and terrified but somehow Rose managed to remain calm. She quickly tied a bandage firmly around Ruby's hand and they set off, Rose driving as fast as she could up the highway to the hospital, and Ruby holding her hand high above her heart to slow down the flow of blood. Ruby had lost the end of her little finger and badly damaged another two fingers. She needed surgery and a skin graft. The surgeon wanted to take skin from her bottom and use it to repair the end of the little finger but Ruby refused to let him take it from her bottom so instead they used the skin from inside her arm. She spent three days recovering in hospital. This of course meant that her guitar playing was now on hold, Ruby was very upset and Rose wondered if raising children and keeping them safe would ever get any easier. It seemed there was always something happening to test her.

APRIL 1974

It had been raining for three days non stop, there were two cyclones further up the coast at Murwillumbah which had caused major flooding and the Wilson River was now rising. Jimmy had taken Fred with him to work in town today and had told Rose to go to town and do the grocery shopping to stock up on extra food in case the river banks broke and the road went under, cutting them off. There were already parts of the road that were under a foot of water. The river was rising in the backyard getting closer to the house, theirs was the only home on the river side, most houses were built further away and had been built up high because of flooding in the area. Rose, Betty and the girls headed into Port Macquarie early, they were only gone for four hours and on returning they found the Pacific Highway cut off with the old bridge almost underwater.

Rose drove on the just completed new highway up to their gravel road which ran underneath the start of the new five hundred and fifty five metre long bridge which had not yet been opened to the traffic, barricades had been put in place to stop people using the new highway, it was still two weeks before the official opening. This new road and bridge had been built because the approach to the old Telegraph Point bridge was located on a corner with poor alignment and traffic congestion caused by the single-lane bridge was compounded by the need for traffic to queue on the northern side of the bridge to allow numerous trains to cross through the highway. While the old bridge itself was above flood level, the southern approach was subject to regular flooding and now it was under water and there was no way across. The rain had been torrential further up in the mountains and had come down in a rush, flooding the area. By building the new road higher with dirt and inadequate via ducts or drainage for the water to flow through, it had changed the way the water flowed in the area and made the flat area of land more prone to flooding. Before the road was built, the water would flow down the Wilson River into the Maria River and out to the sea and the road would stay open, but now the water banked up and flooded the plains, cutting the roads off. The local radio station had been saying the road was open but clearly as far as you could see there was water.

Mr Cutler was standing beside his truck arguing with one of the road workers fixing the barricades in place, he needed to get across to the other side to rescue his cattle from the rising flood waters but his way was barred by the road worker.

"I'm sorry but you can't drive across the bridge." The road worker in his bright yellow vest was trying his best to calm the crowd.

"Why the bloody hell not? It's finished isn't it?" Mr Cutler was losing his patience.

"Yes, but it hasn't been officially opened so I have orders no-one is to use it until then." He was getting frustrated, he also thought it was stupid as these were extreme circumstances but he was doing his job.

"You can tell your bloody officials to get stuffed, get out of my way mate because opened or not I'm going through. I have cattle to save." Mr Cutler jumped back in his truck and revved the engine. "Move those barricades or I'll drive over the top of them."

The worker realised it was no good arguing, the barricades were moved aside to allow the truck and other cars to make their way to their homes.

"Mum, what about our cows?' Lilly was looking up at her mother with a worried look. "What about Ice-cream he can't swim." Her eyes filled with tears.

"It's okay honey I'll go check on them, but first I will take you back up to Uncle Charlie's and you can stay there while I go home and check on the animals." Rose drove the mile back to the service station and called the radio station to tell them the highway was closed before leaving the girls and Betty safely with her Uncle.

"Betty, you stay with the children, I'll go back and check on the animals and William."

"No love, it's too deep and dangerous and you can't swim, just wait for Jimmy to get here he said he wouldn't be long." Betty was concerned for her daughter in law; she was strong and feisty and she knew she wouldn't listen to her.

"I can't, I need to get home and check the pigs and the dogs, I left the dogs tied up by the house. I will be fine." Rose bent down to Ruby and held her arms. "Look after your little sister, I won't be long." She kissed the girl's head and headed back towards the flooding river.

As she clambered down the embankment into the cold, rushing water she wondered what the hell she was doing, she still had not learned to swim and could only dog paddle. The water was up to her waist and she could only just see the tops of the fence posts that ran parallel with the road, she would need to keep them in sight to follow the road. She pushed forward making slow progress along the gravel road now underwater, tripping every now and then in a pot hole in the road. The water was flowing so strongly in areas it was washing the gravel away. In front of her she spotted a red fox swimming through the water looking for higher ground, sticks, logs and other debris floated past her, pushed down from upstream. Suddenly a gush of water running off from a drain caught her off guard and the rocks hitting her feet almost knocked her over. The water was dirty and frothy and a snake glided past her on top of the water paying her no attention, just looking for a safe place out of the flood waters. As she passed by the paddocks of their neighbouring farms she could see the cows up on earth mounds, out of the water. Farmers on tractors trying to move as much as they could before the water rose any higher.

It took Rose almost two hours to walk the two miles home through the flooding waters. William was at the dairy herding the milking cows into the yards. The dairy had been built up on the highest part of the farm for that reason. It was still drizzling rain but there was a break appearing in the clouds. Hopefully it will stop soon she thought.

William yelled out to her "I've got the cattle love and the pigs are okay I haven't had a chance to check on the dogs though."

Rose waded through the paddock that was now a lake to their house, the water was lapping at the verandah but luckily was not inside the house yet. The dogs were cringing in their kennels, wet and afraid. She unhooked the leads and let them off, they bounded happily up onto the verandah jumping on the old lounge that sat at the front. Rose quickly moved any belongings she could inside the house up onto tables and cupboard tops, she grabbed a change of clothes for herself and the girls put them in a bag to carry back through the flood waters. As she looked around her eyes fell on the door frame, it had notches carved into it from previous floods. One was four feet up the frame, she hoped that it would not reach that level, they would lose everything if it did. She could do no more but hope that the water would start going down, and soon.

She fed the dogs and left them on the verandah cuddled up on the old lounge. They would be safe there until Jimmy got back with Fred. He would stay here at the farm while she, Betty and the girls would stay with Uncle Charlie for the night and hopefully they could come back tomorrow. She stepped off the verandah back into the cold water, shivering from the cold. It was no good trying to dry off because the water was too deep, she held the bag above her head and started the long walk back. The rain had finally stopped and the clouds were dispersing at least that was a promising sign. She had almost made it back to the bridge when she saw the backhoe coming through the water with Jimmy and Fred inside, he shouted out to her as he drove past that he would drive up tomorrow to let her know if her and the girls could get through back to the house.

The river went down as quickly as it had come up and by late afternoon the next day they were able to drive back to the house to start the clean up. Mr Cutler was the talk of the town for weeks, on how he had defied the order not to cross the bridge, he had become the local hero and in years to come whenever there was a flood someone would retell the story.

It took days to clear the mess and debris left by the flood. Lilly, Fred and Mitch had fun out in the flooded paddock in an old forty-four gallon drum that had been cut in half lengthways and now had become a makeshift boat for Lilly to be pushed around in.

She squealed with delight as Mitch would push and rock the drum pretending he was going to tip her out. Ruby helped her mother tidying the house, she didn't like getting in the dirty flood water. As the water subsided from the paddocks, the stench of drying mud was everywhere.

Everything was back to normal within the week and Lilly and Fred were helping their father at the dairy with the milking. They were responsible for mixing the molasses and the chaff together to feed the "poddy" calves that had been weaned from their mothers. Lilly loved the taste of the molasses with its thick black, gooey, sweet tasting liquid she would feed some to the calves and some to herself. Fred would shake his head and laugh at her.

"You'll turn into a cow if you keep eating that stuff."

"No I won't, don't be silly Fred." She laughed at the thought, she adored her big brother and she felt more comfortable in shorts and shirts getting dirty with him on the farm than in a dress. One day when her father was yelling at her, he had told her he wanted another boy not a girl, so she tried hard to get his approval by doing what a boy would do and she was turning into a tomboy to please her father. Lilly had left the gate open to the calf pen and two of the calves made a run for their mothers.

"Quick Lilly we need to get them back before they have a chance to suck on their mother's milk, Dad will be furious." Fred took off after the calves just as Jimmy came out of the dairy.

"Bloody hell, you stupid bloody kids can't you do anything right? Do I have to do everything myself?"

Fred had managed to get the calves back in the yard with Lilly's help but they knew they would cop it now. Jimmy had gone back to the dairy returning with the short whip in his hand.

"It's my fault Dad, not Fred's, I left the gate open. Don't punish him, just me, please Dad." Lilly begged her father.

"You'll both get it and maybe next time you'll take better care. You need to learn, now turn around!" Jimmy was stroking the whip in his hand.

Fred took Lilly's hand. "It's okay sis, don't let him see you cry, that's what he wants."

The crack of the whip sounded sharp in the air as it came down, the first one across their backs, Lilly let out a squeal and Fred gripped her hand tighter, then two more cracks to the legs. Fred bit his lip, he would not let his father see him cry. Men that cry are weak, they are sissy girls, that's what his father had told him. Lilly stood beside him trying not to cry but a whimper escaped her lips.

"Now get home and wash up for dinner and tell your mother I'll be down soon and I want dinner on the table when I get there." He turned and walked back into the dairy muttering to himself "fucking, useless kids."

After dinner Fred looked for Lilly to see if she was okay, she was nowhere in the house, he walked out the front and could see her coming back from the dairy, she was skipping and had a big smile on her face.

"Where have you been?"

Lilly giggled. "Dad won't be able to hit us with the whip again, I threw it down the well." She stood there triumphantly with her hands on her hips.

Fred looked at his little sister, she was a gutsy one that was for sure. He hugged her tight. "Come on we have to go have a shower and get to bed, we have school tomorrow and it would be best not to tell anyone about throwing the whip into the well either, okay?"

Lilly nodded and made her way up the stairs into the house. Fred watched her, one day when he was big enough he would stand up to his father and stop him from hitting and hurting his mother and sisters. He was only eleven but in just a few more years when he was bigger and stronger. Fred promised himself he would never be anything like his abusive father.

CHAPTER 17

WEE WAA
JULY 1975

It was school holidays and they were heading off to a cattle & sheep station between Burren Junction and Wee Waa. The town was known to be the "Cotton Capital of Australia" a rural community situated in the rich agricultural heartland of the Lower Namoi Valley located on the north-western slopes of the New England region in New South Wales. They came out here to go pig shooting on one of the large properties owned by an old friend of Jimmy's. They had two cars this trip, Rose drove the old Holden with the children and full of supplies and clothing to last a week while Jimmy drove an old Holden station wagon with the two bull terriers "pig" dogs in the back, which had been modified to hold the pigs once they had caught them. They would spend a week out here, wild pigs destroyed the crops and deprived the farm animals of food and Jimmy could earn good money shooting them. Jimmy had promised the kids that if he made enough money this trip he would treat them to a new colour TV but everyone had to pitch in and help.

It was late afternoon when they arrived at the shearer's quarters where they would be staying and the children were all restless after the long drive over the mountain through the changing landscape, to the station. They started to collect firewood while Rose cleaned and began to prepare their dinner on the old combustion stove.

"Don't forget to wear shoes, those "cats head" burrs will stick in your feet and they hurt and watch out for snakes." She yelled out through the battered old screen door. It was hot and sticky and the flies were swarming around in their hundreds, it was a constant battle to keep them away from the food and your face.

"Yes Mum, we will." Fred shouted back.

Jimmy had been in a good mood all the way across to Burren Junction, he loved shooting and he loved to show off to Rose how good he was with one of his many rifles. She wondered if it was because he kept threatening that if she ever left him he would hunt her down like a pig and shoot her and the kids. She never wanted to test him to find out, she believed he would do it, that terrified her and was the main reason she stayed with him, as well as she had no money of her own to support her and three children.

Everyone was tired after the twelve hour drive which meant it was an early night so they could go out scouting early in the morning for pig tracks.

The next morning just after sunrise, they headed out in the old modified station wagon. Jimmy had pulled the back seats out of the wagon and put a floor all the way through with a wire grill behind the seats and another grill across the back with a gate in it. Once they caught the pigs they would be locked in the back. The tailgate was left down for the three children and the dogs to stand on as they drove around the station.

Lilly in the middle and Fred and Ruby on the sides hanging onto an old rope that had been strung across the top with one hand and the collar of a pig dog in the other hand. They had to have their wits about them because sometimes when going at speed, if they hit a large bump the tailgate would go up in the air and they had to keep it from jumping up otherwise there would be nothing to land on and they would fall off the back onto the hard ground. Rose sat in the front beside Jimmy with a video camera so she could film the pig chase, Jimmy wanted it caught on camera.

"There's some over there, quick start filming Rose." Jimmy swerved the car to the right sharply. "Hang on kids, don't let the dogs go until I tell you." He yelled.

Rose heaved herself out through the open window sitting on the edge of the window, filming with one hand while trying to hang on with the other. The pigs were quick and darted this way and that through the bushes, then turned crossing back across in front of them, there was no real track so they were bashing through the scrub. Jimmy kept close behind them and followed them through the undergrowth clipping a dead tree which burst into shreds showering bark and leaves all over Rose.

"Be careful Jimmy" she shouted "that nearly hit me."

Jimmy wasn't listening; he was too intent on chasing the pigs. "Fred! Let Tiger go."

Fred released the bull terrier dog "Tiger" and he flew off the back of the car after the pigs heading for the big boar. Tiger was fast and focused on getting that pig, he brought his jaw closed around the pig's ear, bit down hard and pulled the pig down to the ground with a thud. Jimmy was out of the car and was shooting at the others as they ran away, he managed to shoot two dead. He turned back to where the old bull terrier was holding his own against the big boar. Jimmy put his foot on the pig's neck to hold him still before shooting him between the eyes. The crack of the rifle made the dog let go and he moved away limping.

"Dad, Tiger's hurt, he's bleeding." Fred was holding the poor dog in his arms, the bore had ripped through his leg with his tusk leaving a gaping wound.

"Come here old boy." Jimmy knelt beside his dog to have a closer look. "It's not too deep, he's a lucky dog, grab the rag out of the car Ruby, I'll bandage him up now and when we get back I'll stitch him up, he'll be fine."

They put the three dead pigs in the back of the car and drove back towards the quarters. Jimmy needed to get the pigs into the cool room to keep them fresh. He would go out and catch more later. He preferred to catch them alive and take them home where he could sell them alive or slaughter them and sell the meat to make extra money. The boss of the farm paid him for every pig he caught or killed and would give him extra if he gutted and butchered the meat up for him to give to his farm hands.

As a treat that night they headed for the town of Burren Junction, a small rural town on the Kamilaroi Highway to have tea at the old pub, finishing off at the bore baths for a swim before returning back to camp. The water bubbled up to the surface at the Burren Junction Bore Baths from the Great Artesian basin bore, it then ran into a series of bore drains then into a pool for swimming while other drains distributed the water around the district for various agricultural and domestic uses. The water was a constant temperature of around forty-one degrees and reputedly offered therapeutic qualities that relieved aching muscles. There were lights surrounding the baths, old drop toilets and a change room. It was a popular meeting place for locals and visitors. There was always a film of green soft moss on the sides of the concrete swimming tank and the bottom was sandy. After a swim and chat with the locals they headed back across the paddock to their quarters.

They got up early to see if they could spot any pigs coming out at sunrise, but it had been a few hours before coming across a sow with six black piglets.

"Fred, Lilly jump off and chase those piglets, Ruby, you hang onto the dogs and stay on the back." Jimmy went after the sow.

Lilly and Fred jumped off the back of the tailgate and ran after the piglets. Fred had caught two and was struggling to hold onto the squirming little things. Lilly was having trouble catching hers. It was quick and darted quickly away every time that she got it cornered. This time she was sure she would get it. She moved slowly towards the little pig as it tried to make a dash for freedom, she jumped and took a dive and managed to grab its legs.

"I got one! Fred, I got one!" The little pig wiggled and squealed in her arms fighting to get free.

"Hang onto it tight then." Fred called back to her laughing.

"Oh look, she's got a funny foot that's why she wasn't as quick as the other ones."

The car came back through the scrub towards them with the dead sow hanging across the top. "Good job kids, you can look after these ones until we get them home so we can fatten them up and kill them."

Lilly's eyes filled with tears "But Dad, they are so little and cute, can't I keep this one for a pet? Please. Oh Please Dad, I could call her Penny. I'll look after it."

Jimmy looked at his youngest daughter standing before him, her hair was all messy with dirt and leaves in it, a scrape on her knee with blood trickling down her leg and tears in her eyes, how could he say no, she had been brave enough to jump off and chase the pig.

"Okay Lilly, but you have to be responsible for it, you will have to feed it and take care of it."

"I will, I promise, thanks Dad." Lilly looked down at her little pig. She had a pet of her own now. "Come on Penny, you can come home with me."

By the end of the week Jimmy had killed thirty four pigs and had five to take home plus the three piglets.

"Okay kids, I've done alright on this trip and the boss has paid well so we will be getting that new colour TV. Come on, let's get home."

It had been two months since they had returned home from the pig shooting out west and today Jimmy was killing the pigs they had brought back with them. The hot water was boiling in the cut in half forty-four gallon drum and was hot enough now to throw the pigs in one by one. Jimmy would lift the pigs in and submerge them for a short time then lift them out onto hessian bags on the ground beside the drum. All three children lined up side by side on their knees bent over the carcass and had to pull all the hair out of the pigs' skin with their bare hands. The water was boiling hot and so was the pigs' skin, their hands burned but they had to keep going until the pigs were cleaned of all hair. Everyone had to help on the farm, it was a part of life to learn about raising and killing animals for food. Once the pig was cleaned of all hair, it was strung up to the rafters in the dairy where Jimmy would behead it and gut it. The kids would have to watch, they hated it, the smell was horrible and Ruby wanted to throw up. The intestines would fall into a bucket under the pig's upside down gutted body, then they had to drag the bucket over to the river and throw them in. They decided they could use the guts as burly to catch eels. The pigs were then hung up by their feet to drain overnight from the rafters in the girls' bedroom, this would allow the meat to soften before being cut up.

Lilly lay in her bed unable to sleep, she slept on the bottom of the bunk bed while Ruby slept on the top. Thud, thud, thud, silence, thud, thud, thud the sound made Lilly uneasy, the sound of the blood dripping from the dead pigs. She could see the shapes hanging there from the moonlight coming in through the window. Thud, splat, thud, splat, the blood dropped onto the newspaper covering the vinyl floor underneath the pigs' bodies. Lilly squirmed in her bed, pulling the pillow over her head trying to drown out the noise.

"Lilly? Lilly, are you asleep?" Ruby whispered down to her from the top bunk.

"No I can't sleep, not with that noise, it scares me."

"Me too, and I can't stand the smell of the blood, come up here with me, we can cuddle under the blankets until we go to sleep."

Lilly clambered up the ladder, careful not to touch the dead pigs hanging close to the bed. She scrambled under the covers with her sister pulling them over their heads to muffle the noise. Their mother had asked Jimmy not to put the pigs in their room, they were young girls, it would give them nightmares.

"Shut up woman, it's the only place to hang them where the dogs won't get to them, and besides it's right next to the kitchen so it's easier for me to cut them up in the morning before I go to work," he gave her a dark, threatening look, she knew not to push it. Her poor girls, Rose hoped they'd be ok. It was just part of their life and everyone knew to get up and have an early breakfast, the day after the pigs were killed because Jimmy used the small kitchen and the kitchen table to cut them up and pack the meat for freezing or selling. One consolation though, they would be getting a colour TV next week.

OCTOBER 1975

Jimmy and Fred were out in the front yard sparring, waiting for Rose to get home with the new colour TV. Jimmy was a great fighter in the boxing ring and had won many boxing matches professionally, he'd been teaching Fred to box. He had fitted the boxing gloves tightly to Fred and explained that a great fighter was strong, quick, skillful and had to be in top condition. The gloves would protect his hands and would help soften the blow.

"Now a basic stance helps you move quickly and effortlessly, keep your left side towards me, stand with your feet about shoulder width apart, hold your left fist a bit in front of the left shoulder and your right fist just to the right of your chin, tuck in your elbows close to your body to protect your ribs like this." Jimmy assumed the position.

They circled around each other, Jimmy pretending to throw a punch, Fred moving back, dropping his hands, he didn't want to fight, especially his father, he knew he would end up on the wrong side of it.

"Come on boy, keep your hands up like this, you need to protect that pretty face of yours." Jimmy had his hands in the position showing Fred how to jab, duck and weave out of the way. He threw a punch which clipped Fred on the ear pushing him backwards. "Come on boy what are you a girl? Have a go, try to hit me."

"I don't want to hit you Dad."

"I said hit me, if you think you can. I'll give you a free shot, come on ya bloody sissy." Jimmy was taunting him now.

Fred shaped up and moved towards his father, he knew he had to have a good go at his father otherwise he would keep pushing him. He moved closer getting ready to have a throw but before he could do a thing his father let go with a combination of lightning fast punches in a row, left, right, left, hitting him in the face and chest knocking him to the ground, winded.

Jimmy stood over him laughing, "Bloody useless, you'll get your head punched in every time if you don't learn to fight dirty." He turned and walked away leaving Fred upset and bleeding from a cut above his eye.

Rose pulled into the driveway just as Jimmy walked away from Fred on the ground, she knew what he had been doing and she knew not to interfere, she didn't agree with teaching violence to the children but if she spoke up she would feel his fist again, he liked using her as his punching bag. Fred looked up at his mother and smiled and nodded that he was okay.

They took the new TV inside and placed it on the cabinet, Jimmy hooked up the wires and antenna while Rose cleaned up the cut over Fred's eye. The children were excited, they would finally have a colour TV to watch. They jostled for places closest to the screen. Of course Jimmy would decide what they would be watching. It was the October long weekend, the fifth of October and the Hardie-Ferodo 1000 was on, it was the sixteenth running of the Bathurst 1000 touring car race. It was an endurance race for touring cars and was held at Mount Panorama just outside

Bathurst in New South Wales. The cars would race one hundred and sixty three laps a distance of over one thousand kilometres. All day they sat memorised to the colour TV watching the cars go round and round the track, until the race was finally won by Peter Brock and Brian Sampson. It was Brock's second win driving his Holden LH Torana, they won by two laps. Brock had lost the previous year when the engine failed on the one hundred and eighteenth lap. Holden took out the top three spots on the podium.

It was the only time in her life Rose would ever watch the race, she found it boring, but the novelty of having a colour TV was too much to miss.

CHAPTER 18

WILSON RIVER 1976

They now had two old motorbikes to use on the farm, they had bought them cheap from the neighbours. Fred was a natural on the bike using it instead of the horse to bring the cows in for milking from the back paddock. He would do wheelies up and down the road and go flying high over the jumps. Lilly also had learnt to ride with Fred's expert guidance, she would just putter around the paddock with Penny the pig trotting along close behind her, that silly pig thought it was a dog, it had been raised with the farm dogs, it slept and ate with them and would also try to help bring the cows in to the milking yard with the dogs. Penny had grown to be huge; she came up to Rose's thigh and would wander into the kitchen with the dogs, leaving little room to move in the small kitchen.

Ruby wasn't interested in riding the bikes, she preferred to ride Flash or Tony their farm horses or put on her record player and sing along, practising harmonies. Rose watched them from the front verandah, riding around and around the paddock. It looked like fun, maybe she should have a go herself, surely it couldn't be that hard, she could drive a tip truck so this should be easy.

"Fred! Fred! Come over here" she beckoned for him to come to her.

"What's up Mum?" Fred pulled the bike up beside his mother.

"I want you to show me how to ride the bike. I want to have a go."

Fred burst out laughing "Really Mum you want to ride the bike? Will your legs even touch the ground?"

"Very funny son, now show me what to do."

Fred put the bike into neutral, put down the side guard to stabilise it and hopped off and left it running.

"Ok, stand on the left side, grab the handlebar and swing your right leg over the seat and make sure your feet are firmly on the ground. That's good, you can touch the ground" he laughed as his mother took a playful swat at him. "Now the lever here on the left is the clutch just like in a car you need to pull it in to change the gear, that pedal there beside your left foot that's the gears, it's down for first up to neutral then up for second, third, fourth. This one on your right is your throttle it's for acceleration and the lever in front of it is the handbrake for the front wheel." He pointed to the peddle beside her right foot "and that lever there beside your foot is the rear brake."

Rose was wondering whether this was a good idea, it all seemed a bit over her head there were so many things to remember. Fred was excited now, he was chuffed that his Mum wanted him to show her how to ride the bike.

"You can start by just going slow in first gear till you get the knack of it, pull the clutch lever in and push down on the gear lever that will put you in first gear, just remember it's one down and five up for the gears and when you let the clutch out do it slowly so the bike starts to roll forward without jerking, if you let it out too fast it will jump forward and just turn the throttle a little to keep you moving along smoothly. If you want to stop, pull the clutch in and brake and remember to put your feet down to hold the bike up."

"Oh this sounds way too complicated Fred."

"You'll be fine Mum, just do it slowly and I'll run beside you until you get the feel."

Rose let the throttle out slowly and the bike moved forward, she put her feet up on the foot rests and Fred ran beside her encouraging her. She managed to ride around the paddock without falling off and even changed gears. Fred stood back and watched his mother riding in circles.

"That's great Mum see I told you you could do it." Fred yelled after her.

Rose was laughing and enjoying the feel of the breeze in her hair, she could do this, she would go a bit faster now, she flicked the lever up one more notch and turned the accelerator hard. The bike took off faster than she expected and she was heading for the barbed wire fence, oh god which one was the brake she was flustered and revved the motor instead.

"Fred, which one is the brake? Freeeeddddd!"

The bike hurtled into the fence and stalled to a halt hanging up on the fence with Rose laying flat on her back underneath it, winded. Fred and Lilly came running.

"Mum are you alright?" Fred and Lilly were beside her, she looked up at their worried faces and burst out laughing, they looked at each other and burst into giggles.

"Well I don't think I'll try that in a hurry again. I'll stick to the horse I think."

Rose had cleaned herself up, luckily she only had a bruised ego and nothing else from her fall from the bike. Jimmy was taking her out tonight for dinner and dancing, it was a treat, they rarely went out together, they were going to meet friends at the Bowling Club in town. She hoped he wouldn't drink too much and end up causing a fight, for once she would like to go out and have a nice time without arguments. They met Terry and Karen at the club and enjoyed a great evening of gossip and dancing. Jimmy was a good dancer and she loved it when he whirled her around the dance floor, they didn't get to dance much anymore, they worked such long hours. Everything was going well until another guy came over and asked Rose to dance, she declined she knew better than to antagonise Jimmy. She could see by the look on his face that he was not impressed and he would more than likely berate her over it even though she had declined the offer to dance. They said their goodbyes to their friends and headed for home. Jimmy was silent most of the way and she could tell by the tightness in his body that he was angry.

"Who was that guy that asked you to dance?" His question came from between clenched teeth.

"I don't know, I've never seen him before."

"Are you sure of that? He looked like he knew you."

"I don't know him Jimmy, I didn't accept anyway so why are you angry?"

"You're mine, and no one else will dance with you or touch you! Understand?" Jimmy's voice was raised and his mouth was in a tight smile.

"Oh for god sake Jimmy you're being a bit dramatic aren't you? Why can't I dance with someone else? It's only a bloody dance."

Rose was sick of his possessive, jealous side. He didn't trust her even though she had never given him reason not to. She knew he'd had an affair, she had found a pair of women's underpants in his car after he hadn't come home one night, and when he did turn up the next morning he smelt of perfume and there was lipstick on his shirt. Rose didn't bother to ask him about it, she knew it would only mean denial and a fight and it would all be her fault anyway. She hoped that maybe he would run away with someone else so she could be free from this nightmare.

Jimmy bought the car to a stop in the front driveway and reached across to grab Rose but she was too quick and was halfway out the door, he flung his door open and raced around the side, knocking her down with a blow to the back of her head, he pinned her down on the front lawn and grabbed her by the throat squeezing tightly.

"Don't fucking back-answer me you bitch, when will you ever learn to keep your mouth shut? Maybe I'll keep it shut for you permanently."

He tightened his fingers around her throat, cutting off the air supply, Rose tried to pry his fingers away, clawing at him, his grip was too strong, his eyes burned with emptiness and anger and her lungs had started to burn with pain, her eyes were bulging, she could feel everything becoming hazy as she was slowly losing consciousness. This was it, he was going to kill her here on the front lawn of their home, oh, her poor children. Suddenly he released his grip from her throat and as if some demon had taken over his mind he lashed at her with open fists hitting her in the face three times before standing up towering over her, he gave her a kick for good measure.

"Don't think you're getting away from me that easy, you slut." He snarled at her, got back in the car and drove away leaving her laying there breathless and crying.

The next day Rose drove into town taking Lilly with her, she pulled up outside the store and gave Lilly some money. The bruise spread across her face, her cheekbone puffed up until it was tight and shiny and the swelling pushed her right eye half closed, Rose had tried as best she could to cover it with makeup.

"Go in and buy me the biggest pair of sunglasses you can find, I need to cover up my eyes, I can't let anyone see the bruises." Rose had a scarf around her head and pulled it around as much as she could to hide the marks on her face.

"Mum, why do you let Dad do this to you? Can't we just leave?" Lilly had tears streaming down her face, she hated her father, how could he do this to her Mum.

Rose took her daughter's hand. "Honey I wish it was that simple but it's not. Your father would come after us and that would only make it worse, besides where would we go and how would we be able to afford to pay for anything? Now go grab me those glasses so we can go shopping."

Lilly knew how violent her father could be, they all knew. It hurt her children to see what he did to her but they felt as helpless as Rose did. Once when he was hitting Rose in the lounge room Ruby ran into the room and jumped in between Rose and Jimmy crying "stop hitting Mum" Jimmy in his rage picked Ruby up by the shoulders and threw her across the room. Rose yelled to Ruby to go to her bedroom, trying to keep her out of harm's way, Ruby was scared and hurried away but she could still hear him hitting her mother through the thin walls. Ruby lay on her bed crying at the sound of her mother being hit, she felt so helpless. She loved her father but hated him as well, how could he be so violent? More than once she had lay in bed and imagined ways to get rid of him, like they did in the crime novels she loved to read, maybe poison?

The next day she asked her mother "why do you put up with it Mum? Why don't we just run away, leave him?"

Rose sadly replied. "I couldn't support us on my own, and besides I feel safer knowing where he is than spending my life looking over my shoulder." Ruby understood, but was so sad for her mother.

Jimmy kept his rifles and revolvers in the house, he had his revolver beside his armchair at all times and when they watched TV, the field mice often came in through the gap under the front door and as they would scurry across the floor in the lounge room Jimmy would grab his gun and shoot them leaving a hole in the floor or wall.

Rose asked him to stop shooting in the house but he ignored her, he thought it was fun besides he liked to frighten the children. Lilly knew her mother was right, if she ever did try to leave him, he would come and find them and god knows what he would do to her when he did.

16th December 1976

Dear Daniel,

I received your letter Monday and I am pleased to hear you are well. I'm well now but still a bit sore in the tummy after my operation, I need to rest up for another week. We had a few windy days this week but it's still hot and we had a hailstorm at home on Sunday, the hail stones were as big as marbles, the kids ran around collecting them. The kids finish school today for the holidays. Ruby has a job over the holidays, she is working at Woolworths in the Port Plaza. I don't know what we are doing for Christmas but it seems we will be working all the time. I don't know when I'll get up to see you as I never seem to find time to do anything lately.

Thank you for the cheque for our Christmas presents. I got Jimmy a shirt, Lilly got new coloured pencils, I got a wooden salad bowl, Fred got a shirt and Ruby hasn't spent hers yet. The new Coles is a big shop and on opening day there were cars and people everywhere. At ten thirty there were three thousand people in the shop and they closed the doors and were only letting two in at a time. All those other shops next to the RSL that we were working on are finished and open too.

Well I'd best go as I have to get the accounts out this week.

Love Rose

CHAPTER 19

TELEGRAPH POINT
JULY 1977

Fred hated going to school, he was bored and didn't like all the work they gave him. He would rather be out driving the backhoe with his father or working on the farm. He didn't want to be a teacher or a doctor; he enjoyed manual labour and wanted to get his hands dirty. He had been summoned to the deputy principal's office and was now standing outside the office waiting. The door opened and he was asked to come in and sit down.

"Fred, I have been told by your teacher that you are not paying attention in class, you've been disruptive to the other students and your grades are slipping. What do you have to say for yourself?" Mr Graham looked at him over his glasses.

"School is stupid, I don't want to be here." Fred mumbled back at him.

"School is an important part of your life Fred, how do you expect to get anywhere in life if you don't work hard?" His tone was condescending and his brow was furrowed with disgust. "School is not stupid and do not say that again, have some respect for the teachers who are trying to teach you."

"I will work hard but I want to be out working now, I have no interest in history or geography. I don't want to work in an office or be stuck inside."

"Well that's not possible, you are fourteen and still have two more years of school, so I suggest you knuckle down and make the best of it. Now go back to class." He dismissed him with a wave of his hand and went back to the papers on his desk.

Fred raised himself from the chair and walked towards the door, two more years of school like hell, he thought school was stupid, he would talk to his parents tonight about leaving. Neither of them had completed school and they were doing just fine.

"I tell you Mum I'm going to punch that bloody Mr Graham if he gives me another lecture, he is so high and mighty, why can't he understand that I don't want to be at school? I want to get out and work now." Fred was frustrated with the situation.

"Fred, you need an education. It will help you get a good job when you leave school." Rose had heard this protest from Fred many times over the last month.

"Well you and Dad didn't finish school, so why do I have to?"

"That was different Fred, your father had no choice he had to help on the farm that's why he left early and as for me, well I had your sister Ruby to look after so I had to leave. I wanted to stay at school but I didn't have a choice, you do! Just give it a chance please?"

Fred didn't want to disappoint his mother but he hated school. "I'll try but if he calls me back to the office again I'm gonna give him one just like Dad taught me."

Rose shook her head. "Violence is not the answer Fred and you know that, now go do your chores."

Jimmy's earthmoving business was doing well and he had a big shed in town now for his equipment and an office where Rose did the book work, answered the phone, paid bills and booked in the jobs. Rose was busy doing the accounts when just after one o'clock the phone rang.

"Hello, Rose speaking."

"Hello Rose, this is Port Macquarie High School, we need you to come to the high school immediately, there's been an incident."

Oh my god! Rose thought Fred had gone and punched the deputy principal, that's all she needed. "What! What happened?"

"Your daughter Lilly has fallen over at PE and we think she has broken her arm, you need to come and get her and take her to the doctor."

"Oh thank god, is that all? I thought it was something worse." Rose was relieved a broken bone would mend.

"Um, excuse me? We think that a broken arm is quite serious." The voice on the line sounded reproachful.

"Oh yes it is, sorry it is bad, I'll be there right away." Rose hung up the phone, relief washing over her. She would talk to Jimmy tonight about Fred leaving school, she couldn't risk him doing something he would regret the rest of his life and if he wasn't happy at school he wouldn't try. Rose grabbed her bag, locked the office door and headed to get her baby girl from school.

Rose had not written to her father for over a month, it seemed she was always so busy. Also the fact she had been unable to use her right hand for the last two weeks, the cut on her hand from where Jimmy, in one of his rages had sliced her with his pocket knife was still healing. She was lucky that's all she had, he was actually trying to slash her throat, it was only her quick thinking in putting her hand up to her throat to protect herself that the knife had sliced her hand open. She had to get four stitches and once again lied about how it had happened, she had told the doctor that she had sliced it on a bit of thin steel on the truck.

She was never sure what to write to Daniel, it was more out of a sense of duty than love that she wrote to him and stayed in contact. As far as she was concerned Martin was her father, he was the one that had raised her as his own. She had a few moments free before heading to work, she made herself sit at the kitchen table and pull out the floral writing paper with its pretty little roses in the corner that Daniel had given her for her birthday. She stared off into space tapping the pen on the table, where do I start and what do I say?

10th August 1977

Dear Daniel,

It has been ages since I have heard from you and as I have a few spare minutes, I thought I would write. We have been flat out. I have been in the truck full time, we are carting gravel straight from the river to the D.M.R at Cooperabung mountain. Hope this finds you well as we are all well here. Lilly fell at school last month and broke her left arm. She only had it in plaster for two weeks but still has a bandage around it.

It has been cold at night the last few weeks and we have had some big frosts. It killed some of my plants near the tank stand and the banana trees look sick. My rock lily and bush orchids all have buds on them. I have a few daffodils out and have pansy and poppy plants in. Fred won the prize for the best and fairest player in football at school.

We are selling our business here, a bloke is supposed to take over at the end of the month. We are trying to get money to buy a wheat growing place halfway between Manilla and Barraba, fifty two miles from Tamworth. It is two thousand three hundred acres. We have a new car, a Ford Falcon, it is yellow with a bone vinyl roof. The Fairlane broke down, a lug end bearing came off and ruined the motor. It would cost twelve hundred dollars to do it up but they traded it in as it was.

I am going to Sydney on the twenty-first of this month. I'm taking Ruby down to a beauticians course, we will be there for a week and are going down on the bus. Did you hear that Dennis Campling died on the twenty-eighth of July? He had a heart attack and was only forty six. The kids and Julie all took it hard and it was a big funeral.

We sold six head of cattle yesterday. The prices are up to what they were. We have sold all the pigs too. Ruby started her exams for her school certificate. She is going to Maclean rowing in a regatta in three weeks. Her team won a medal at the regatta in Port Macquarie in June. There is another regatta here in October.

The place we are trying to buy out west has a nice big house with four bedrooms and a gauzed verandah and a big yard and garden.

Hope we get it as it's a nice place. Our bull is big now and the three of the stud cows should calve any day now. The kids have two budgies, a green one and a blue one.

Well I will have to go now as I have to go to work and drive the truck.

Bye for now love from Rose xxx

NOVEMBER 1977

Lilly sat in the mulberry tree where the lower branches forked, there were hollows here, she could sit in with her back supported and her legs wrapped around the branch. She was always happy here, dreaming of something or someone, often humming or singing a vague tune that came into her head. The old tree had a gnarly old trunk and she loved its glossy, heart-shaped leaves and pendulous branches that spread out wide offering shade on a hot day. The foliage was thick and dense and great for feeding her silkworms. The fruit had started forming now, starting with green flowers and developing into red fruit that would turn purple and black ripe for the picking. They were juicy and sweet and would leave a stain if the juice fell on your clothes. Sometimes her siblings and cousins would have mulberry fights and end up with stains all over them, much to the disdain of their parents.

It was one of her favourite places to be alone but it also made her sad because underneath the tree her old horse Tony had been buried. He was a beautiful horse, Pa had given him to her and he stood sixteen hands tall, had a dark brown coat with a white star on his forehead. Tony had been a gentle horse she could climb all over him and he never once tried to buck her off. He was already old when she got him and well trained, whenever she had to bring the cows in from the back paddock she would nudge him forward in the direction and then go along for the ride he knew what he had to do. But sadly he had gotten old and sick and she had come home from school one afternoon and he had fallen into the drain and unable to get out he had drowned. Her father had brought the backhoe home and dug a hole for him under the tree so that she could always be close to him.

Jimmy was an excellent horse rider and had broken in a new horse for her, Dusty, he was seventeen hands tall, had a red coat with a white stripe down his nose, he was too frisky for her and Lilly was frightened of him and did not want to ride him. He had already bucked her off twice, luckily she hadn't been hurt. Well it was no good sitting here daydreaming, she had to go and catch Dusty and ride him around the paddock to get him used to her and the saddle. Her father had made it quite clear when she had told him she was afraid of Dusty that she was not to be a sook and a crybaby and to just do it. Lilly wanted her father to be proud of her, he never showed much affection to her or her siblings, if only she could get him to say she had done a good job.

Her back was still hurting from the flogging he had given her last week, at least the welts had gone down now and the bruising had turned to yellow. The memory came flooding back and made her shiver.

"You will do as you are told, don't back answer me girl!" Jimmy was yelling at Lilly. "You tell that bloody bus driver Tom exactly what I said, the old bastard."

"Dad I don't want to." Lilly stood with her head down. They were in the backyard, her mother was hanging the washing on the line and Lilly had been playing with the dogs. Why did she have to do her father's dirty work? He was the one with the problem with the bus driver, not her.

"I don't want to," he mimicked her. He was right up in her face, he grabbed her arm and squeezed tight making her cry in pain. "Do as you're told, you stupid girl." Jimmy pushed her away and started walking towards the house.

"No Dad, I'm not going to, I will get in trouble. You tell him yourself." Lilly stood defiantly.

Jimmy grabbed the mop from the back verandah and strode towards her. "You will do as you are told you little bitch, you're useless, just like your mother." He swung the mop and hit her across the back with the handle, raising it again and again hitting her across her legs and back as she fell to the ground. Lilly looked at her mother who was making her way towards them and shook her head pleading with her eyes not to. She knew that her father would hit her mother if she tried to stop him and her mother had already had enough abuse at the hands of this man. Jimmy stood over her as she lay crying on the ground.

"Now get up you little bitch and apologise."

Lilly tried to get up but everywhere was hurting she pushed herself up from the ground standing her legs felt like they would buckle.

"I'm sorry Dad." It was barely a whisper. Whack the handle hit her again knocking her to the ground.

"Not good enough, try it again and make it good otherwise I will hit you until you say it with meaning, you will do as you are told you ungrateful little bitch."

Lilly's body felt like it was on fire, welts had appeared on the top of her legs and they were burning, she pushed herself up from the ground, she could see her mother frozen to the spot, tears running down her face, she smiled at her Mum and nodded it was okay. As she stood in front of him, she straightened herself up as best she could and stared straight into his eyes, she ground her teeth hard and clenched her jaw.

"I'm sorry Dad for back answering you, it won't happen again." Lilly would not let him break her.

Jimmy nodded, threw the mop down on the ground and walked away heading for the dairy. Lilly waited until he was out of sight before collapsing on the ground in tears, Rose ran to her side cradling her youngest in her arms.

"Oh my baby, I'm so sorry you should have let me step in and stop him."

"No Mum, you know he would have hit you then and I still would have copped a flogging, better just me, not you too." Lilly hated her father so much right then, why did he have to be so cruel? One minute he could be loving and caring and the next turn into a monster.

The sound of a dog barking brought Lilly back from the memory, the old red kelpie was below her looking up at her and barking. She jumped down from the branches and headed to the barn to get the bridle and saddle with the dog close on her heels.

Dusty was so far behaving himself as she trotted around the paddock, turning him this way and then circling back, he seemed to be getting used to the bridle and saddle, maybe he would get better as he got older, he "pig rooted" a few times and tried to buck her off his back but Lilly dug her thighs into his side and hung on tight. Suddenly he took off in a gallop heading for the fence, she tried hard to turn him back, pulling on the reins and yelling at him to woo up, but he wouldn't listen, he was too strong for her and as the fence loomed in front of her she knew she had no choice, they would have to try and jump it, there was no way he was going to stop. Dusty saw the fence and hesitated briefly then lifted his front legs and jumped, suspended in mid air over the jump Lilly felt relief they would make it, but Dusty's back hoof caught the fence, his front legs crumbling, he stumbled and fell, throwing Lilly to the ground, she rolled and looked up as the large red horse came down on top of her legs, crushing them sending pain from her ankle up, she curled into a ball as the horse stumbled to get up his hoofs narrowly missing crushing her head before galloping off across the paddock.

"Mum!" Lilly screamed from the ground, she tried to get up but couldn't, the pain was burning in her legs and her right ankle. "Mum, help!" she was crying uncontrollably now, she hadn't wanted to ride the stupid horse, she had told her father he was too strong for her and she couldn't control him. Now her father was going to say it was her fault, not the horses.

Rose had been inside on the phone talking to her mother when she heard the screams. She bundled Lilly up and drove her to the doctor, then for X-Rays. Luckily nothing was broken, just sprained. Her self confidence and ego were bruised and the fact she had let her father down hurt even more.

9th November 1977
  Dear Daniel,

I received your letter the other day and I'm pleased to hear you are well. We have had a couple of storms. Had a good one on Monday afternoon and got some good rain and a bit of hail as well, it made everything look greener. We have a few veggies in too, some lettuce, beetroot, carrots, onion, radish they are just coming up.

Ruby went to Taree rowing Sunday and they got second. She is going to Maclean this weekend to compete again. Another of our Hereford stud cows had a calf, the old girl that wins the ribbons at the show. Lilly had a spill off the horse last week. It went to jump the fence, got his hoof caught and fell, throwing her off and falling onto her legs.

She couldn't stand so I took her to the doctor and he thought her leg was broken so I had to take her for an X-ray but it was only bruised and her ankle sprained. She is okay now but she is a real handful always on the go or into something. We have a doctor here now at Telegraph Point. He lives up on the Plains Road. He is very good and it's rather handy having a local doctor and not having to drive into Port Macquarie.

Jimmy has almost twenty acres ploughed up to plant sorghum. He blew a lot of stumps out, and we brought the backhoe and truck home at the weekend and cleaned them up. The truck is getting fixed next week. The starter motor burned out on it, it's still under warranty but that won't pay for lost time. We hope to have it back tomorrow. We went to Taree to dig out a swimming pool on Monday but couldn't do it as it was solid rock when we got down about two feet. They had to get a big machine with rippers.

The flies are bad here and ticks too, we have been treating the cattle every week as they are covered in them. Mostly grass ticks and bottle ticks. Jimmy's mum and dad didn't get away last week, they are leaving today for their holiday. There are a lot of fish jumping in the river at night. The boys have been fishing the last couple of weekends in the river just up from the bails and caught a couple of nice bream and two big crabs.

Well there's no more news for now so bye.

Love Rose xx

CHAPTER 20

Rose drove the Louisville tip truck towards the front gate of the high school, the girls had missed the bus and as there was only one bus into town, before heading off to work, she had to drop them both to school.

"Drop us down at the bottom gate Mum, I don't want anyone to see me getting out of a truck." Ruby, now almost seventeen, was not impressed that she was being dropped to school in a truck, how embarrassing, it was especially embarrassing trying to climb down out of the truck in her very short uniform.

"No Mum pull up out the front where everyone can see me getting out of the truck. I want to show them how cool my Mum is driving a truck. One day I'm going to be just like you." Lilly was ecstatic, she loved being in the truck with her mother, the fact that she could drive this huge machine as well as tip loads off the back made her so proud.

"Mum please don't." Ruby was nudging Lilly to shut up.

"I don't have time for this. I have to get to Wauchope to get a load of gravel and drop it off before going to work on the new break wall." Rose pulled the big old yellow Louisville up at the front gates. Ruby scampered down and quickly disappeared. Lilly turned to her mother with a huge grin and kissed her goodbye before climbing down to meet her friends, turning and waving goodbye.

Rose drove out to the quarry picked up her load and headed back to town, oblivious as to what was going on behind her, a few cars went passed and beeped their horns, it wasn't until she had turned into the job site to drop her load that she noticed a police car pulling up behind her. She jumped down from the truck to open the tailgate as the officer approached.

"Hi Rose." It was Terry, one of the local police, everyone knew everyone in a small town like Port Macquarie.

"Hi Terry, what's up?"

"Well it seems you have been dropping gravel all the way back from Wauchope and you have damaged a few windscreens."

"Oh really, but I'm only half loaded I can't see how?" Rose tipped her load and there was the problem, a hole the size of a golf ball, one of the large rocks she had been carrying for the break wall must have pierced a hole in the bottom tray. "There's the problem, I'll get it fixed, sorry about that."

"I'm sorry Rose but the cars that were travelling behind you have put in a complaint and at this stage you have cracked about thirteen windscreens. I'm going to have to issue you with a fine." Terry wrote out the fine and handed it to her. "You better get that fixed as soon as you can." He smiled and waved goodbye.

Rose looked at the fine. It was a summons to appear in court, that's all she needed, hopefully the day would get better, she was already running late and she got paid by the load on the break wall, she had better get moving, the hole would wait until tonight. You had to be alert when reversing the truck along the break wall with only a few feet either side of you, get your wheels over too far and you risked rolling the truck into the ocean on either side. Rose had no problems reversing what made her laugh were the men who would stop to watch her in amazement driving the big old tip truck. Why did it seem so unbelievable that a woman was driving a truck, she would laugh to herself, it wasn't that hard. The men were gathered at the end digging around; they had found some of the wreckage of the PS Ballina; it was one of many ships that had operated on the NSW North Coast during the 1860s and 1870s. Owned and operated by the Clarence and Richmond Rivers Steam Navigation Company, the largest shipping company operating on the north coast at that time, it carried freight and passengers to Sydney on a regular basis stopping at ports along the way including Port Macquarie on an "as needs" basis.

In February 1879, the vessel became grounded on the Port Macquarie bar and was entirely swamped and broke in two. Her cargo had already been thrown overboard in an attempt to float the vessel. No passengers or crew were lost. In 1908 the Ballina's funnel was regarded as a shipping hazard as it was sticking out above the water, however attempts to remove the wreck from the river entrance by detonation proved unsuccessful. Now it had been unearthed again with the building of the break wall.

Great, that meant no more work for the day, she may as well get back to the yard and leave the truck so the hole could be fixed before she caused anymore damage and hopefully she would get home earlier today.

As Rose rounded the last bend towards the house she noticed a police car out the front. Oh god what now? Fred and Johnny, his friend from down the road, were standing there with their heads down as the police officer was obviously giving them a talking too.

"Hi Rose, meeting twice in one day and once again not on a good note." Terry smiled and nodded towards the boys.

"What have they done?" Rose wasn't sure she wanted to hear this.

"Well it seems the boys have been fishing." Terry cocked one eyebrow.

"What's wrong with fishing, surely they couldn't have done anything wrong there?" she looked questionably at Fred who looked very sheepishly at her.

"Um, well it's how they were fishing Rose. The boys had decided to blow the fish out of the water with gelignite! They have told me that they had found some up in Johnny's dad's shed. Mr Clarke got quite a fright as he was driving past, not so much the dull thud of the gelignite but the fish that came raining down on his car as he drove past on the road, he almost ran into the corner fence post, he thought the world was ending, fish falling from the skies." Terry looked back at the boys and spoke with a stern voice.

"I won't do anything about it this time boys but this is your one and only warning, no more playing with explosives." Terry was trying to stop the smile he could feel creeping across his face. Silly young buggers but he could see the funny side of it, it reminded him a little of some of the silly things he had done as a kid. He hopped back into the police car, leaned out the window and said. "You better go pick the fish up off the road too boys, you might have to eat them for dinner" he smiled and drove away.

Rose looked at both boys. She could not deal with this right now, not after the day she had just had. "Okay you two go pick all the fish up off the road and then you can go home Johnny and tell your father what you have been doing." The boys took off before she changed her mind, what would Jimmy say to Fred about this?

AUGUST 1978

It had been an eventful month for Rose with her children, there always seemed to be something going on. Ruby had been driving for just over three months and they had bought her a little old Corolla to go back and forward to work at the hairdressing salon in town where she was doing her apprenticeship. She had come home late after working one Thursday night and didn't want to wake anyone up so she had turned the headlights out on the car as she turned in off the road to park on the front lawn. With the headlights off she had not seen her brother's pushbike, lying on the ground in front of the verandah, as the car wheels ran over the bike and made a crunching sound it scared her and she forgot to hit the brakes, slamming into the front verandah, the whole house shook and woke everyone up.

It seemed like that little car was jinxed, two weeks later Ruby and Lilly had left to drive up to the local shop to buy some bread and Rose needed a cup of coffee, she had just settled down at the kitchen table when Lilly came running through the door.

"Mum quick, you have to come quick, we've had an accident."

"What are you hurt? What about Ruby?"

"We are okay but she ran off the road about a mile back and hit the big post on the corner of the cattle yard. She can't get the car started and it's all smashed in on the passenger's side. I was lucky I saw it coming and pulled my legs up otherwise they would be crushed." Lilly was gasping for breath. She had run the mile back to get her mother.

"Come on then we will have to take the backhoe and tow it back." Lilly climbed up beside her mother and sat on the wheel arch of the backhoe as they drove to where Ruby was waiting for them, Lilly explained that Ruby went to lean across to pick up a cassette tape and just as she did the car hit a pothole and the wheel jerked out of her hand and spun them into the post. Ruby was standing beside the car in tears. She knew her father would be angry with her for smashing the car.

"Oh Mum, I'm sorry it was an accident."

"It's okay darling as long as you are both okay that's all that matters. Come on, I'll reverse the backhoe up and we'll hook the chain under the front of the car so I can tow it home."

Rose wrapped the chain under the front of the car securing it to the hoe on the back. She climbed up into the seat and pulled the lever to raise the car but she had pulled the wrong lever and the bucket slammed down onto the bonnet of the car putting a big dent in it. Rose looked at the girls and burst out laughing, the girls stood horrified and looked at each other then at their mother who was in fits of laughter, they also started to laugh, could it get any worse?

"Just tell your father it happened in the accident, no need for him to know that I did it." They towed the little blue Corolla home leaving it at the side of the house where Jimmy would be able to check it over and see if it could be repaired.

Fred had been out riding his motorbike and had fallen off on the gravel road, flying over the handle-bars landing on his elbows, scrapping along the gravel taking off the skin, he had managed to get back on and ride home for help but the only one there was Lilly. She tried as best she could to clean him up, a flap of skin was hanging from his elbow and it was full of small bits of gravel and dirt and would not stop bleeding. Lilly had wanted to train to be a nurse when she finished school but after that incident she knew it was not for her.

CHAPTER 21

OCTOBER 1978

"But Mum I don't want to leave here, I want to stay with Pa and all my friends. Why do we have to move out West?" Lilly was very upset, she didn't want to move to a farm out at god knows where, away from all she had ever known. "It's my fourteenth birthday in two weeks and I won't have any friends to share it with me."

"Lilly you will make new friends, we don't have a choice you know that. Your father has decided he wants to run a large property with sheep and that's that. I don't want to go either but sometimes we have to do things we don't like. It will be an adventure, come on honey we have to get going, grab your bag and jump up into the truck. I don't want to be driving up the mountain in the dark."

Rose hugged her girl. She didn't want to leave either but they had no choice. Ruby was seventeen and had signed up as an apprentice hairdresser. She would be staying behind to finish her hairdressing course and would be moving into town in a share flat with a married couple, close to her work. Of course Jimmy had decided the move was what he wanted without discussing it with anyone. Rose should be grateful, at least they had stayed in the one place for thirteen years, but it seemed Jimmy had itchy feet again so they were on the move to Coonabarabran out over the Great Dividing Range on the New South Wales Central Western Slopes. The area was known for its wool, wheat and timber but also for the beautiful mountain range the Warrumbungles which arcs around the town to the west, north and east. It was also known as the Astronomy Capital of Australia with the Siding Spring Observatory and the famed Anglo-Australian optical telescope located there on top of the mountain.

They were moving to a three thousand acre property twenty miles out of town near Ulamambri. Jimmy had big dreams, he was sick of the small farm on the Wilson River and driving backhoes he wanted more. They would have sheep and pigs as well as plant crops of sorghum and wheat. The farm had all the machinery they needed to sow and harvest the crops. There were dams on the property as well but at the moment they were only half full. Why did he have to come out here now with a drought on? Rose put the truck in gear and headed up the road to make the trip over Walcha mountain, it would take them about eight hours to get out there. The truck was loaded with furniture and belongings, they had put a tarp across the load in case it rained. Once she had dropped all this off they would have to come back for another load while Jimmy and Fred stayed at the new place getting everything organised.

The house was at the top of a long dirt driveway sitting on top of a small hill. It was a big old house with a large dining lounge room with a fireplace, three bedrooms and a room built onto the large L shaped verandah, Lilly picked the room on the verandah and Fred had chosen the smaller room out the back of the sun room. The kitchen was a good size with a wood stove and the window overlooked a neglected vegetable patch. The laundry was in a shed out the back. They would put an electric fence up around the house to keep the sheep and cattle out of the yard. They had spent a few days unpacking their belongings and making the house nice before Rose and Lilly headed back in the truck to pick up another load.

They were late getting away and Rose knew she would have to drive down the mountain in the dark. It was bad enough in daylight with its hair pin bends and steep drops. They stopped at Walcha and had a bite to eat before heading off for the last leg of the drive. It was dark as they approached the bends and they had seen no other cars on the road, the truck headlights lighting up the road ahead, it was a very dark night. It was only a half moon so there was no light filtering through the dense treetops. Lilly was getting fidgety in her seat and uncomfortable.

"Mum?"

"Yes dear."

"Did you ever wonder if there was anyone up there in the bushes?"

"Um no, I hadn't thought about it Lilly."

"What if there's someone up there watching us, following us, waiting for us to pull over and then they jump out from behind the trees and attack us."

"Oh Lilly don't be silly, there's no one up there." Rose glanced into the darkness at her side.

"Um okay" Lilly yawned "I'm tired I'm going to sleep" she climbed down onto the floor of the truck curled up and promptly fell asleep.

Rose now felt very on edge about what Lilly had said, she still had a hundred and fifty miles to go, it was gloomy and dark and a mist had rolled in across the road reducing visibility and making the forest seem even more eerie than it already was with storm clouds gathering, dark and ominous. The densely packed trees loomed up high above, their branches interlocking into its neighbours like giant arms, the tall trees blocked out the moon and stars creating long shadows across the road and the forest floor was lost in darkness. Her eyes flickered over the thick dark bushes, she started to see shapes in the undergrowth and move-ment, what if someone was up there in the bushes? She had to stop this, her imagination was running away with her, focus on the road and just get down the mountain and back out into the open flat country, there was no way she was going to pull over either. As she drove along the winding road she kept her eyes fixed on the white centre line, guiding her down the mountain, too afraid to look sideways in case someone was lurking behind a tree ready to jump out. Lilly certainly had a good imagination, she would make a great writer one day.

CHAPTER 22

COONABARABRAN
FEBRUARY 1979

They had settled into their new life easily enough, Lilly had made new friends and would stay in town once a week with her best friend Alicia so she could play in the night basketball competition. Fred had also made friends with some of the young boys on the neighbouring farms and they would go motorbike riding on the weekends. They had planted the sorghum in October and it would be ready to harvest next month. It wouldn't be as good a crop as they had hoped for due to the lack of rain.

Rose was finishing packing a few things for herself and Lilly before going to bed. They were going back to Telegraph Point to see William, he had caught a cold which had turned into pneumonia and he was now in hospital. Lilly was very sad she wanted to see her Pa, he meant the world to her. They would leave to head back to Telegraph Point early in the morning and Jimmy and Fred would come down in a few days.

It had just past midnight when Jimmy sat bolt upright in bed and let out a loud gasp which woke Rose, he was staring wide eyed at the end of the bed.

"What is it Jimmy?"

"It's Dad," barely a whisper escaped his mouth.

"Yes, I'll see your Dad tomorrow when I get there."

"No he's dead, he just appeared to me at the end of the bed, as if he was saying goodbye." Jimmy was still staring at the foot of the bed. "He was smiling and he raised his hand up as if to wave, then he just vanished."

"Don't be silly, no one has called us, if anything had happened they would have phoned by now. Go back to sleep." Rose lay back down and pulled the covers up, she was concerned, Jimmy did not believe in the supernatural, so something had spooked him.

There was a rumour that the house they were living in was haunted, at times you could feel a presence, like someone was standing behind you, yet there was no one there and a coldness brushing your face which made you shiver, her thoughts were interrupted by the phone ringing. Jimmy jumped from the bed to answer it, he talked in a hushed tone for a moment before he came back into the room.

"That was my sister, Dad passed away a few minutes ago."

Rose sat with her mouth agape, so he really had seen his father's spirit, Lilly would be devastated that she had not gotten a chance to see her beloved Pa. No need to get up early now she would need to pack more things and organise some time off school for Lilly so that they would be there for the funeral.

It was a large funeral, people came from all over to pay their respects to William, he had been a well respected and much loved man in the community. Lilly had broken down in the church and was inconsolable, Rose's good friend Karen had taken her back to her house while everyone else went to the cemetery. Rose stood with her arm around Betty as she said her last goodbye to her husband.

"You know he knew he wasn't going to make it through the night, I told him that you were coming down and that "chicken" was going to be here the next day to see him, he looked at me and smiled and said I would love to see chicken but I won't be here. Tell her I love her and I will always be with her in her heart." She paused and stifled back a sob. "I didn't think anything of it at the time, I thought it was just the drugs they had given him for the pain, but he knew, I woke through the night I could feel his presence just before he passed, it was like he was in the room with me holding my hand. Goodbye my love." They stood for a moment longer before turning and walking back to a waiting car.

COONABARABRAN
JUNE 1979

The jarring of the truck was hurting Rose's ribs, Jimmy had been drinking the night before and once again found a reason to hit her, she wasn't even sure what she had done this time to deserve this bashing. Rose was working for the local council driving the water truck on the roads they were repairing. The grader would grade the road, then the rollers would flatten it and then she would follow dampening the soil with a fine spray from the trucks back hoses. She was filling up the water tank, so took the chance to write to Daniel, she would call her mother tonight after dinner.

Dear Daniel

Just a few short notes to let you know how we are going out here. I hope this letter finds you well. Lilly is doing well at school and has been selected to go away to state for javelin, discus and the fifteen hundred metre race. I've taken her to Tamworth and Gunnedah to compete and she is getting quite a few trophies and medals now. She runs every afternoon after school around the farm with her dog Rusty close behind, he got too close to her the other day and she trod on his foot with her running shoes which have sharp spikes, he was okay though. Fred is busy on the farm and on the weekends he has a few friends that come over and they have built a motocross track out the back of the farm so they can race their motorbikes around it.

Ruby has moved into her own flat in Port Macquarie she is working in a hair salon there, she has a hair-dressing apprenticeship. Jimmy has a garden going over near the chook pen. It has beans and melons up, the pheasant has laid seven eggs so far and the guinea fowl is laying too. I've been getting ten to twelve eggs a day. I'm working driving the water truck for the council and I'm writing this at work while the tank fills. We have had a few hot days and today looks like it will be hot.

When Jimmy first went to Sydney to see the specialist we went by car down through Mudgee, Lithgow and Katoomba. First time I have been that way, it's lovely over the mountains. Jimmy has bought more pigs, eight white sows and a boar. Lilly has a pet lamb and it loves the flowers on the rose bush. I had a lovely lot of sweet *pea flowers but they are nearly all gone now. Fred sold his old bike and bought a new one, a Suzuki PE 250.*

I had to get a new washing machine as the old one died. It used to give you electric shocks when you used it, I bought it in Tamworth the other day when I took Lilly to compete in her running. The place looks lovely and green and the barley is a nice golden colour at present. No more news for now so I'll say goodbye. I hope this finds you well.

Love Rose.

Rose wondered how Fred and Lilly were doing back at the farm, they had finished baling the hay and Jimmy had taken a load of lucerne bales across to Gunnedah and had told them to finish picking up the rest of the bales from the bottom paddock.

Lilly sat up in the driver's seat of the big old Massey Ferguson tractor, she could only just reach the pedals, she loved driving the big tractor. The trailer had been hooked on behind with a bale conveyor attached to the side, the shoot would guide the rectangle bales onto a conveyor belt up to where Fred was waiting on the back so he could stack them. All she had to do was drive slowly in a straight line, line up the bale with the shoot of the conveyor belt until they filled the trailer then they would take them to the barn to stack. Their father had told them he expected it all to be done by the time he got back from Gunnedah.

"Okay sis I'm ready let's get started." Fred stood waiting for the first bale; it went up without a hitch, one after the other they picked up the bales as they went round and round the paddock. The stack was getting higher and higher.

"Come on can't you drive any faster than that? You're driving like an old woman." Fred laughed.

"Old woman really, you want me to go faster, no worries." Lilly pushed the accelerator pedal down and the big tractor surged forward picking bale after bale up she was going so fast that Fred could not keep up, and the bales which were falling all over him and off the sides of the trailer. He fell on top of a bale laughing, he should know better than to dare his little sister, she never turned down a challenge.

"Okay, okay, I take it back, now slow down, you're going to have to come back around and pick those ones up again. We better get this done before Dad gets back otherwise we'll cop it."

DECEMBER 1979

"Mum, can we go out for a horse ride tomorrow? I'd like to have a look at the caves we've been told about out the back of the property in the scrub." Lilly had finished her dinner and was waiting for everyone else to finish, she knew better than to get up from the table, she had copped a clip up the back of her head from her father before for leaving the table while people were eating.

"That sounds like fun, sure we can take a picnic with us. Is that okay Jimmy?" Rose looked at her husband, he had been in a good mood lately even though the drought was affecting the crops.

"Sure I don't need you for anything, but you better be careful of the Yowie." He smiled and his eyes held a cheeky glint.

"Dad they are only stories and besides, that's miles away further up in the Pilliga scrub." Lilly had heard something about these so-called ape men but they were just stories.

"Don't be so sure of that, it was only last week that a truckie was carting stock across between Narrabri and Barradine, he pulled over to check the load, he was checking the tyre when he heard a noise on the other side of the truck. He went to investigate with his torch in hand and ended up face to face with a ten foot hairy ape man, he froze to the spot in disbelief, then bolted to the open door of the cab and drove off flat out. When he got to Narrabri he got out to check the load again and a piece of timber had been broken off and pulled out from the trailer and he said it was too high above the ground for a normal person to reach." Jimmy had heard the other property owners talking about it when he had taken a load of hay to town.

"Sure, okay we will keep a look out then." Lilly giggled, what a load of nonsense.

Rose and Lilly saddled the horses and Rose carried a pack on her back with some sandwiches, cake, fruit and water for them to have later. Rose was riding the chestnut, his coat was a copper colour with a white stripe that ran down his forehead, he stood fifteen hands tall, Rose stroked the base of the mane down the withers and then his upper shoulders, he was a beautiful, placid horse. Lilly had opted to ride one of the Shetland ponies that they had on agistment on the farm. He stood only thirty five inches but was strong and sturdy with a deep girth.

"Are you sure you want to ride the Shetland? Wouldn't you prefer a bigger horse?" Rose knew how temperamental these ponies could be, she knew Lilly had become wary of the big horses since her fall.

"No Mum I want to ride this one, he's short like me." Lilly had finished putting the saddle on the little horse and was climbing onto his back. "Come on, let's go." She gave him a kick and away they went with short, bouncy strides making Lilly's brown curls dance around her shoulders.

Rose threw herself up into the saddle and followed her out the gate. Fred shouted out to them as they went through the gate.

"Watch out for the Yowie's out there!" He grinned mischievously as everyone had heard about the sightings of what they called big foot or Yowie's in the area especially around the Pilliga scrub. "You better run if you see a big black hairy thing coming for you."

"Don't be ridiculous Fred, there's no such thing." Lilly yelled over her shoulder as they followed the track heading for the caves.

The area was dominated by Pilliga sandstone, a coarse red and yellow stone. The sandstone outcrops with basalt-capped ridges were common in the south, while the Pilliga outwash areas in the north and west are dominated by alluvium from flooding creeks. In the west dry sandy creek beds were common and usually only flowed after significant rain. In the east is a heavily eroded sandstone mountain range. The cypress pine covered the area with its dark grey bark and grey green foliage, "she oaks" and eucalypts scattered throughout and small prickly shrubs. The air was still, birds chirped and every now and then, there would be a rustle in the bushes with wallabies bounding away as they made their way along the sandy track.

"Come on, no stop it, turn around, we are going this way, stupid horse." Lilly was getting frustrated with the little Shetland pony. It kept stopping and refused to move forward, it wanted to turn around and go home. It was a constant battle to keep him moving towards the cliffs. They would take a few steps forward then he would turn and head home Lilly was going around in circles.

"I told you that you should have ridden one of the horses."

"I'll make this bloody pony go where I want to even if I have to get off and push it."

Rose laughed, she didn't know who was more stubborn Lilly or the pony. Rose was enjoying the ride through the bush enjoying the smells and sounds. The tall iron bark trees with their rough bark and dark red sap, scribbly gums, wattle trees with their yellow flowers. The blue flax lily plants were scattered all through the bush, some were up to a metre high, with dark green blade-like leaves and blue flowers that turn to indigo-coloured berries in summer. After half an hour of coxing and frustration on Lilly's part they reached a small clearing, over to their left they could see a sandy outcrop and what looked like an opening amongst the rocks.

"Look Lilly I think that's it there, lets hop off and give the horses a rest and go investigate."

They tied the horses to a tree, the horses seemed to be restless and tugged at the reins, the chestnut was pawing the ground and snorting, Rose gave his neck a rub and a pat. The track was surrounded by burr daisies with its yellow flowers, rough speargrass and bandicoot grass. As they walked along the track Rose noticed that it was extremely quiet, not even a breeze, there was no movement or noises.

"Mum, does it seem really quiet to you? There's not even a bird making a sound." Rose nodded looking back at the horses who were becoming more restless by the minute, something was spooking them. Suddenly there was a snap! The sound of twigs breaking and rustling sounds coming from around the side of the hill. Rose looked around, she couldn't see anything, but her instincts were telling her there was something out there watching them, she could feel the hair rise on the back of her neck and a chill ran down her spine. Suddenly in front of her a flock of glossy black cockatoos took off out of the shrubs squawking, the sound of something crashing through the undergrowth was coming closer and whatever it was it was big. Lilly just caught the glimpse of a large black hairy beast running through the bushes coming their way, it let out a blood curdling piercing shrill screech that sent goosebumps up Rose's arms.

"Bloody hell Mum it's a bloody yowie! Look there, see? It's black and hairy coming around the side of the hill, run!" Lilly was already on her way back to the horses who by now had sensed the danger and were trying to pull free of their reins.

The noise got louder and they could hear loud grunting snorting noises. Rose turned and ran as fast as she could, she didn't look back, they untied the reins, jumped on the horses and bolted, the little Shetland pony didn't need any coxing this time and Lilly had to hang on for dear life. The horses galloped all the way back to the farm house they were not stopping for anything. Jimmy could hear the commotion and the horses coming from a mile away and was standing outside the shed when they came flying into the yard, stopping in a cloud of dust.

"What the bloody hell are you trying to do bloody kill the horses for Christ's sake." Jimmy was not impressed. The chestnut was frothing and covered in sweat and the poor little pony looked like it was about to keel over from exhaustion.

"We couldn't stop them if we tried, there was something out there that spooked them, they took off and would not slow down."

"Dad, Dad I saw a yowie! It was big, black and hairy and was crashing through the bush after us out near the cave." Lilly was beside herself from the adrenaline running through her and her lucky escape.

"Don't be ridiculous Lilly there are no yowies out there. Come on Fred grab the rifle and the dogs, we'll go have a look."

It was after dark before Jimmy and Fred returned with something in the back of the ute. "There's your Yowie, we went to exactly where you told us, your backpack was still lying near the tree, we walked around the side and this is what came running towards us." In the ute was a huge wild boar, he was black and hairy and much larger than normal. "So you can see it's not a yowie, just a wild boar and a bloody big boy at that. You're lucky he didn't catch you with those tusks he would have ripped you or the horses to pieces. We found a spot where he's been sleeping near there and he's got a cut on his leg which looks infected that was probably making him even angrier so when you two came around the corner near his den he came at you."

Lilly and Rose looked at each other and burst out laughing how could they have gotten sucked into the yowie tales.

CHAPTER 23

COONABARABRAN

JANUARY 1980

The headaches had been getting worse, Rose could hardly see through the pain, it felt like someone was squashing her head, she had put up with it for four days but now it had seemed to have turned into a migraine and her vision was blurring. Jimmy had dropped her to hospital that morning and they had admitted her for tests. The doctor had asked her if she had had any knocks to the head recently and she had told him the truth about the bashings that Jimmy had been giving her. She had made the doctor promise not to say anything to anyone because Jimmy had threatened if she left he would hunt her and the children down and kill them and she believed him. It was against his better judgement not to inform the police but he must respect her privacy, he had seen it all too often before. The best he could do was to sedate her for two days hoping the pain would subside.

Loretta and Martin were on their way out to visit and Loretta was determined to take her eldest daughter away from Jimmy once and for all. Loretta had discussed it with Rose on the phone before leaving Kempsey and they had devised a plan to get her away. Jimmy had been told that Lilly and Rose would come back with them for a holiday but unknown to him they would not be returning. Fred would stay behind and follow in the next few weeks once Rose had set herself up somewhere.

Rose hugged Fred and whispered in his ear. "It won't be for long, I'll find a place to live and Grandfather will come back for you. Make sure your father doesn't find out or there will be hell to pay." She kissed his forehead, said goodbye to Jimmy and left with her parents.

Her mother had grabbed more of their clothing and had put them in the car when Jimmy was out in the far paddock on the tractor. They headed up the Newell Highway to Narrabri, they weren't going back to Kempsey just yet they were going to Bundaberg in Queensland for a week to visit her little sister Alice and her husband. They stopped overnight in Goondiwindi just across the Queensland border before driving the final leg to Bundaberg.

They had enjoyed four days of sunshine and sightseeing around Bundaberg renowned for its Bundaberg Rum. The sweet smell of molasses hangs in the air around the distillery and museum, they had even done the tour to see how the rum was made. They had wandered through the botanical gardens and taken a day trip out to the islands where Lilly went snorkelling. They were just sitting down to breakfast when the phone rang.

"Hello, what are you serious? Hang on, I'll get Dad." Alice handed the phone to her father. Her face had gone white and her hands were trembling. She couldn't believe what she had just heard.

"What's wrong?" Rose had a bad feeling about this.

Her father hung up the phone and turned to Rose. "That was your brother George. He went around to the house to check on it for me and it seems that Jimmy has got wind of you leaving and had turned up at the house. He had broken in through one of the windows and was sitting inside waiting for you to turn up. George got the fright of his life when he came through the door and saw him sitting on the lounge pointing a rifle at him demanding to know where you are."

Rose was shaking. "Is George alright?"

"Yes he's okay, just a bit shook up. Jimmy told him to tell you that if you don't come home now he will hunt you down and he will shoot your mother and me if you don't go back with him." Martin sat beside her on the lounge holding his daughter as she lost control and burst into uncontrollable sobs. "You can't go back to that Rose, you know he will give you another bashing for leaving."

"But Dad, I have to go back. If I don't he will kill you and god knows who else, anyone who gets in his way. I couldn't live with that." Rose knew she would never be able to escape Jimmy, the only way would be to die herself but then what about the children who would look out for them, she couldn't do that to her children. If she could just last a few more years until they were grown and had left home and had made their own lives, maybe then ...

Rose stood up, "Come on let's pack, I need to get back before he does something stupid." She held up her hand as her mother started to speak. "I know what you're going to say Mum but I can't risk it, I know what he is capable of, come on let's go we should be able to get back by tomorrow if we leave soon and I need to find out where Fred is."

They drove most of the way in silence. Rose knew that she had to try to reason with Jimmy hoping that the bashing she would incur when they got back to Coonabarabran would not be too bad. They pulled into the driveway of her parents' house, the door was open but there was no movement. Rose entered the house making her parents and Lilly wait outside, Jimmy was sitting on the lounge, the rifle still on his lap, there were empty beer bottles at his feet. He looked up at her as she entered the room, the sneer on his face and the evil glint in his eyes made her shiver.

"So you came back, where's Lilly?"

"She's outside with Mum and Dad. I wanted to talk to you first." Rose kept her voice as calm as possible, she kept her hands clasped to try and stop them trembling, her heart was pounding so hard she felt sure he could hear it.

"There's nothing to talk about, you're coming home with me and if you don't I'm going to kill your parents, then Lilly then you." He picked up the rifle and cocked it, putting a bullet into the barrel to confirm he meant what he said, fixing his eyes on her.

"Jimmy can't we talk, surely you're not happy with the way things are?" Her voice cracked, she took a deep breath and continued she had to try and talk sense into him. "Please Jimmy don't do this."

"Like I said, there's nothing to talk about, you're my wife for better or worse and you will do as you're told. So what's it going to be?" Jimmy pointed the rifle at her head and smiled. "Don't think of calling the police either or there will be a shoot out, I've got nothing to lose."

"Okay Jimmy I'll come home with you please put the rifle down. I'll get my things from the car."

Rose turned and walked outside to her parents, holding her breath hoping to god he wouldn't shoot her in the back. Once outside the house she took a deep breath and sighed. "I'm sorry Mum and Dad I have to go back with Jimmy, it's the only way that I know you will all be safe, please try not to worry, we'll be ok."

Loretta nodded, she knew what Jimmy was capable of, they would just have to try another way to get Rose and the children free from this evil, cruel man before he ended up killing them all. They placed the bags into Jimmy's car, Loretta hugged her daughter tight she hoped that it would not be the last time she would see her. They drove back to the farm in silence. Rose knew better than to say anything, it wouldn't matter what she said anyway he would turn it around and start an argument. Lilly laid down on the backseat of the car and tried to sleep, she knew to keep quiet, she had seen what her father had done to her mother over the years. One day she would help her mother escape, how she didn't know that yet but she would work out a way to get her away from him. She couldn't understand how one minute he could be kind and the next he turned into a monster. They never went without anything as a family, there was always food on the table, a roof over their heads and they would have a holiday once a year. But all that meant nothing when you were made to feel stupid and useless everyday of your life by someone you looked up to and was supposed to help guide you and protect you in life. How could you love and hate one person so much at the same time? All Lilly wanted was for her father to say he loved her and was proud of her.

JUNE 1980

Rose and Jimmy were leaving today, moving back to Kempsey to live, leaving Lilly and Fred here on the farm alone. Fred had turned seventeen yesterday and passed his driver's licence. He had been driving machinery since he was about twelve years old so there was never any doubt he would pass his driving test. Lilly was also a competent driver, most kids who grow up on farms are taught to drive at an early age, Jimmy had taught Lilly to reverse the old F250 ute out through the gates with only an inch either side of the car. Jimmy stood up in the back of the ute yelling instructions to her and abusing her every time she got it wrong. Rose had been into town and set up accounts at the local chemist and grocery store for them, the bills would be sent to her and she would pay them once a month. The lease on the farm didn't run out until December and Lilly was half way through year ten with her exams coming up in October just before her birthday. Fred and Lilly would stay here on the property until the end of the year while their parents went back to Kempsey to set up a new home and start up the earthmoving business again. Lilly knew her mother had no choice in the matter, her father was taking her away against her better judgement but Lilly had assured her mother she was capable of finishing school plus helping out on the farm until then.

Rose hugged her one last time she didn't want to leave her, she was only fifteen and a half, she knew Lilly was quite mature for her age, she had grown up so fast and seen and heard way more than most girls her age should, she knew Fred would look out for his sister.

"If you need anything just call okay? Take care of your sister and no fighting." Rose hugged Fred, he was a calm, sensible young man and getting so tall and solid and muscly.

"We'll be fine Mum, don't worry about us, we'll drive down in a few weeks to see you. I'll make sure this one does as she's told" he gave Lilly a playful nudge.

"It's okay Mum we have it all worked out, I'll go to school and when I get home I'll do my chores before cooking tea. I can help Fred and he'll help me." Lilly tried to sound confident but inside she was crying, she didn't want her mother to go. They were twenty miles from town and they were both still kids even though Fred had been working like an adult for the past three years. Lilly would be doing all the household chores, the washing, ironing, cooking and cleaning while Fred would take care of the farm and whatever livestock was left until they too would leave at the end of the year. They would take the seven hour drive once a month down the mountain to visit their parents for a few days if it didn't interfere with Lilly's school work.

"Come on Rose hurry up we need to get going, they'll be fine now let's go." Jimmy was getting impatient, he couldn't understand the fuss over leaving them behind, god he was out working when he was thirteen.

Rose gave both the children one last hug "I love you two, take care of each other and call me if you need me."

"We will Mum , it's okay, we'll be fine as long as Lilly doesn't poison me with her cooking." Fred laughed as Lilly shoved him.

Lilly adored her big brother. He had taught her to ride a horse and a motorbike and she knew he would always look out for her. It was only five months before they would move back with their parents at Kempsey and she had exams to study for she was sure it would go by fast.

Fred and Lilly worked as a team over the next few months, Fred gave Lilly more lessons driving the car and had taught her how to do a handbrake turn on a dirt road in the car, using the handbrake locks the rear wheels, and when turning, will help rotate the back end of the car more quickly than a normal turn.

They went into town once a week to get groceries and sometimes went to the movies with their friends. Lilly turned sixteen in October, she wished her mother could be with her but she was still down in Kempsey and her sister Ruby was due to give birth any day now and she wanted their Mum with her. They went to town and had dinner at the Chinese restaurant with their closest friends to celebrate this milestone birthday then to the movies. Lilly studied hard and completed her exams while Fred sorted getting the last of the livestock sold and finished packing up the farm. They rode their motorbikes and would put the music on in the lounge room which was now empty of furniture and dance as if no one was watching them.

CHAPTER 24

Rose was pleased to have Fred and Lilly back with her. It had been hard the last six months with them being so far away and alone. Being back closer to her eldest daughter Ruby who was now a mother herself and being busy working to set up the business again helped some of the time pass by quickly. Ruby had married at eighteen and at the age of nineteen had given birth to Rose's first grandchild, a gorgeous dark haired girl.

Rose loved being a grandmother but with working every day and Jimmy's constant demands she had little time to see Ruby and her new granddaughter, even though they were only a forty minute drive away in Port Macquarie. Lilly seemed to have grown up so much, she had wanted to stay at school to do her higher school certificate but Jimmy had refused to pay for the schooling and told her to get out and get a job and support herself and stop bludging off him. Lilly had started work as a checkout assistant at the local Food for Less store in West Kempsey. Fred was now operating a bobcat working with his father.

They had bought five acres in South Kempsey and had started to build a house but at the moment they lived in a small caravan with a shed built on to the side. It was cramped with all four of them there, but Rose didn't mind, she loved having her children with her. All the cooking was done in the van or outside on the barbecue, Jimmy and Rose slept in the van while Fred and Lilly had rooms partitioned off with curtains in one part of the shed and there was a lounge area with a TV. The laundry and bathroom were outside in another smaller shed.

Fred had started dating Victoria, a lovely girl, she was a quiet, well mannered, pretty girl with a beautiful warm smile and they suited each other well. Lilly also had a boyfriend Patrick and they both loved music and would sit for hours with Patrick playing guitar while Lilly sang. Jimmy had been busy building up his earthmoving business and they now had a backhoe, bobcat and two tip trucks. Jimmy was in demand as a backhoe operator; he had a reputation for being the best on the coast and took great pride in his work.

Rose loved being back in Kempsey, her mother and father were living only five minutes away and all her brothers and sisters lived in town as well so she would catch up with them whenever she could or whenever Jimmy would let her. Jimmy had come home just after midnight last night, drunk again and he bought two of his mates with him. Rose was sound asleep but he woke her up and made her get out of bed to cook them something to eat. His friends looked embarrassed and said they were okay but Jimmy played the big man and said his wife did as she was told, when she was told. His drinking had been getting worse over the last few years. There was still physical abuse but the verbal abuse was becoming increasingly frequent and now he would insult her in front of people calling her an idiot and useless bitch. Rose knew not to say anything and just let it go if she didn't want to cop a flogging.

Rose and Lilly had taken a drive up to Bellingen last weekend to visit Daniel and they had stayed the night with him at the house. Daniel had sold most of the land around the house and had only kept the house block. The house was old and needed some repairs and he still boiled his water in the old copper out the back. The electricity had been put on but only for the lights and a few power points, Daniel said he liked it that way. The big old grey cat called "Man" lay on the back verandah in the sun most of the day, sometimes he would follow Daniel when he went for a walk down the road. They picked macadamia nuts to take home from the big tree outside the house. Rose and Lilly wandered down to the creek following the overgrown path. Moss draped vines formed curtains between trees which were themselves covered in moss and sucker plants. On fallen old logs grew ferns and strange coloured, funny shaped fungi. There was a pungent smell of rotting vegetation and damp earth, the light only just managed to reach through the dense trees where the creek still flowed, bubbling over the rocks disappearing around the bend.

Daniel still loved his photography and had the negatives developed into slides, he didn't own a TV so they spent the evening with him as he proudly showed them slides projected on his white lounge room wall. He took amazing photographs of nature, waterfalls, flowers, insects and animals. Lilly found it boring and Rose had to hide her boredom and pretend that she was interested. Daniel had never remarried after her mother left and had lived alone ever since. He looked frail and old, he would be eighty four soon and Rose knew the day would come she would have to take care of him full- time, she was his only relative. When they left she promised to come back and pick him up soon for a visit to see Ruby and the baby and meet his first great grandchild, she could see the loneliness and sadness in his eyes and she felt dreadful leaving him.

DECEMBER 1981

Fred and Victoria had become engaged three months ago and planned to marry in the January of the next year. They had bought a caravan to live in and had set it up opposite the family van so they could have some privacy, they had built a little room off it as well to give them more space. The new house was progressing slowly, not as fast as Rose would have liked because Jimmy kept changing his mind on how he wanted it, so it was a constant change of plans. Rose kept busy driving the tip truck during the day and managing the accounts on the weekends.

Lilly and Jimmy clashed all the time, her youngest daughter was strong willed and could be quite stubborn at times and she had started to stand up to her father. The last argument they had Lilly had stood her ground in front of her father and had yelled at him "well you taught me not to take shit from anyone, so I'm not taking your shit anymore." Jimmy had told her to get out and not come back.

Lilly had moved in to stay with her grandmother Loretta, it made more sense, she could catch the bus to work each day and she only had to see her father occasionally, they were talking again now but Lilly usually came to visit her mother when her father was out. Lilly kept begging her mother to leave but Rose knew that was not possible. Jimmy would never let her go.

Rose woke with a pain in her chest. She sat up quickly and her heart was racing, she could feel it pounding in her chest so hard she felt it was going to burst, a wave of nausea came over her, she was here alone, panic set in, was she having a heart attack? Jimmy had left early for work and Fred and Victoria had gone away for a few days. Rose put her head between her legs hoping the nausea would pass, she was only thirty six too young for a heart attack. She dressed and drove herself to her mother's.

"Rose what's wrong? You look pale." Loretta was concerned she could see her daughter was not well.

"I don't know Mum, my heart is racing and it won't slow down. I feel sick and dizzy and I'm short of breath." Rose was slurring her words and she found it difficult to breathe.

"Come on, we are taking you to the hospital, something is wrong and your speech is affected."

Loretta called out to Martin to come quickly; they bundled her into the car and drove her to the hospital. Once they reached emergency there was a mad rush to get her into Intensive care, the palpitations were getting faster and stronger. The doctor hooked her up to the heart monitor, her heart beat was erratic, this was not good.

"Get me the defibrillator we need to shock her heart and try and get it back to a normal rhythm. Give her some medication now to sedate her so she won't feel the pain."

Rose was now drifting into unconsciousness from the medication, the paddles were placed on her chest she could hear talking, "clear" then a jolt of fire in her chest. Her heart was slowing down, coming back to a normal rhythm, that's all she remembered as she drifted into unconsciousness.

When Rose awoke she was hooked up to an ECG machine, she had wires and patches all over her chest monitoring her heart beat and rhythm. The doctor was there talking with her mother.

"Well hello, it's nice to see you awake." He smiled.

Rose tried to speak but her mouth was dry and she couldn't form the words.

"Don't try to talk, just rest. You have what is called Paroxysmal Atrial Tachycardia. It's a type of arrhythmia that occurs when electrical signals starting in the heart's atria fire irregularly. This affects the electrical signals transmitted from the sinoatrial node, which is your heart's natural pacemaker. Your heart rate will speed up, this prevents your heart from having enough time to fill with blood before pumping blood out to the rest of the body. As a result, your body may not receive enough blood or oxygen. We need to do more tests once you're feeling better, you may not need medication, it means just changing your lifestyle."

"What causes it? She's only thirty six." Loretta was anxious for her daughter.

"There's no obvious cause but some are anxiety, stress, physical exhaustion, emotional issues, too much alcohol or caffeine. We will keep monitoring you and like I said we will do some more testing but if you feel any symptoms like persistent palpitations that feel like pounding, galloping or fluttering, chest pain, dizziness or fainting, shortness of breath, light-headedness, fullness in the throat or neck you need to get straight to a doctor or the hospital." He patted her hand. "Now get some rest, we will keep you overnight and monitor you. I'll come see you again in the morning and all going well, you should be able to go home."

No words were exchanged between mother and daughter but Rose knew what her mother was thinking, this was Jimmy's fault.

CHAPTER 25

MAY 1982

Finally Rose was in her new home, it had taken two and a half years to get it finished, now she had made new curtains and had set about making it a home. Rose was proud of her new brick home with its large open plan lounge and dining room, a large kitchen with a breakfast bar, four bedrooms, two bathrooms and laundry. There was a large verandah all around the house and she loved sitting on the back verandah with a cup of coffee looking over the paddock with the ducks on the dam and cows grazing. There was a chicken coop with ten chickens which gave her fresh eggs every day, she had a vegetable patch and a herb garden.

Fred and Victoria were still living in the caravan at the back and had married in January, they were both working and saving their money so they could buy a place of their own and one day start a family. Rose liked having them close and while they were there Jimmy was less likely to hit her. Lilly had returned home to live after Rose's heart scare and had made a sort of peace with her father. She had passed her driver's test and had saved her money from working and bought her first car, an old second hand EH Holden. It was gold with a white vinyl roof.

Rose finished washing the dinner dishes and cleaning the kitchen. Jimmy had gone down to the shed to do some work on the tractor, she had made changes to her lifestyle to keep her heart condition under control, they had found she had an extra nerve in her heart so she had to be careful not to bend up and down quickly, keep her anxiety under control and watch her alcohol consumption. She was tired now and needed to go to bed, but first she would sit and write to Daniel then she could post it on her way to work tomorrow.

She felt bad that she didn't see him much but she was always so busy.

Dear Daniel,

Just a short note to let you know the news. I hope you are well and your leg is better. Everyone here is good. The house is finally finished and we have moved in. It would be nice for you to come and stay for a while, I could pick you up from the train if you're feeling up to it. We have a spare bedroom and the kids would like to see you. I've had a cold for the last week but I'm finally getting over it now. The weather is up and down and it still keeps raining every few days. I worked six days straight down at South West Rocks driving the tip truck. I went down this morning but it rained last night so we didn't work. Today was fine so I should be back at it tomorrow.

I had three stitches in my finger a few weeks ago. I was tying up the dogs and they started fighting and one of them bit me. Well best go to bed and get a bit of sleep as I have to get up at five. Bye for now. Love Rose.

CHAPTER 26

MARCH 1983

Daniel had taken ill last month and had seemed to age very quickly, he was incapable of caring for himself so Rose out of a sense of duty had packed up his clothes and a few possessions and brought him down to live with them. His leg had gotten worse and he was finding it quite difficult to get around. Rose knew that her mother did not want to see him and wanted nothing to do with him, she knew something bad had happened between them but her mother refused to discuss it, so Rose let it be. She had nursed Daniel at home for as long as she could but as his health had deteriorated she had no choice but to take him to hospital. Daniel passed away in his sleep peacefully a week ago. At least he had been able to see his latest great grandchild, Fred and Victoria had given birth to a big, healthy baby boy last month.

Now Rose was at his home in Bellingen, she was his only relative and it had been left to her. She was busy cleaning out the rooms and packing up mementos to take with her. Most of the furniture and belongings she would give to charity. She looked around the room, nothing had changed in all the years she had been coming to visit, it was funny that she had no attachment to the house even though she had spent the first four years of her life here, she did not recall it. It had no sentimental value to her so she had decided to sell the house, hopefully a young family would buy it and make it into a loving home. It needed a lot of work but it had a lovely big yard with trees and an amazing view across the valley.

Rose had been busy all day packing and cleaning, she had wanted to do this alone, she was staying the night and finishing the last of the cleaning tomorrow, the Salvation Army were coming to pick up the furniture and clothing tomorrow at lunchtime. Rose had found a box containing all the letters she had written to him over the years and two very old exercise books that had what looked like Italian writing and badly written English in them. She wondered who's they were and why he had kept them? She poured herself a glass of wine and wandered out to the back verandah and sat in the old wicker chair to watch the day draw to a close. In the paddock stood the white trunked eucalyptus trees with their long sinewy branches, the cows were setting down for the night on the green grass that they had cropped low by their grazing.

The purple wisteria vine was tangled through the beams on the verandah and disappeared around the side. The old shed was falling down and probably needed to be demolished and the once thriving vegetable patch was now overgrown. The low mountains of the Great Dividing Range were a hazy-blue with a few round peaks here and there. The mountainside was covered in trees and the smell of eucalyptus was in the air, the sun was setting over the mountains turning the clouds into colours of yellow, pink and orange. The air was almost still except for a soft breeze, she could hear the water cascading over the rapids in the creek. There was a drifting smell of woodsmoke mingling with the night blooming flowers, the leaves rustling slightly on the trees. Rose caught her breath watching the day going to sleep as the sun sank behind the jagged peaks of the ranges. Lights from the houses in the valley twinkled through the trees, as the sun finally faded away and the dusk crept in, the sound of hundreds of birds erupted breaking the silence, the cicadas joined in rubbing their legs together in a frenzied percussion.

As she sat there silently, she wondered what sort of life her mother must have had living here with Daniel and what had happened that was so bad she would never talk to her about it? How different her life would have been if her mother had stayed with Daniel. Her mother had her reasons for not discussing it with her and she respected her privacy but Rose had a sneaking suspicion that maybe her mother had also been abused at the hand of Daniel. Maybe one day she would tell her about it.

CHAPTER 27

"I told you Jimmy I am not coming back, I can't do this anymore." Rose had left and gone to stay with her mother; she would no longer put up with the abuse. All three children had left home and were getting on with their lives and now she would too.

"Please Rose I promise I will change, don't leave me please." Jimmy was begging her.

"No Jimmy, I'm not coming back, you won't change, I don't love you in fact I hate you, I wish you were dead." Rose's body was still hurting from the bashing she had received two days ago. She had packed some clothes and left, she would not return this time no matter how many promises or threats he made.

"Well if that's what you want that's what I'll do then." Jimmy stormed out slamming the door behind him. He jumped in his car and drove off with the tyres squealing heading towards their home.

As Jimmy turned into the street that ran down to the house he pushed hard on the accelerator the car responded with a powerful surge, he hurtled down the road and instead of taking the sharp right hand corner he slammed the car into the power pole. The sound of crashing metal hitting the pole was deafening, Jimmy's head hit the windscreen as it shattered cutting his forehead, the blood trickled down his face, the hood crumpled under the force and the impact pushed the engine back through the dashboard and the steering wheel jammed into his chest, he felt a burning pain in his ribs, then silence as he blacked out.

Rose was sitting at the kitchen table having a coffee with her mother when the phone rang, her father answered, he turned to look at Rose, his face anxious.

They had heard the sirens go past only a few moments ago now they knew why and who.

"What is it Dad?"

"There's been an accident, it's Jimmy, his car hit a pole on the way to your house, he is unconscious and they have taken him to the hospital, they need you there now."

Rose's first thought was this was her fault she had told him she wished he was dead and now he might be. Her father drove her to the hospital, they were ushered through to the waiting room and told that he was alive and in Emergency, someone would come and get them when he was able to have visitors, the waiting area was flooded with bright light and the pungent odour of antiseptic. The next two hours were agony for Rose as she kept replaying the fight over in her mind, she had conflicting feelings of regret for wishing he was dead and relief that she might finally be free of this abusive monster.

Rose stayed by his bedside that night, the doctors had told her he was lucky, he had a few broken ribs and the cut on his head was not deep, he should make a full recovery. Jimmy struggled back up to full consciousness. Despite his injuries, he was able to talk, his cheeks and forehead were cut from the shattered windshield, he rolled his eyes, trying to focus on her, smacked his cracked lips, unable to produce saliva for all the painkillers administered through the IV needle in his arms. His tongue was swollen. He looked frightened, diminished. "I'm sorry, I can't even get that right, I can't even kill myself for you" he said with difficulty, then fell back to his morphine pillow.

As he lay in a morphine state of delirium he started to mumble and twist in the bed. "No Mum, don't hit me, please Mum, why did Frank die? Am I going to die too? I'm scared Mum please don't belt me with the cord, don't lock me out in the dark, I'm sorry Mum, I'll be good I promise."

Rose had no idea what he was talking about, had his mother abused him? Rose could not believe it, Betty was a good hearted woman she could not believe she would have done such a thing. She knew Jimmy was twelve when his older brother Frank had died at the age of sixteen. Jimmy never spoke about it, when he was better she would ask him what really happened. Rose wondered whether he really was having flashbacks or was it just another ploy to get her to stay? Was he looking for sympathy? Rose felt she had no choice now but to stay and take care of him after all she felt responsible for the accident.

Two weeks had gone by and Jimmy was home, he had recovered well from the accident and his ribs were still sore and would take time to heal. Jimmy finally opened up to Rose and told her about his brother Frank who died at the age of sixteen he had a congenital heart disease and was a bleeder, his veins would rupture at any time, and he would bleed under the skin, sometimes the skin would break and blood would fly out everywhere he ended up needing skin grafts to cover the holes. Frank and Jimmy had shared the same bedroom and Frank was his hero; he would follow his big brother everywhere and wanted to be just like him. When Frank died, he was scared in the room alone. He was only twelve and didn't really understand why his brother had died, no one had explained it to him. When he would cry, his mother would lock him in the bedroom alone telling him to be quiet and if he didn't she would belt him with the strap.

She would call him a cry baby and that he would never be as good as Frank, he was stupid and useless. Rose thought, maybe this is where it began? Why he did what he did and said what he said to her and the children all these years. It was what his mother had said and done to him. That was still no excuse for his actions. Rose found it hard to believe that Betty would have done the things Jimmy was claiming of her and she was no longer alive and could not defend herself. Rose knew that Jimmy would make things up and would tell her stories that in the end even he believed they were true. Rose made the decision then, she would stay long enough to get him back on his feet, she would not let him guilt her into staying longer, she had endured too many years of pain and suffering at his hands. She would never love him again and she would never forgive him, she would wait for the right moment and then she would leave him forever.

CHAPTER 28

SEPTEMBER 1986

So much had happened in the last two years since Jimmy's accident. Ruby had two children now, a girl and a boy. Fred had two children, also a boy and a girl and Lilly had married and just had her first child, a strong baby boy. Jimmy had been away working up in Queensland for the last month, they had hardly spoken over the month and when they did it usually ended in a fight. He would be home today to see his new grandson and he said he wanted to talk to her, she hoped he would finally let her go. She had promised herself she would wait until the children had left home and started their own lives then she would leave Jimmy. Now that all her children were grown and getting on with their lives she needed to be free and start over again and find some happiness and peace.

They sat on opposite sides of the breakfast bar in the kitchen. Rose waited for Jimmy to speak, she hoped he would say he wanted to end the marriage first she knew if it was his idea he would accept it, but if she told him she was leaving he would not agree, it had to be his decision.

"Rose I've done a lot of thinking and it's time we got a divorce, I know you're not happy and neither am I so I'm going back to Queensland to stay and work. We will sort out selling the house and paying off the debts over the phone."

"Okay, I'm fine with that." Rose was so relieved she could hardly breathe, finally she would be free.

"Right so we are both free to do and see who we want. Okay then, I'll see you later." Jimmy stood up and walked to the front door, he turned, smiled then drove away.

Rose could not believe it was that simple he was letting her go, no fighting, no angry words. Her body and mind felt as if the worries about her family and the shackles that had tied her to her unhappy life for so many years had been finally hacked free, Rose felt liberated and optimistic for her new future. No more broken promises, no more broken bones and no more abuse.

What Jimmy didn't know was that Rose knew about the woman he had shacked up with in Queensland and she had been praying that he would leave her for this other woman. Rose felt sorry for the other woman, if she only knew what she was getting herself into, but her main focus now was on herself, she couldn't be worried about someone she didn't know.

Over the next two months Rose started to sort out all the details to finally get herself free from Jimmy, she couldn't believe he would let her go so easily, deep in her gut she knew it was not going to be that simple. The phone would ring in the middle of the night and when she would answer she could hear breathing on the end of the phone but no one would talk, then they would hang up. Rose knew it was Jimmy calling to see if she was home, he had told her she was free but she knew he would not really let her go.

HAT HEAD
NOVEMBER 1996

Rose had come down to spend a few days with her parents in the caravan at the little seaside village of Hat Head, she had just picked up her order of fish and chips for lunch at the take away food shop and was on her way out the door when she bumped into Tom. They had known each other for years from around the work sites, he was a plumber and a single Dad to seven boys.

"Hello Rose, what are you doing down here?" His smile was warm and he had laugh wrinkles at the corner of his eyes.

"Hi Tom, I'm down here staying with my parents for a few days to relax, taking a little break." Rose liked Tom; he was tall, strong, with dark wavy hair and a gentle disposition. He had always been courteous and respectful whenever she had seen him on the job sites.

They chatted for several minutes about the children and what they had been doing since they had last met. All the while Tom helped himself to the hot chips Rose was carrying. The conversation was easy and cheerful.

"Um, would you like to go out for dinner tonight?" Tom was bashful and hopeful and there was a twinkle in his eyes.

"You mean like a date?" Rose gazed down at her hands, it had been a long time since she had been on a date and Jimmy had repeatedly told her no man would want her, she couldn't believe it.

"Yes a date, we could have dinner and a few drinks at the club, if you'd like?"

Rose thought for a moment, why not? Jimmy and her were separated and in the process of a divorce. Tom seemed like a nice guy and it was only dinner and a few drinks, she couldn't help but warm to his charming manner.

"Sure, I'd love to, I'll meet you at the club at six o'clock." She smiled and headed back to the caravan park with what was left of their lunch.

As Tom watched her walk away he couldn't believe his luck. Rose was a beautiful woman, strong and hard working, he had heard the rumours about the way her husband used to treat her and he promised himself if she gave him the chance he would look after her for life. He knew at that moment he had met his soul mate and he would marry her one day.

Rose took her time getting ready for her first real date in a very long time, luckily she had packed a good dress and shoes just in case they went out anywhere. She applied her makeup sparingly and styled her short dark hair, put on her little black dress that flattered her slim waist and her black pump shoes. Loretta smiled as she watched her daughter dress, she was happy that finally she had freedom and a chance to find some happiness, she just hoped that Jimmy would stay away from her daughter for good now.

Rose could not believe what a fantastic evening she was having with Tom, he was so easy to talk to, they laughed and chatted like two old friends, even though

Tom said he had two left feet he whirled her around the dance floor to the music of the local band like a natural. It had been such a long time since she had experienced such freedom, such connection with the music, she felt sparks and her heart was pounding as he held her close in his arms as they danced, she felt like a giddy young girl in his arms. The club was closing and the last of the patrons were heading home, Tom took Rose's hand and walked her out to the carpark. The night sky was brilliant, the stars were bright and twinkling down on them like fairy lights. Tom put his arm around her waist and pulled her closer, his eyes twinkling like the stars, he hesitated looking deep into her eyes as if gauging if she was feeling the same way he was, Rose smiled, that was all he needed he bent down and kissed her gently on the mouth, his lips were soft and tender, bliss washed over her as she melted into his embrace, wishing the moment wouldn't end.

"I'd like to see you again, would you like to go out with me again sometime?" Tom shuffled from one foot to the other a little nervously waiting for her answer.

Rose had not felt like this in a very long time, she felt light headed and giddy and she hadn't even had much to drink, he made her feel warm and tingly all over. She really liked him and it had been so long since a man had made her feel that way.

"I'd really like that," she kissed him and headed back to the van feeling like a giggly teenager, she couldn't wait to tell her mother all about her date.

CHAPTER 29

KEMPSEY
JANUARY 1987

Rose and Tom had been dating for two months, Rose had still not told Jimmy that she had been seeing someone she was not sure of his reaction. Even though he was with another woman himself, Rose felt he would not let go easily. Lilly had dropped in yesterday afternoon with the baby to say hello while Tom was there having coffee and in her usual cheeky fashion had asked him what his intentions were towards her mother and that he better take care of her or else he would answer to her. In Tom's good natured way he played along and promised to be a true gentleman with her mother. Of course Lilly had to have the last word and on her way out the door she turned and shouted over her shoulder. "You two kids make sure you use protection now, I don't want any more brothers and sisters" she laughed and left.

Rose was busy in the kitchen preparing dinner, Tom was coming over tonight for tea. The phone rang and she felt a shiver go up her spine. She knew it was Jimmy before she even answered, she was going to tell him about Tom before someone else did. "Hello."

"Hi Rose it's me Jimmy. What are you doing?"

"I'm just working in the kitchen, preparing dinner for tonight."

"I tried calling you last night and there was no answer. Where were you?"

Rose paused and took a deep breath. "Jimmy I have been seeing someone, I was out on a date last night."

"What! What do you mean you're seeing someone, you're my wife." he scrreamed down the phone.

"Jimmy we have been separated for four months and I know you are living with a woman up there. We agreed we would get a divorce." Rose tried to keep her voice calm but she could feel his anger coming through the phone.

"Is he there now?"

"No, no one is here, it's just me." Her voice trailed off, she was losing her confidence.

"I'm coming back, don't leave there until I get home. I don't want you, but by hell no one else will have you either." Jimmy's voice was ominous and threatening.

Rose cringed at the underlying meaning in his words, she knew she had to get out before he got home. Why was he doing this? He didn't want her, he'd asked for the divorce. She phoned Tom in tears and told him what had happened.

"I'm on my way, I'll come and get you, grab some things and you can come and stay with me. I'll take care of you Rose, he won't hurt you again while I'm alive. I promise." Tom hung up the phone and grabbed his keys, he would not let Jimmy anywhere near Rose ever again that was for certain.

Rose phoned Lilly to tell her what had happened and to be wary, her father was on the war path again, she grabbed a few clothes and waited for Tom to pick her up.

Lilly was hanging the nappies on the line when she heard the phone ringing and ran inside to answer it. "Lilly, you'd better get over here."

It was her father on the phone, her heart dropped. "Why Dad, what's wrong?"

"It's your mother, get over here now." The phone clicked and there was silence.

Oh no! He had done something to her mother? Lilly picked up her three month old sleeping baby, put him in his capsule and ran to the car. It was only a five minute drive to her parents but it felt like an eternity. Why didn't she call her brother before she left home to ask him to meet her there, too late now, her only concern was to get to her mother before anything happened. She could tell by her father's voice that he had been drinking and she dreaded what she would find when she arrived. Lilly carried the capsule inside her parents' house and placed the sleeping baby in the hallway where she could hear her father in the study scratching around and talking to himself.

"Mum!" Lilly called out for her mother, fearing the worst.

"The fucking bitch isn't here. Where is she?" Jimmy was standing at the door holding a rifle he stumbled against the door frame.

"I don't know Dad. I thought she was here."

"Well she's fucking not, the slut, she's been whoring around with some bloke. I suppose you know all about it too you little bitch."

"Dad, there's no need to swear at me and call me names. Besides you and Mum called it quits last year and you are getting divorced, so why does it matter to you if she is seeing someone else?"

"Of course you would take her side, you're a fucking slut just like your mother." he spat the words at her. "You get that bitch on the phone now or I'll shoot you and that bastard child of yours."

"I'm married, he is not a bastard and I am not a slut, how can you speak to me like that? I'm your daughter."

"Are you?" Jimmy levelled the rifle at her head. "Call your fucking mother now."

"Okay I will but only if you promise to speak to her rationally and not yell and swear at her." Lilly dialled Tom's home number her mother had given it to her in case of an emergency and this was an emergency.

"Hello, Tom speaking."

"Hi its Lilly, can I speak to Mum please." Lilly tried to keep her voice calm even though her insides were doing somersaults.

"Hi Lilly, are you alright?" Rose tried to calm her shaking voice.

"Mum, I'm at the house. Dad is here and he wants to speak to you."

Jimmy wrenched the phone from her hand. "Where are you? You get back here now you fat cow, I'm your husband and you will come home right now."

Rose felt her heart go into her throat, Jimmy had Lilly at the house and she probably had the baby with her, she had to try and talk sense into him, she could tell by his slurred words he had been drinking and she knew Jimmy well enough that he would have the rifle with him.

"Jimmy I am not coming home, we are over, you agreed last year that we would get a divorce, you have moved on and so have I, now let Lilly leave."

"She's not going anywhere until you get back here, if you don't come back now, I'll shoot her and that fucking bastard kid of hers and it will be your fault." Jimmy slammed the phone down and sneered at Lilly. "You better call her back and tell her not to call the police either cause if she does I'll guarantee no one will leave this house alive, there will be a shoot out and you will get the first bullet."

Lilly never doubted a word her father said she had seen him in fits of rage before. She could see he had been drinking heavily. There were empty beer cans laying all around the floor and he had two rifles on the desk fully loaded as well as the one in his hand.

"Mum, it's me again, Dad said don't call the police or he will shoot it out with them." Lilly's voice was shaking and Rose could hear the fear in her voice.

"I won't, I've called your brother Fred he is on his way. Try not to antagonise him Lilly, I won't forgive myself if anything happens to you and the baby."

Jimmy grabbed the phone from Lilly again "Hurry up ya fucking bitch, I'm losing my patience and tell that bastard who's fucking you to show his face if he's got any balls, I know you're with him."

Rose put the phone down, she could not listen anymore, she broke down in sobs unable to control the fear that was going through her. Jimmy had told her many times that if she left he would hunt her down like a pig and kill her and now her baby daughter and grandson were in his firing line.

"Rose let me go, maybe I can talk some sense into him." Tom's heart was breaking watching Rose go through this, he would gladly put his life on the line for her.

"No Tom, he would shoot you as soon as you walked in the door. Fred will be there soon and Lilly has been around her father long enough to know what to do and say. I just hope" she couldn't bring herself to finish the sentence, the thought of what Jimmy might do was unbearable.

Lilly watched her father fill the chamber on the rifle and lock and load it, he had made her sit down on the chair in the office, she could see her sleeping son in the capsule in the hallway. Even with all this commotion he was still fast asleep she prayed he would not wake and cry, god knows what her father would do. She had to stay calm and try to reason with him.

"Dad, you know it's no good talking when you've been drinking, Mum is too scared of you, she won't come while you're threatening me or her."

Jimmy looked up from polishing the barrel and grunted.

"Dad, you and Mum have been unhappy for years, why drag it out any longer? Move on and find some-one else. Just let me leave with your grandson and I'll come back tomorrow and bring Mum and Fred and we can all sit down and talk about it reasonably." Lilly stood up and started to walk towards the door.

"You're not going fucking anywhere you fucking little slut, get back here and sit down." Her father was screaming at her now.

Lilly turned to find the rifle only inches from her head, her father was looking down the barrel at her, an evil glint in his eye and his finger hovering on the trigger. Lilly knew the rifle was loaded and that if he wanted to, he could end her life right there and then.

So many things ran through her mind: her baby, her husband, how would her mother cope with her death, she would blame herself. At that moment Lilly fully understood why her mother had stayed and put up with the physical and verbal abuse for all those years because what she feared Jimmy would do was exactly what was unfolding right now.

Lilly had a choice to make, stay or try to leave, her protective motherly instincts kicked in and in that moment she remembered something her father had told her. She bent down and picked up the baby capsule stared back at her father defiantly and with as much strength and commitment as she could muster.

"Well Dad, you taught me a lot of things in my life and one of them was to stand my ground and not to take shit from anyone. I am not a slut, I am not stupid, I am not useless and I can be whatever I want to be, and one thing is for sure, I am never going to be anything like you. I'm not taking any more of your shit, so if you're gonna shoot me and your grandson in the back like a coward then do it, because I'm leaving." Lilly's legs were like jelly, she walked out to the car placed the capsule in its holder and got in the car and drove away. It wasn't until she was up the road and out of sight of the house that she pulled over and broke down, her body shaking, she had called his bluff and had lived to walk away, she needed to get to a phone and call her mother and let her know she was ok and call Fred to stop him going to the house.

CHAPTER 30

HAT HEAD

APRIL 1987

Jimmy had finally let Rose go, he would not let her return to the house to get any of her belongings, he had told her if you're leaving you go with only the clothes on your back. He had sent boxes out with Fred with her clothes and on opening them she found he had smeared grease over most of her clothes destroying them. It had come to light over the last few months that Jimmy had been spending more than he was earning and wasting money on stupid "make it rich" schemes. Now the bank was taking the house and everything in it to sell and repay the debts. After all the years of working as hard as any man, Rose was left with nothing and was forced to apply for bankruptcy, Jimmy had been smart and put most of the loans and vehicles in her name, he didn't have to repay a thing and walked away with a clean slate.

Rose didn't care though, she was finally free from him and happy, she was madly in love with Tom. He treated her like a princess, he absolutely adored her. Rose had never felt so loved in all her life, she was wary though, could any man really be nice? Rose was still having nightmares about Jimmy and would wake up screaming during the night and when Tom tried to hold her she would push him away thinking it was Jimmy attacking her. Tom would hold her and rock her, telling her she would be safe and no one would hurt her ever again. Rose would never feel totally safe from Jimmy, the only day she would feel safe was when she saw him with her own eyes cold and dead on a slab.

Life in the sleepy little village of Hat Head with its beautiful beaches, sand dunes, rainforest and wetlands was just what Rose needed to begin to heal and start her new life. Everyone was friendly and welcoming and Tom's sons had all accepted Rose into their fathers life. Their two families blended as one and her children were all so happy to finally see their mother truly loved and adored as she deserved to be.

Often Tom and Rose would pack a picnic lunch and take the Korogoro walking track which circled the headland of Hat Head. Along the walk there were coastal views of both Smoky Cape and Crescent Head, the track took you through stands of paperbark and casuarina trees, endangered native kangaroo grass and wildflowers dotted the area when they were in season, particularly white flannel flowers. In autumn and spring they would stop and watch the whales migrating up and down the coast, and the Korogoro Arch and Cave, a formation which could be explored at low tide. They would emerge through the windswept banksias greeted by a refreshing ocean breeze and find a spot to sit and enjoy the spectacular view while they enjoyed their picnic lunch before heading home.

Their other favourite walk was to Connors Beach where they would sometimes go fishing. Rose especially loved this walk in the warmer months when the vibrant paper daisies and pea flowers bloomed, dotted among the gnarled banksias and heathland. The track wound through rainforest and sheltered gullies with spectacular views before gently winding down to the beach.

Tom was taking her fishing, she hadn't done a lot of fishing but she did enjoy it, they scampered down the rocks at The Gap onto one of Tom's favourite places, there was a great fishing hole just below them that always had fish in it, he had told her how many big fish he had caught off these rocks and not to worry if she didn't get any bites or catch a fish, you're a beginner, be patient. They had thrown their lines out and Rose had only just had time to sink under the water to the bottom when she felt an almighty tug on the line.

"I think I've got one." She squealed with delight.

"I doubt it, you probably got a snag on the rocks love, give it a tug."

"No, no I've got a fish, look it's trying to get away, it's pulling on the line."

"Bloody hell I think you're right, well come on then reel it in, let's see what you've got." Tom was impressed with this diminutive woman, he was madly and hopelessly in love with her, she may be small in stature but she had a huge heart. He would love her and shower her with affection, make her feel safe and hopefully one day she would be able to forget all of the bad things that had happened to her. He would try, that was for sure, he laughed as he watched her fighting with the fish, she pulled and wound the reel trying to pull in her fish, finally landing a big jewfish.

"Well love, that is impressive I must say, especially for your first fish, I guess I better up my game then." He pulled her close and hugged her tight, he was never ever going to let her go. "You're the best thing that's ever happened to me Rose, I thank the gods every day for bringing you into my life, it was the best day of my life when you agreed to go out with me. It's like I won the lottery." Tom bent and kissed the top of her head. "You're the most beautiful girl in the world and you're mine and I'm going to marry you one day my love."

"No Tom, I'm the lucky one." Rose tilted her head up and met his lips with a soft, warm kiss, this is how love was supposed to be, she finally felt truly loved and appreciated.

CHAPTER 31

Rose now worked at the local bowling club a few days a week behind the bar, she liked working there, everyone was friendly and the time passed quickly. Tom would come in some nights to have a drink and catch up with his mates while he waited for her to finish work. Rose looked after their finances now, Tom preferred it that way, he had been into the club the last two nights, each time asking for twenty dollars to buy a couple of drinks, Rose would hand over the money. Tonight he approached the bar grinning.

"Hey beautiful, can I have twenty dollars for a drink?" he grinned that cheeky smile of his and gave her a wink.

"No you can't, I've given you twenty dollars the last two nights," she joked.

Tom reached into his pocket and pulled out a wad of hundred dollar bills. "That's okay I got paid for a job today, I have my own money," he laughed and waved the notes at her.

Rose reached across the bar and in one swoop snatched the money. "You did have your own money now, here's the twenty dollars you asked for."

Tom laughed and took the twenty dollars. "You're worth every penny of it my little flower."

It was three years today since Tom and Rose had started living together and Rose had decided to make a special candlelight dinner as a surprise for them tonight. She was busy in the kitchen when Tom grabbed his lunchbox and thermos to set off for work, and as every other day, he stopped and kissed her on his way out.

"Can you pay the power bill today love, I forgot and it's overdue, I don't want them to cut the power off."

"Okay, what time will you be home for dinner?"

"Probably about six, all going well on the job site today, I'll see you tonight. I love you gorgeous." He blew her a kiss as he went out the door. "I'm going to marry you one day my love."

Luckily today she would finish work at two, so she had time to get home and prepare his favourite dish for the romantic meal she had planned for tonight. She took extra time setting the table with candles and flowers. Rose wanted it to be perfect, the last three years had been the best of her life, she felt totally loved, safe and secure.

As Rose cut the vegetables she thought of some of the fun times they had had over the years. Like the time he had taken her fishing near the Groper Hole and every time he threw out his line all he kept catching were little crappy fish not good for eating and she kept reeling in big brim. He looked at her and laughed and said "If you catch any more like that I'm going home or I'm gonna push you in."

Or the time he had been over at the club with a few of the boys and was late coming home and a little bit tipsy, he knew he would be in trouble, so as he was walking along the side of the house he thought he had better bring her some flowers, so he grabbed the nearest ones he could see in the dim light, straight out of the pot, dirt and all, he walked in through the back door with a sheepish grin holding the flowers in front of him.

"A flower for my little flower."

Rose, trying not to laugh, replied "It's not a flower it's a bromeliad and get it outside you're dropping dirt all over the carpet." How could she be mad with this wonderful, loving man, he made her laugh every day. It made her laugh recalling the time she had ridden the push bike to work and Tom had called in to the club and had one to many drinks with the boys. When it was time to go home he offered to ride the bike home and she could drive the ute. Rose laughed telling him he wouldn't make it home on the bike. Tom scoffed, I'll show you he said and off he went weaving his way along the track over the pedestrian bridge, knocking his knuckles on the sides of the bridge scraping off skin, unable to get up the hill he threw the bike on his shoulder and carried it up the back way behind the houses. Trampling all the cabbages in his neighbour's vegetable patch, the next day the neighbour was over complaining how the dogs had crushed all his plants. They never did tell him the truth.

Rose had the table set and the meal was ready to dish out as soon as Tom arrived home. She had put on the pretty green dress he had bought for her for Christmas and pulled one side of her hair back with a comb. Rose didn't bother with makeup Tom had told her she didn't need it, she was a natural beauty. She could hear the sound of his work truck coming along the straight, she lit the candles and dashed around and turned all the lights off and waited for him to come through the door. She could hear him muttering and cursing as he came up the back steps. On entering through the back door he called out to her.

"Rose I told you to pay the bloody power bill today, looks like they've cut the power off."

Rose walked over and flicked on the light switch, the lights burst on in a white flash lighting the romantically set table for two. Tom looked at the table then back to Rose before he could utter a word.

"Well that's the first and last time you will be getting a candlelight dinner."

CHAPTER 32

MAY 1993

The years seemed to fly by. Rose had been with Tom for over six years now. They had settled into a comfortable routine. Between them they had a blended family of ten adult children and their families and as Tom would always say they are "our children".

Everyone got along so well and they often dropped in to stay and go fishing, the grandchildren loved their Pop, he would take them fishing and taught them how to catch the beach worms and bait the hook, throw out their lines and how to take the fish off the hook, he would roll around the lounge room floor wrestling with the younger ones, then they would sit up on his lap and he would tell them funny stories making them laugh, always telling them how much he loved their Grandma and that one day he was going to marry her. Rose and Tom had a cheeky, playful banter between them and could not imagine life any other way. Lilly and her two boys were over for the afternoon, Rose overheard Tom telling Lilly "I'm going to marry your Mother one day."

Rose thought "my oath you will". The next day she went up to the Kempsey court house, filled in the appropriate paperwork, booked the date and when Tom got home from work she sat the papers down in front of him.

"What's this love?"

"Just sign there." Rose pointed to the spot for him to sign. "You keep saying you're going to marry me, well I've booked the courthouse for next month so you can do just that."

Tom grinned and without hesitation signed his name, he didn't need to think twice he wanted more than anything for Rose to be his wife. He grabbed her around the waist, picked her up and twirled her around the room. "You're stuck with me, my little flower."

JUNE 1993

Rose and Tom stood in front of the judge facing each other holding hands at the Kempsey Court House. It was a small intimate wedding with their children there to witness the commitment between them. Rose wore a royal blue skirt and matching jacket, the jacket had white beading on the front with a circle and then strips fanning out like sunlight rays. A small blue hair piece with white beading and flowers. Tom was dressed in a light blue suit and a royal blue tie to match her dress. The ceremony was underway and the room was full of love and smiles.

"Tom, do you take Rose to be your lawfully wedded wife, to love her, comfort her, honour and keep her, in sickness and in health, forsaking all others, as long as you both shall live?"

"I sure do."

"Rose, do you take Tom to be your lawfully wedded husband, to love him, comfort him, honour and keep him, in sickness and in health, forsaking all others, as long as you both shall live?"

"I do."

"You may now exchange your vows."

"I love you Rose, I take you to be my partner; to have and to hold, from this day forward. I give to you my unending love and devotion. I will help you when you need it, and step aside when you don't. I promise to be true to you, to cherish you, and to share my thoughts, hopes, and dreams with you. I look forward to spending the rest of my life with you, my best friend. I will love you forever."

"I love you Tom. You are my best friend. Today I give myself to you in marriage. I promise to encourage and inspire you, to laugh with you in times of joy, and comfort you in times of sorrow and struggle. I promise to love you in good times and in bad, when life seems easy and when it is hard, when our love is simple, and when it is an effort. I promise to cherish you, and to always hold you in the highest regard.

These things I give you today, and all the days of our lives."

Tom placed the ring on Rose's finger. "With this ring I thee wed."

Rose was trembling with excitement as she placed the ring on Tom's finger. "With this ring I thee wed."

The judge smiled, "It is with great pleasure that I now pronounce you husband and wife. You can kiss your bride now Tom."

Tom pulled Rose to him and smiled "Well you're stuck with me now my little flower." He took Rose in his arms and every moment he'd lived before this moment faded away, as he dipped her back and kissed his dark haired beauty, he knew his life had truly begun.

The reception was held at the Hat Head Bowling Club, their friends had set about decorating it and organising the food and music. Everyone loved Tom and they were so happy he had found a perfect partner in Rose. Their children had told them not to worry about the wedding cake they had it all organised, this should have sent alarm bells ringing for Rose but she was too happy to give it another thought. The meal was finished and the band was warming up when Tom tapped his glass to get everyone's attention.

"I'd just like to say a few words before I take my beautiful bride on the dance floor for our first dance as husband and wife. You all know my story and the struggles I have been through in my life and you also know how my life changed the day I met this amazing woman here." Tom looked down at Rose whose smile was lighting up the room. "The first day I asked her out I knew I would marry her one day, she is the light of my life and I thank my lucky stars every day that she walked into my life and agreed to take me on." Tom looked out at his children. "To you my children and that's all of our children, they are not hers or mine, you are all our children, one family together, I thank you for combining as one and loving us both. We are truly blessed to have such wonderful children that love and support us, we love you all. Okay my little flower, now let's have that dance."

There were tears and laughter as they took to the floor, the band started up with what would be their song "You're My Best Friend" once they had finished it was time for the cake. Their combined children were standing in front of the cake table laughing.

"Okay you lot what have you been up to?" Rose had just realised she hadn't seen the cake, she had trusted the ten children to organise it.

They laughed and moved aside. Sitting on the table was a large white cake with ten miniature prams on it with the wording "Sorry Mum and Dad, we are all coming back home to live." Tom and Rose burst out laughing. The cake was perfect just like their love for each other and their family.

THE HONEYMOON
JULY 1993

The weather was cold and blustery when Rose and Tom left for their honeymoon, it may have been cold and bleak outside the car as they drove along but the love and warmth inside, left them without a care, they were heading down the coast taking two weeks to get to Victoria to stay with Tom's sister for a few days before making their way back home. They spent their time leisurely driving down the coast highway stopping into little towns and beaches and enjoying their first real holiday together, staying overnight at quaint motels and enjoying sunset meals by the sea. Through the coastal towns to the inland farms and mountains turning off at the Mornington Peninsular south east of Melbourne travelling past all the farms, wineries and small towns with its beaches and scenic views. The eastern shorelines were lined with mangroves and mudflats before tapering down to Sandy Point at its most southeasterly point. The mudflats gave way to sandy beaches then to rocky points further south where the peninsular meets Bass Strait. They decided rather than drive through Melbourne and around the bay, to take the ferry across from Sorrento to Queenscliff then to Torquay where they stayed the night, before heading off on the two hundred and forty four kilometre drive along the Great Ocean Road.

It was windy and freezing cold when they stopped along the Great Ocean Road to admire the towering rock formations of the twelve apostles, the massive limestone structures towered forty five metres above the Southern Ocean, their beauty and size left Rose awe struck, the forces of nature, wind and sea had gradually eroded the softer limestone, forming caves in the cliffs which became arches and when they collapsed, rock islands were left isolated from the shore.

They stopped for the night in the town of Warnambool, a pretty coastal town on the Princess Highway and the end of the Great Ocean Road. They spent two days here exploring and enjoying the laid back friendly hospitality. Next stop was Horsham to Tom's sisters where they enjoyed three days of sightseeing and good company before making their way back through Gundagai, it was raining so heavily they could hardly see the road ahead through the windscreen. They found a little motel and stopped in for the night. The next morning they set off up to Dorrigo and down the winding mountain road stopping along the famed waterfall way to admire the waterfalls in full flow from all the winter rain, finally arriving back at their beach side home after three weeks.

CHAPTER 33

Loretta lay sweating and weak in the hospital bed with her daughter Rose beside her. She slowly opened her eyes and whispered, "I have to tell you something, this is very important."

"Please, Mum, don't try to speak. Save your energy," Rose urged.

"No, I have to tell you, please let me finish." She gasped for breath. The cancer had taken most of her strength, but she knew she had to tell Rose the truth and there was not much time left. She had kept the secret way too long.

"I don't know how to tell you this. I have wanted to tell you so many times but I couldn't find the words. You know your father?" Rose nodded, "Well, he wasn't your real father." Rose was silent. She didn't know what to say. Was her mother having delusions from the morphine? Could this be true? She tried to focus on what her mother was saying.

"You know that I had an arranged marriage to your father, but I didn't love him. He was a cruel man. When the war was on, there was an Italian prisoner of war sent to our farm to help us. You've seen his photo in my album." Rose nodded, not sure what to say. Her mother continued.

"Your father was away a lot and I became close to Lorenzo. I taught him to read and write English." She paused, "It's a long story and one that I don't have the time or the strength to tell you now," her voice was just a thin thread, her hand touched Rose's, her fingers long and soft. "It's written in my diaries for you to read. You'll find them in the bottom draw of my dresser. We fell in love and ... well ...!" Loretta stopped and took a deep breath, Rose noticed she looked embarrassed.

"It's okay. Mum, I understand. The Italian is my real father, isn't he?" Loretta nodded, she had tears running down her face.

"I should have told you years ago. I don't know what happened to him, I don't even know if he's still alive. I hope I have not left it too late to tell you. I'm sorry. Rose, can you forgive me?"

Rose looked at this woman, who had given her life and who had sacrificed so much for her. How could she feel anything but love?

"Mum, it's okay. I understand and there's nothing to forgive." Rose took her mother's frail body in her arms and they both wept until Loretta fell asleep exhausted.

Rose sat beside her mother's bed, watching her peaceful sleeping face. She had so many questions still to be answered. She knew she had to find the man who was her father. Did she have sisters and brothers? Why had he not come back for her mother and her? So many things now made sense. Now she finally understood why she had never been very close to her father.

August 1996

Rose sat at the kitchen table, she needed answers but where to start? She thought her best bet was the Italian Embassy in Australia. Hopefully they could help her locate her father in Italy. Rose hoped that she could find out the answers before it was too late to put her mother's mind at rest, she knew her mother felt regret for not telling her the truth earlier. She prayed the embassy could help locate him and she hoped that he would receive her with open arms, she had so many questions.

To The Italian Embassy
    Canberra
    To Whom It May Concern

I am writing to you in the hope you may be able to help me find my father. He was an Italian Prisoner of War and spent time on a farm in Bellingen NSW between 1944 to 1946. His name was Lorenzo Cammalota from Verona and he would have been about twenty seven years old at the time. This is all the information I have. I would be grateful for any information you could supply.

Regards

Mrs Rose Francis

Rose looked at the address on the envelope that had arrived today, it was from the Italian Embassy she was almost too afraid to open it. What had they learned about her father?

Italian Embassy Canberra12 Grey St,Deakin ACT 2600

13th September 1996

Dear Mrs Francis

I am writing in reference to your letter regarding information on Mr. Lorenzo Cammalota, a prisoner of war during the 1939/1945 conflict. Unfortunately this embassy is unable to provide you with this information, however, your request has been forwarded to the Municipality of Verona and the Distretto Militare (Recruiting Office) also in Verona.

I will not hesitate to contact you again as soon as a reply is received. Yours sincerely,

Giulio Timoni Counselor.

Rose's heart dropped. She would have to be patient and hope that the office in Verona could find some information about her father. Christmas had now come and gone and still no word about her Italian father. Her mother was getting frailer by the day, the cancer was taking all her strength and she slept most of the time with the help of painkillers. Rose thought that maybe she was hanging on until she heard word about Lorenzo, so she could die in peace knowing that he would get to see his little girl again.

Finally a letter arrived, hopefully this would contain better news.

5th February 1997

Italian Embassy Canberra 12 Grey St, Deakin ACT 2600

Dear Mrs Francis, We have received information concerning Mr Lorenzo Cammarota (and not Cammalota) born in Verona, who appears from the matriculation documents assumed in the Municipality of Verona to be taken prisoner during the 1940-45 war, he was a soldier in the Italian Armed Forces and a prisoner of war in Australia during the 1940/1945 conflict.

From the informations received by relevant Italian Authorities we inform you that, unfortunately, the above mentioned person and wife have died.

Yours sincerely,

Giulio Timoni Counselor.

Rose sat outside the hospital staring at the letter, her father had died, now she would never get to meet him or have the answers to her questions. A tear rolled down her cheek for the father she never knew and for her mother who had kept this secret all her life, she knew that her mother would be disappointed. She had to go inside, her mother was expecting her. Rose spent every day at the hospital now, at her mother's side as the disease ate away at her body. Rose took a deep breath and made her way down the hospital corridor to her mother's room as she entered Loretta turned and smiled at her.

"Any news from Italy?' her voice was just a whisper.

Rose sat beside her mother and took her frail hand in hers. "Yes Mum, they've located him but unfortunately he has passed away."

"Oh Rose I am so sorry I should have told you years ago, now you will never get to meet him." Loretta's eyes welled with tears, why had she kept this from her daughter? She should have told her sooner.

"It's okay Mum, I'll keep looking, maybe there is still family there I can still find my answers."

CHAPTER 34

Ministeroperi Beni Culturali E Ambientali
  Archivio Di Stato Verona
  7th March 1997

Dear Mrs Francis,

I read with attention your letter under-standing how much is your wish to know all about your father and family. Unfortunately the war originated a lot of situations like your own.

I'm sorry to inform you that this office cannot comply with your request because we don't keep certificates of birth of Verona and his province, and so it is impossible for us to check if there is a person with family name

Cammarota with that date and place of birth, we conserve only military documents until the birthdate year 1911.

For documents after that year you have to ask the Distretto Militare di Verona - Via September - 37100 VERONA for a "Foglio matriculate di Lorenzo Cammarota, Verona" with this application I think you could have good probability of success.

I made a search in the telephone directory of Verona's province and I found some families named Cammarota in Verona, but no one with the name Lorenzo.

I'm sorry about the impossibility to help you with more informations about your father, but we have not the document you need.

With Best Regards

Il Diretto Reggente.

On the nineteenth of March, Loretta lost her battle with cancer and passed away with her family at her bedside. Martin rarely left Loretta's side and the children had to make him take a break, he was devastated to lose the love of his life, they had shared so much together she had been his one true love and he could not imagine life without his dark haired Italian beauty. Rose and Alice had stayed every night sleeping on mattresses on the hospital floor staying close to their mother for the last several weeks so she would never be alone while the other siblings stayed during the day. Loretta looked at her children and her loving husband one last time, closed her eyes and as she took her last breath she smiled, she had lived a good life surrounded by love and family, she would see them all again one day.

Rose felt her mother's hand go lifeless in hers, she knew her mother would have no more pain and had gone on to a better place, but that did not make the pain any easier to bear. It had been heartbreaking to watch her once vibrant mother waste away to nothing from the ugly cancer that consumed her. Rose felt lost now, she had confided in her eldest daughter the secret her mother had told her and Ruby was encouraging and supporting her in her search. Now her mother had gone she would be unable to share any news on her search, she had hoped to find out more about

Lorenzo and his family before her mother died. She was sure that no one else in her family knew anything and she didn't want to ask her father Martin if he had any information that might help, she wished she asked her mother more questions. So many questions left unanswered for now.

Loretta had left her children a letter.

To my six children, Rose, Max, Daphne, George, Charlie and Alice. I would just like to tell you how much I love you all and you have been a wonderful family to me. I love you all and hope God showers you all with blessings and when God calls me home you will understand. I will always be in loving distance and one day we will meet again.

Love mother xxx

Italian Embassy Canberra12 Grey St,Deakin ACT 2600

24th March 1997

Dear Mrs Francis,

From Information received we inform you that Mr Lorenzo Cammarota, born in Verona has two daughters. Their addresses are attached.

CAMMAROTA Rosa, CAMMAROTA Angelica

Yours sincerely,

Giulio Timoni Counselor.

Rose had received addresses from the Italian Embassy for two women whom she believed were her half sisters and now it was time to write and find out the truth. She had no idea if they knew about her and she hoped they would keep an open mind to what she was about to write to them. Her only wish was that her mother could have known she had found the family.

Dear Signora Angelica

Sono serivere lettera in Inglese non capisco Italian, voi capisco inglese mia chiamo Rose Francis no 52 annie oggi.

I have been searching for Signor Lorenzo Cammarota and the Italian Embassy in Australia have given me the information that both he and his wife have passed on and that you are his daughter and have kindly given me your name and address.

During the second World War when Signor Lorenzo was in the Armed Forces he was a war prisoner and he was transported to Australia around 1942 or 1943. He was sent to my parents farm in a small village called Gleniffer in New South Wales, a state of Australia and was there until the war ended in 1945 when he returned home to Italy. My mother was Loretta, my father was Daniel, I was named Rose.

I have always known of Lorenzo and his photo was in my mother's album. Late last year when my mother was told she had cancer and only a few months to live she told me that Lorenzo was in fact my real father, and she gave me the photo, two linen towels and a hand knitted silk scarf that he had brought out from Italy and given to her for keepsakes.

Mother said he knew about me and loved me. I was born on the 31-03-1945 while he was in Australia and that she wrote to him for a while after his return to Italy.

I also have two notebooks he used to write in, while he was learning English, on the front of one of these books written in pencil is my birthdate and the word figlia.

I truly hope this letter does not upset or distress you as that is not my intention. I would so much love to find out about my father and his family, where he lived and his life. To learn all about my family and heritage.

My mother passed away only two weeks ago and I received a letter from the Italian Embassy just one week later informing me I have two half-sisters. I have been looking forward to finding out more about my father and the news of your existence coming so close to losing my mother has lifted my spirits.

I hope you are not too upset by this news. I would dearly love to hear from you and look forward and hope for a reply. I am enclosing a copy of the photograph I have of your father and one of myself. I have also written to your sister Rosa

My best regards Rose

Rose sealed the envelope with hope and love, tomorrow she would go to town to send it, all she could do now was once again wait for a response.

April 1997 A Letter from Italy

Rose excitedly opened and read the letter written in broken English and post marked from Italy.

17th April 1997

Dear Rose,We are those who you called your sisters.

We ask your pardon if we seemed to you a bit cold. We can understand what you have proved when your mother told you who was your real father, but now is your turn to understand our feeling in front of your really unexpected letter. If the revelation was a bolt from the blue for you, it would be a real bomb for us who knew our father and his behaviour. We ask you to understand how we feel now and please do not misinterpret us. If what you write us is true, we ask you something, more than a photo and an address written by our father.

You wrote us that you have got some notebooks where our father took English notes and on the front of one of these books there are your birthdate and the word figlia written on it. You added that your mother wrote to our father for a while after his return to Italy, have you got some letters that justify their relationship and where he spoke about the existence of their daughter? If you have them please send us a copy to understand a bit more and to have an answer to many questions we wonder.

Why didn't your mother tell you anything during all these years? Why didn't our father recognise you as his daughter and come back to Italy after your birth? Please help us to under- stand and make clear the whole situation. If everything you told us is really the truth, we will be happy to give you information about our father and his family and why not to meet you too.

We just tell you that Lorenzo Cammarota was the sweetest, most affectionate father in the world and he loved his family so much to give his life for them.

We are looking forward to hearing news from you. Lots of love

Angelica and Rosa

May 1997

Rose re read the letter several times, they did not believe her, they didn't accept that she was their half sister. How was she going to prove it? The letters that her mother had received all those years ago had been destroyed, all she had were photographs and one with his old address on the back. That didn't prove anything, why didn't she ask her mother more questions? It was too late now. The only thing she could do now was to sit and write them a letter and pour her heart out to them and hope that they would give her a chance to get to know them and find out more about her father.

Sunday 4th May 1997

Dear Angelica and Rosa

Thank you so very much for your letter. I do under-stand your feelings and doubts and I'm sorry if I caused you any hurt and did not mean to bring dishonour to your father or family it's just that when mother told me,

I felt a need to find out about him, the family and the country. It was an answer to some questions and doubts I had through my life why I never felt close to the man I called father, even though there was a small photo I've always had a feeling about it and often over the years would look at it and wonder "is that my real father?" I never knew but just felt there was something but one does not like to have other than pure thoughts of their mother so I never had the courage to ask.I do not have any written proof of what I say. I don't know what became of the letters. I can only suppose they were destroyed many years ago. I don't know if your father recognised me as his daughter perhaps just between mother and himself. I do know he went to the hospital when I was born. Circumstances of the time prevented too much being said. The morality of those years these things aren't done or if they were they weren't talked about so people kept their true feelings hidden and got on with the lives they were expected to live.I do know your father had no choice but to go back to Italy as the Army picked up all prisoners to be sent to back their homes. The only way he could have stayed was to go into hiding and become an illegal immigrant. Mother said she wanted to go with him but had no money, a young baby and no way to travel.

I don't know why she never told me before, I can only surmise that she didn't want to cause trouble or maybe she thought I would lose my love and respect for her. In the last few weeks before her death I told her I'd found your father and that he had already passed and she said "I'm sorry I should have told you years ago maybe you could have had a chance to meet him." You say he was sweet and affectionate, mother said he was very quiet and gentle. I do wish I could have met him.

My mother's marriage was arranged to a much older man. It was a marriage in name only. She was with him for many years and I was the only child. Your father lived in the house with them so I think perhaps two lonely people formed a relationship that should not have been, something that had to be kept hidden. The man I knew as my father many years ago told my now ex-husband about the relationship between mother and your father. That I was your father's child. My ex-husband sometimes brought this up when we had an argument and this added to my doubts. I didn't want to believe this of my mother so I kept it all inside and still didn't ask and now it's too late, I wish I had.Mother remarried when I was seven and had five more children and I have a wonderful step father, two sisters and three brothers none of who know any of this. I wouldn't risk upsetting or hurting their memories of a lovely wife and mother if I wasn't sure it was true. You may wonder with all this family why I want to find my real father. It's just something I feel I need to know, I'm very proud of my Italian heritage.

My mother's family also came from Italy from Val-Malenco. All my life people have asked me if I'm Italian and now they ask my daughters the same thing and until recently I thought it was because of my mother's side of the family. Please believe me I don't want to cause any upsets or trouble in your lives and if you don't want your family or friends to know of this I'd still like to write to you just be known as a friend or pen friend.

A bit about myself. I am fifty two years old. My eldest daughter Ruby has a daughter and a son she is thirty five. My son Fred is thirty three and has a son and a daughter. My youngest daughter Lilly is thirty two and has two sons. I have remarried and live in a little seaside village called Hat Head about three hundred kilometres north from Sydney, our state capital and about one hundred and twenty kilometres from where your father spent his time in Australia. I don't work now so I spend my time at home enjoying the garden. I like knitting, crocheting, tapestry and even trying folk art painting.

To my letter and for your understanding in a difficult situation and I look forward to a further reply from you.

Lots of love Rose

CHAPTER 35

VERONA – ITALY
10th MAY 1997

Angelica had gone to see her Aunty Annettea, she knew that her father and sister had been close, maybe she would know something. As usual her aunt was in the kitchen cooking.

"Hello my little angel, what brings you here to see your old aunty?" Annettea kissed her niece on both cheeks and ushered her into the kitchen, the aroma of tomatoes, onion and basil cooking wafted through the air.

"I need to ask you a question and I'm not sure how to start." Angelica felt uncomfortable with what she was about to ask her Aunty, she didn't know if she really wanted an answer, she shuffled from foot to foot.

"Just ask it Angelica, you know I will always tell you the truth."

"We have received a letter from a woman in Australia who says she is our sister. Did Papa ever mention anything about a child? Do we have a sister in Australia?"

Annettea stood silent for a moment, finally she could tell the secret that Lorenzo had asked her to keep all those years ago. "Mio Dio" she sighed, "make us a coffee, I need to get something from the bedroom and we will sit down and I will tell you what your father told me many years ago."

Once they were seated at the table Annettea opened the box she had retrieved from her bedroom, it was dusty and tattered.

"When your father came home to Italy from Australia he told Mumma about a woman he had fallen in love with and a child they had together. He wanted to bring them here to Italy to live, he loved them very much. Your Nonna would not hear of this, she refused to let him go and she did everything she could to stop him, there was little money so it became impossible. She forbade him to ever mention them again to her. They lost contact over the years and finally your father had to let them go. Before he married your mother he gave me this box. It has a couple of photos in it and a few little knick knacks. He asked me to keep it safe, he told me his story in the case that one day his daughter came looking for him. He always loved her and thought of her often. He wanted her to know that he did try to come back for her."

Angelica sat with her mouth open in disbelief. It was true, she had a half sister. This woman in Australia really was her sister, she looked at the photo. It was the same photo that Rose had sent to them. Annettea patted her hand.

"This is good news, another sister, I have hoped and prayed that one day she would come looking for us, now we must make her welcome because that is what your father would have wanted."

"I have to go tell Rosa, I will be back tomorrow. I want to know more." Angelica didn't wait for the reply; she was out the door and on her way to her sister's house.

Rose was out in the garden when she heard the phone ring, she made a dash for the phone, almost knocking over the side table on her way past.

"Hello?"

"Hello, is that Mrs Rose Francis?" The voice sounded Italian.

"Yes it is."

"Mrs Francis I am an Italian interpreter and I have Angelica and Rosa Cammarota on the other line who would like for me to tell you something important." Rose had butterflies, they were ringing her from Italy, what did this mean?

"Are you there?"

"Oh yes sorry go ahead please." She could hear two female voices talking excitedly; she had no idea what they were saying.

"Mrs Francis they wanted to tell you that they spoke to their Aunty Annettea and she knew about you,

they believe you. You are their sister and they look forward to getting to know you. They will write soon."

Rose had tears streaming down her face, they believed her, they accepted her, she may not get to meet
her father but she would be able to meet her half sisters
and maybe find some answers. She decided right then
that she would save and make the trip to Italy to her
father's birth place no matter what it took.

"Tell them thank you, thank you."

"They said bye for now." That was it a click on the
end of the phone they were gone.

Tom came out from the bathroom. "Who was that
love?"

"It was Italy, my sisters, they believe me." Rose was
still standing with the phone in her hand unable to
fully comprehend what had just happened, tears of
happiness streaming down her face. Tom flung his
arms around her and kissed her head.

"Well my little flower I guess you better start saving
for a trip to Italy to meet them."

A few weeks later Ruby was staying with Rose for
a holiday. Rose had been keeping Ruby up to date
on her Italian family and Ruby was so excited for her

mother. Rose had now told Fred and Lilly about her Italian family but had not yet told anyone else in the family. She wanted to protect her father Martin, she was still unsure how much he knew.

They arranged a phone call with Rose's Italian sisters while Ruby was staying, using a translator service. It was incredible to speak to each other for the first time, to hear the voices of sisters she had never known. They were so sad that Rose had not known their father, there were tears from Angelica and Rosa, tears from Rose, tears from Ruby and even the translator on the phone was crying as she listened to their story and helped them to get to know each other.

Rose felt such relief when they ended the call, finally she would meet her family, finally that thing she couldn't put her finger on was now within reach. Tomorrow she would sign up to study the Italian language so she could speak with her sisters when she made the journey to Italy to meet them.

28th May 1997

Dear Rose,

I am very sorry about answering you late but I need a translator because I can't speak English. I'll do my best to reply as quick as I can. I know it is important my letter and you are looking forward to receiving some news from us. You have sincerely answered to my questions and I thank you very much for this. I'm happy your mother and you are able to have a new life after your first marriage broke.

I'm the youngest of family's children and Rosa is the eldest one, but we are not alone there are two brothers. Carlo who is forty five, he's not married and has been living with me for five years since mother died (I will speak of him in one of my following letters) Luigi who is forty two, he's married, he lives in my village and he's got three children. there is also my Aunt, my father's sister named Annettea who is seventy-four, she is widowed and has three children, my cousins.

What can I tell you about my father? He was a very honest man and very proud of what he had, even that it was very little. He suffered very much in his life, on one hand lots of suffering and sorrow but on the other everybody loved him. Dear Rose I can assure you that his life was very miserable just as his eyes were. As I know him I can assert that even if he never said a word about your existence, he has always kept you in his heart, perhaps this is one of the reasons he had sad eyes. I find it strange that my eldest sister is called Rosa so similar to yours Rose and my middle name is Loretta like your Mother. I think it was our father's way of remembering you both.

Many times I've heard him saying that if he could, he would go back to Australia. Now I can understand why. He has never mentioned he had another child and I supposed that as your mother did, he didn't want to reveal to anyone because he was afraid of losing his family's respect and love. His life was very simple as he was, he taught me many important principles, respect of myself and other people, pride to be what I am, not to be ashamed of my condition, not to fear anything, to be brave in facing all life problems just as he did in the end, to love life and this teaching has had a lot of importance to me.

I am thirty four, I am married and have three children, boys. I live in the same village in which my parents and grandparents were born. It is a small village in-habited by only eight thousand people thirty kilometres from Verona. I would like to get a job but there is no one to care for my children or brother. My family is big and I don't have much spare time.

Now I would like to let you know my feelings about you while I'm writing I am very serene, but don't judge me wrongly. I don't feel affection for you because you enter in my family only at this point in life. I ask you some time to get used to you, to appreciate you and why not? To be fond of you. I will be very glad to hear from you and I'll be happier if we can meet one day.

Here are some photos of my family, I've written the names on the back. Please answer me as soon as you can. I'm looking forward to receiving other news from you.

Ciao Love Angelica

2nd June 1997

Dear Rose

I am Rosa, I'm answering to you alone and not with Angelica only to try and explain my feelings. I've read

*your letter again and again for me it has been derang-
ing to know about your existence and now there is a
great confusion inside my heart. I am a strong tempered
woman used to overcome all difficulties that life brings
around and I had many also big ones but now in front
of what is happening, I feel like a frightened child. I
wish my father was still alive to answer my questions
I'd like very much to know why he didn't recognise you
officially. I'd like to know why, as I am the oldest among
my brothers and sisters he would never confided to me
his secret even though he had placed all his confidence in
me and I never disappointed him as a daughter.*

*My father used to tell me I was his right arm and
that when he looked at my face it was like seeing the sun
rising. Thirteen years have gone since his death, and I
miss him so much as the first day. I loved and respected
him and maybe his silence about you was in order not
to give us sorrow or maybe because of the fear to lose his
family's love and peoples respect. However my questions
will never find an answer.*

*Dear Rose, I think the only thing we can do now for
respect to our father is to accept our being sisters and keep
the secret inside our hearts. You can write to me any time*

you want to, the way you write to a sister. I will always answer to your letters even if I don't speak or write English and I have to ask the help of an interpreter.

Dear Rose I still would have many things to tell you but I am not in condition to write any longer. Forgive me and give a little time and we will learn to know and love each other a bit. I send you a photo of mine and write something about myself.

I am nearly forty-eight, I have been married for twenty seven years to a wonderful man. I have a son and he is twenty two. I don't have a job. I spend my time taking care of my house, my garden and doing other typical woman works, such as embroidery and sewing and I love reading.

a hug with love Rosa

JULY 1997

Rose had made the decision to go to Italy to meet her family and had booked her flight for February the next year. She had signed up at TAFE and was studying speaking Italian and she was doing quite well. Now she had to talk to her father and tell him what she had found out. As she drove to Martin's farm she wondered did he know about her real father? She would soon have the answer.

"Hi Dad." Rose embraced her father and kissed his cheek. "Dad, I need to talk to you about something and it's really important."

"What's bothering you love?" They sat on the old seat on the front porch.

"Dad, my father wasn't Daniel, my real father was an Italian prisoner of war named Lorenzo."

"Who have you been talking to, your Aunty Kathy?"

"No Dad, Mum told me when she found out about her cancer. Did you know? Does Aunty Kathy know too?"

"Yes love, I've known about Lorenzo from the very first day I met your mother." He took her hand in his. "Your mother wanted to tell you so many times but she didn't know how, she was worried how you would react and she didn't want to hurt you. Lorenzo also sent your mother letters and a belt he had made for you and inside the belt he had put a note saying "ask your mother about your father" she took it out before giving you the belt. There was a lot that happened back then that she didn't talk about much, it was too hard for her to talk about those days on the farm with Daniel. Maybe you should go see Aunty Kathy and chat to her. She will be able to fill in the blanks for you or at least some of them."

"Well Dad I have found the family in Italy, Lorenzo has passed away but I have sisters and brothers and I'm saving to go and visit them in Verona next year, I just wanted you to know."

Martin hugged his daughter. "I'm so pleased for you Rose, maybe you will find some inner peace when you get there."

Rose went straight to her mother's sister Aunty Kathy and asked her about what she knew of her father, she told her all about the abuse her mother had suffered at the hands of Daniel and how she never wanted to marry him but her father had forced her, she had no choice in the matter, she told her about the love that Lorenzo and Loretta had for each other and his promise to come back for them, but they lost contact and it wasn't until many years later that he wrote her telling about his mother's deception, hiding Loretta's letters from him. By the time he found out they had both moved on and married other people. One thing she stressed to Rose was that her mother always wanted to tell her but could never find the right words or the right time. She didn't want her daughter to think any less of her for falling in love and conceiving a child with someone who wasn't her husband. Rose now understood why. It didn't matter, she loved her mother and nothing she could have done or said would have changed that. She was her mother after all.

LETTERS FROM ITALY

August 1997

Dear Rose,

Thank you for sending me your photo's, I will keep them in my family album. The first letter you sent me was badly translated by my nephew so I misinterpreted your feelings. Then I asked for translation to another person and now I can understand what you write.

When I received your second letter I plucked up the courage and I asked my Aunt Annettea if my father had a daughter while he was in Australia. She told me it was true and the story of what had happened. This is why I thanked you for your sincerity. What you don't know is that the day my father came back from Australia, when he was at the front door, he said to his mother. "Look Mumma! This little girl looks like you, she is my daughter, I'll go back to her." and showed her the photo, the one of you and your Mother. But he had no money and his mother who was a very severe woman didn't allow him to leave again and she tried all ways to stop my father from returning for you. So as time went on he was obliged to give up his dream to see you again. When he married my mother, he gave the photo to his sister Annettea asking her to keep his daughter's photo while he would keep her in his heart. You have the same eyes and the same smile our father had, perhaps this is the reason you looked like me a lot when you were my age. I look like him a lot physically but I also have the same character. In various situations I give space to my feelings, I listen to my heart and my reason is put aside.

I think our daddy knows we've found each other or better perhaps he helps us in someway to get in touch with one another, so beyond finding a bit of him in us, you have found a bit of all that love he felt for you.

I am one hundred and fifty seven centimetres tall and I am very thin even if I eat a lot. I have always been very lively and joyful, when I am sad if I have some trouble I try to hide it inside myself. I started working when I was fourteen years old in the field, then I worked in a factory until twenty nine, I can sew, knit and crochet. During the day I do housework and look after my children, my garden isn't very large so I don't spend much time gardening. I am instead very busy with Carlo. I told you he is forty five and I don't know who can look after him. He had a terrible accident when he was young and he cannot speak or walk, he has to be looked after. In the last year he has gotten worse and worse. He is always in bed because he can't sit anymore and I find it difficult to feed him. This doesn't cause me any trouble because I have chosen to keep him with me. I promised my parents while they were alive that I would keep him until his death, sometimes Rosa helps me.

I started going to the disco when I was very young, I like dancing very much, even now I dance but it happens very rarely. I met my husband going to the disco when I was fourteen. I was twenty when we married. I was twenty two when I first became a mother. My husband Antonio is now thirty eight and he is a very sweet man and he loves me very much. He helps me with our children and with Carlo a lot. He is home from work only in the evening and Sunday, he works one hundred and twenty kilometres from our house so he goes out early in the morning and comes back late in the evening.

My children are excited about having family in Australia and have told their friends and I have told my Aunts and friends. I would like to know more about you and my nephew and nieces even if they are at my age more or less. I thank you for giving me hospitality in case I could come to Australia. I don't know how or when But I hope to manage and to organise a journey through the places my father spoke about.

Even if you don't speak Italian, come over all the same, we will find a way to understand each other. You will be welcomed in my house as will be your family. Our father worked as bricklayer in a building enterprise, the house where I live is simple but I am proud as my father built it with his own hands and many sacrifices. Luigi, my brother, has accepted you as his sister, he doesn't write you because he can't speak English and he doesn't know anyone who can help him. He reads your letters and he wishes to meet you as I do.

There are many things I want to tell you and time by time I will do. I send you Luigi's and his families greetings, Aunt Annettea sends you hugs and a kiss for you.

Lots of Love Angelica

P.S. On the telephone I tried to tell you I received your letter and I wished to hear your voice again. I told you I loved you and I waited for you to come to Italy. Forgive me if I disturbed you but hearing your voice gave me great emotion.

My dearest niece

It was a great joy when I returned home from the mountains on the 16th July when ten minutes after I arrived the postman bought your letter. You can imagine the great joy it was for me that my darling brother Lorenzo's daughter finally came looking for her father. I have kept his secret for so long, he would be very pleased to know that his family has accepted you. He loved you very much and wanted to bring you and your mother here but it could not be.

Just think that so far away I have a dear niece that is true blood of my blood, but don't believe my dear that your aunt Annettea never forgets about you, I thought a lot about you, will you come to Italy? I am very pleased that you are all in good health, you and all your family and so do all of us greetings from all your Italian families.

Now I send you greetings and many kisses to you and your husband

your aunt Annettea who always thinks of you XXX

20th August 1997

Dear Rose

I answer your letter with some delay, I beg you to excuse me, I had to wait for my son to return home to translate for me. It seems I have had similar reactions to you in the discovery of the truth, also my stomach has done whims.

For ten days I have not succeeded to sleep and not even eat, I cry day and night. Then I begun to reason of why had happened. I was helped by my husband and my son and when I have spoken about you the first time to my son, he after listening to me has smiled and told me "Mum you are very fond of all your family, widen your arms and greet this new sister who asks you only some of your love." I assure you Rose, hearing these words from a twenty two year old boy gives me much strength and I thought of what had to be joy of our father when you have been born and his desperation when he had to leave you. In that time each defines has collapsed in me and I started to accept you as my sister. We are not up to judge our father and your mother's past. As for me Dad will always be the marvellous man and the god I adore.

Dear Rose,

Even though I am not very religious I also believe in something, they are perhaps looking down on us from up there and they help us, our bloods are of two sisters that will know to love each other for love and respect to our father.

You told me you had your first child at sixteen, you were young and we are convinced you are a strong person if you had the courage of leaving your husband and making a new life as soon as your children have been adult and married. We are in full summer and there is terrible heat and the nights are also hot. I am pleased you will come to our country to meet us. Now I greet you and embrace you with all my love and kisses.

Rosa

Dear Rose,

Who is writing this short letter is your brother Luigi. I received your cards and your presents for my children with pleasure, but I am really happy to know I have another sister. I saw your family in the photo you sent us (my brother in law, and my nephew and nieces) I am very proud of them. Our father loved you with all his heart even if he never could manifest it. I am full of joy thinking that in March you are coming to Italy to visit us. I hope this time will pass quickly. I am sending you all my family's and my love

   Ciao Luigi

CHAPTER 36

SYDNEY

OCTOBER 1997

Lilly ran through the airport terminal looking for her mother frantically, she had received a call early that morning, Tom had had a heart attack and had been flown by emergency air ambulance to Sydney's Prince Henry Hospital, her mother was put on the next available commercial flight. Lilly lived in Sydney on the northern beaches and was the closest to be able to be there for her mother, she knew how much her mother loved Tom and this would be upsetting her terribly. Lilly caught sight of her mother coming down the escalator waving at her to get her attention. Rose saw her youngest daughter and made her way through the busy terminal.

"Oh Mum, is he going to be okay?"

"I don't know darling, I won't know until we get to the hospital, they were talking about putting a stent in his heart, it's a tiny tube that the doctor would insert into the blocked passageway to keep it open. The stent restores the flow of blood he is in the operating theatre now."

"Come on, the car is this way, we should just miss peak hour traffic." Lilly grabbed her mother's hand and led her across to the carpark, paid the parking fee and eased the car out into the busy Sydney traffic. It was a half hour drive to the Prince Henry Hospital and Lilly tried to keep her mother's mind off her fears and what Tom must be going through by pointing out the sites and talking about what she had been doing.

They sat waiting in the lounge area for news of how Tom had gone with the surgery remembering some of the funny things Tom had done, like the time Lilly had made him a sponge birthday cake it was iced in blue icing and as he cut into it the knife had bounced back out, he couldn't cut it and he didn't want to hurt her feelings and kept trying to cut it until everyone burst out laughing, Lilly had made it out of real rubber sponge from a cushion and had iced it as a joke. Or the time he was working on a job and was swearing at everyone wanting to know who stole his "bloody pencil" and it was in his mouth. Tom would always say to Lilly and Ruby "when you two girls are here it's like having your mother in stereo, god your so much like her."

They had been in the waiting room for an hour trying to distract themselves from worrying about Tom and finally the doctor appeared and assured Rose that all had gone well and he was recovering nicely. They had put a stent into his collapsed artery and he would be as good as gold, in fact he would be able to return home tomorrow. Rose broke down in tears. She had been holding it in for so long, the thought of losing Tom was too much, she had only just found her soulmate after all these years, she didn't want him to go so soon.

"It's good news Mum, you know Tom is a fighter and his love for you will keep him going for many years yet. You have your love story and it doesn't end here." Lilly hugged her mother trying to stay strong, finally her mother had the love she deserved, she had suffered for over twenty five years at the hands of her father before finally leaving him and finding the love of her life with Tom. They were so good together and so in love, Lilly prayed that Tom would recover and have a long life with her mother, the life they both deserved.

Rose stayed the night with Lilly before returning to pick Tom up for their flight home. Tom was in good spirits and her mother finally looked relieved. Lilly hugged and kissed them both at the airport departure area.

"Take care of yourself Dad." She kissed his cheek.

"I will love, don't worry I'm sure your mother will have me under the thumb and keep me in order. It'll take a lot more than a heart attack to get me to leave her side."

They made their way to the departure lounge, they still had an hour before their flight so they grabbed a coffee and sat watching the planes coming and going through the window, waiting for their flight to be called.

"Which plane do you think is ours love?" Tom had only ever been on one flight and that was the air ambulance to Sydney two days ago and he didn't recall much of that trip.

"Well that's my bag going on that one there, so it must be that one." Rose pointed to the small thin plane, it looked like it was an eighteen seater.

Tom's eyes widened "Christ if it gets any smaller we'll be flying home on a bloody magpie."

Rose laughed he was back to his old self again, she nestled into the crook of his shoulder and thanked her lucky stars he was still with her.

NOVEMBER 1997

Dear Rose,

I am very sorry I haven't written before but I am sure you will understand the reason. Carlo was a brother and a son to me, during the last few weeks he suffered a lot. I can affirm he died sweetly, from sleeping to a coma when the heart attack arrived. I went to the doctor after his death because I felt as if I was becoming dead, a month has already passed but I miss him so much. I was with him night and day, I didn't look after myself or my family and now I wonder if it was worthwhile as he is not here anymore.

I comfort myself thinking that I could keep my promise I made to my parents, Carlo died in his house, in his bed with his brothers and sisters near him. Last Saturday I took away his furniture from his room. I'm trying to find a bit of serenity anyway, but the emptiness he left in me is very big.

Thank you for the earrings and bracelet you sent for my birthday, they are very beautiful. I like the doily you made with your hands a lot. I am very glad to receive your presents and it is important to me is the fact you choose them with your heart.

I don't think to be a special sister as you wrote in your card, I would like to thank you for your love that I perceive in your words.

I bought your present to our aunt and she told me she prepared one for you too but wants to give it to you when *you come to Italy next year. Thank you again and a big hug.*

Your special sister Angelica

CHAPTER 37

TRIP TO ITALY
MARCH 1998

Lilly and Ruby were so excited and a little appre-
hensive as they stood with their mother outside on
the viewing platform at Sydney International Airport.
Rose was about to board a plane for Italy to meet the
family in person but first she was doing a tour. Rose
had only ever been on short one hour flights from Port
Macquarie to Sydney, now she was going on a twenty
two hour flight to the other side of the world on her
own. Her Italian lessons had paid off and while she
would not consider herself fluent in the language, she

was hoping she could understand and speak enough to get by.

"I can't believe you are doing this Mum, you've never been out of the country and your first trip is alone to the other side of the world and you're doing a tour. Make sure you keep your passport safe and send a message when you get there." Lilly was almost in tears, she was excited her mother was going to meet her family in Italy but she was going alone.

"Yes Mum, make sure you call us when you get there, you know we will worry about you." Ruby also was in tears.

Rose looked at her two grown daughters standing in front of her both crying, she was excited and nervous about this adventure and couldn't believe she was doing it, and alone. Tom had declined to go with her, he had told her he would rather her go over twice with the money her mother had left her, rather than taking him and doing only one trip, besides he wasn't too keen on travelling too far from home these days.

"Stop worrying you two, I will be fine, I'm a grown woman and I will manage, besides the first week I am on a guided tour and the next four weeks I will be with the family. Luckily I have learned a little of the Italian language and way of life, I can understand "poco" and hopefully by the time I get home I will know a bit more."

Rose's flight had just been called for boarding, she hugged her daughters and took a deep breath before heading down the walkway to customs, she stopped and turned, waved to her two crying girls and called "ciao" before taking the steps towards finally meeting her new family. Rose wanted to make sure she didn't forget anything about this trip she had written in her little diary as she sat on the plane she pulled it out to make more notes.

TRAVEL DIARY

Left Kempsey catching the coach over to Port Macquarie to catch my flight to Sydney, it still doesn't seem real. Fred and Victoria and the grandkids came to see me off, there was a tear or two. Then as we take off heading for Sydney it's now getting real I'm heading to Rome … leaving Australia, that's still a dream. Arrive Sydney airport late, put on a holding pattern.

A teary goodbye with Ruby and Lilly then on through customs it's really happening, I'm really going to Italy.

Just landing in Melbourne to fuel up then on to Singapore. Flying over Australia, I can see Ayres Rock then heading towards Derby it's still light outside as we pass over. No getting out now and going home. I'm really going to Italy. Australia is behind us and we are headed for Singapore. Crossed the equator sometime around eleven thirty pm arrived in Singapore at midnight, a quick stopover before departing at two twenty am.

Thirteen hours and twenty minutes to London from here. It's eight thirty am Sydney time and we are not halfway from Singapore to London yet. Seems like we've been going forever. Flying over India, Iraq and Germany. Flying over Istanbul the lights go on forever.

Landed in London at Heathrow Airport and finally made it to British Airways gate and ready to leave for Rome. Heathrow airport is such a big place it took me an hour to get from our landing gate to here. I finally believe it after hearing the Rome flight called. Watch-

ing it all as we take off. Oh Shit! I'm in England, half a world away from home. It's daylight and fairly clear, just flew over Dover headed to Casilis, Paris then down the west coast of Italy. Can't see anything, we're at forty thousand feet above the clouds. A few tears as I get closer and think of it all.

On the ground in Italia. I've made it, all those sleepless nights worrying about clothes, airports and all, I have made it. Now to the hotel to start the tour.

Saturday night – Tour Rome by night and dinner in one of the restaurants down a quaint laneway. Musicians wander the streets singing to the patrons. I still can't believe I'm finally here.

Sunday – a trip around ancient Rome, the Vatican City visiting the Sistine Chapel and seeing the masterpieces of Michelangelo was amazing, The Panthenon, The magnificent Colosseum where games were held and the gladiators fought, then the Roman Forum the old streets have the original paving stones from the time of Julius Caeser, St Pauls. The Trevi Fountain is beautiful, they say if you throw one coin over your left shoulder with your right hand it will ensure you will come back to Rome, two coins thrown will ensure romance with

*a Roman or three coins thrown will ensure marriage.
I only had to throw one as I already have the love of
my life waiting for me back home. I made a wish to
return to Rome again. The fountain dates back to ancient Roman times, since the construction of the Aqua
Virgo Aqueduct in 19 B.C. providing water to the Roman baths and the fountains of central Rome. It's said
that the Aqua Virgo, or Virgin Waters, is named in
honour of a young Roman girl who led thirsty soldiers
to the source of the spring to drink.The fountain was
built at the end point of the aqueduct, at the junction
of three roads. These three streets (tre vie) give the Trevi
Fountain its name, the Three Street Fountain.*

*We went to the Roman Hills and had dinner in a
quaint little restaurant the food was sensational. We
wore joggers to walk around the city on the uneven paths.
I can't believe the Italian girls, they ride vespas in little
short skirts and high heels, park and then walk on the
cobblestones with ease. I could not wait to try my first
Italian coffee, I ordered a latte, when it came out it was
a cup of hot milk, a lesson learned if you want a latte in
Italy you need to say "cafe latte".*

Monday – Siena through the countryside full of peaches, olives, grapes. Little towns very old houses, there are caves in the hills from Tuscan times. Lombardi, Umbria Orvieto we stop for lunch and walk around town then on the rail up the hill. Tuscany to Siena a gorgeous medieval town. Tuesday afternoon a walking tour. I am sharing a room with a lovely girl from America, Jane who is about fifteen years younger than me. We get along well and she is good company.

Tuesday – Siena to Florence. Tuscany's such a beautiful area, green hills, grape vines, olives. Monetigirni, a small walled town on a hill surrounded by green flats, Colle Val De Elsa, the medieval town of San Giminamo was so pretty I loved this little town with its cobbled streets. Castilian Cittadina in Chianti it is a beautiful area full of rolling hills and picture-perfect farmhouses and wine we stopped for wine tasting at Castello Vicchiomaggio beautiful country, Tavanzzu Monastery.

Wednesday – Florence, Piazza St Croca, Wandered through some of the oldest streets to the Arno River to cross the Ponte Vecchio, Signorina Piazza, The Accademia to see Michelangelo's David, whose beauty and size have to be seen to be believed. Duomo Square to the cathedral and its world-famous dome - one of the largest on earth., National Museum, San Lorenzo had a magnificent exhibition of Michelangelo's.

Climbed the hill to the church of San Miniato al Monte with an enchanting view of Florence. Shopping is glorious, I still can't believe I am in Bella Italia!

Thursday – The Appennes Mountains run north to south along the Italian peninsular they call them Italy's backbone there were lots of tunnels through the hills on the motorway they have very good roads here.

Friday – Pisa stopped to see the leaning tower, Montecatini and Alto. Lucca Roman Aqua ducts, mountains with snow appears. Lots of hills around, leaving for Venice, there is snow high up on the Appenenies Mountains.

The coach broke down and we were given a lift by a passing coach, we only lost one hour and twenty minutes. There are lots of grapes in rows and its plain and very flat, Veneto is across the river, lots of agriculture flat country.

Saturday – Venice is very beautiful, it has no roads, just canals, of course we went for a gondola ride. The Grand Canal thoroughfare is lined with Renaissance and Gothic palaces, so many little bridges crossing the canals. The central square, Piazza San Marco, contains St. Mark's Basilica, which is tiled with Byzantine mosaics, and from the Campanile bell tower there are views of the city's red roofs. Spanning the Grand Canal, the Ponte di Rialto is Venice's most popular bridge, its the one I had seen in all the photos of Venice. One more sleep and tomorrow I meet my Italian family, I'm so excited.

It was just past eight o'clock when the phone rang in their motel room, Jane answered, had a brief conversation before hanging up.

"That was the front desk your family is downstairs waiting for you."

Finally she would meet her family, her emotions were running high, anticipation, excitement, fear of how they would greet her. Rose picked up her bags and smiled. Finally she would have answers.

"Can I come with you to meet your family Rose? After listening to your story I would love to see them." Jane was excited for Rose, it was such a beautiful story.

"Of course you can Jane."

As they entered the lobby Rose was expecting to see just her two sisters and brother. Instead she was greeted by about fifteen of the family: her sisters, brother, nieces and nephews, there were hugs, kisses and tears all around. Even Jane had tears watching this momentous moment of family meeting for the first time.

Angelica hugged her new sister and in very broken English cried "finally we meet, you have Papa's eyes and smile, welcome to our family, your family."

Rose said goodbye to Jane with a promise to stay in touch before they all bundled back into the three cars and headed for Ronco all'Adige.

Dear Diary,

The whole family came to meet me in three cars. Everyone was so pleased to see me, we all cried and embraced. I felt like I was home. Arrived in Ronco and went to see Aunt Annettea who kept hugging me and saying "you look so much like your father", they all say I have his eyes and smile and my eyes are the colour of his. Rosa said he always had sad eyes and talked of going back to Australia but never said why, and in quiet moments to himself would often cry and tell them he was worried about work and Carlo. He died from a stroke a blocked artery in the neck. For seven years he worked in France for six months of the year as there was no work in Italy. Aunt Annettea said over the years when they were alone he often spoke of me wondering how I was and what had happened to me. He never learnt to drive, he rode a bicycle everywhere.

Ronco is a farming village, mostly apples. There is a little village every few miles and the country is flat and a lot of fog which doesn't lift until about lunchtime. Luigi is really nice, only my height, he likes vino and a smoke. Their homes are lovely with big rooms, king size beds, marble floor tiles, marble bench tops and beautiful furniture, leather chairs. I'm being spoiled, I'm not allowed to do anything. Both Rosa and Angelica have dishwashers, so no washing up by hand.

Thursday we went to Verona airport to change my ticket and drove through the old part of Verona. It's a beautiful city with mountains around with snow capped tops. To Juliet's balcony, the house is an attractive brick and stone building with ivy covered garden walls and a small courtyard and a small balcony overlooking the courtyard. The entrance is covered with love letters from romantic souls searching for everlasting love. There is a statue of Juliet and the legend is when you rub her breast it will bring you good luck in love. Then to the Arena, the third largest Roman amphitheatre in the world. Its outer ring is made of pink and white limestone. They have operas there now. Wandering through these streets I had thoughts of my father strolling along this same cobbled street years before.

Friday went to the street markets in Albergo a village about six kilometres from here and from there too you can see the mountains and the town of Soave where they make wine. There are acres and acres of apple, peach and pear trees all just starting to flower.

Friday we went to visit my father's grave, it was a very sad and happy moment for me to finally have found him, I am sure he is looking down on me and smiling knowing I finally came to find him. That night we went to Luigi's for tea, his wife and girls are lovely. Tomorrow we are going up into the Alps region of Valmalenco where my mother's family originated from. I'd like to *see if I can find the family home. It's ironic that my mother's family lived so close to Lorenzo yet they met in Australia.*

Today we packed a picnic lunch and drove to Lake Garda the largest fresh-water lake in Italy, the water was crystal clear blue and is surrounded by mountains. Sirmione has a fort with a moat around it, we had ice-cream there it was divine. Riva del Garde is spectacular there was a medieval fortress bounded by a canal. The Varone waterfall had to be seen to be believed you had to walk inside a cave follow a walkway to the lower part of the waterfall which is inside the cave, well its actually a gorge, the sound was deafening, the water was bubbling and frothing and a spray of fine mist. To get to the upper cave we walked through a tunnel in the heart of the mountain to a balcony where the water rushes down here falling to the bottom pooling before falling to the lower cave. It was amazing. Limone was a picturesque town with churches and shrines and had small pebble beaches. It was so beautiful with flowers everywhere and the snow on the mountains.

So many places visited and so much vino, the family gave me a special party for my birthday with all the family here together. We have managed the language difficulties with much hand waving and laughter, my Italian is getting a little better. I have learnt so much about my father and his family and his beloved Italy and I will be sad to leave.

Rose sat on the plane on her way back home to Australia. The last five weeks had been truly amazing, she took pen to paper and wrote down her thoughts into her diary.

What a wonderful emotional experience. The worry about going so far, catching the right planes and the thrill of it all. As the plane came into Rome I had a very warm feeling and as we touched down my thoughts were "I'm Home." I loved the country and felt as though I belonged and meeting the family in Venice very teary and very beautiful so much feeling and love from people I didn't know of until a year ago. They welcomed me to their family and homes treated me like royalty. There was no shame or anything on their part and I was introduced to everyone as "my sister from Australia."

Aunt Annettea hugged and cried every time she saw me and would pat my cheeks and say "Lorenzo's little girl has come home" she was very upset when I had to leave, everyone was. It was a teary goodbye at Venice. I saw so many lovely places and things in Italy, it's a beautiful country. I want to go again as soon as I can. My one great wish is to be able to live there for a couple of years. Ciao for now Italia, I will return.

CHAPTER 38

All Martin's children surrounded his bedside, Rose wiped the sweat from Martin's brow with a damp cloth as he lay in the hospital bed, she knew he didn't have much time left on this earth and soon he would be joining their mother, the love of his life. Martin had lost some of his spark when Loretta had passed away, they had been inseparable and had shown their children what marriage was all about, love, laughter, compassion, compromise and family. Rose was so grateful to this man who had treated her like his own daughter all these years, he had always been there for her whenever she had needed his help or advice. He had supported her in finding her Italian family and had encouraged her to be the best she could be.

Martin had been ill for a while and had not told his children, he did not want them to worry or fuss over him, the cancer took hold quickly it had not been a long illness. He opened his eyes and looked at Rose.

"Hi honey, not long now and I'll be with my beautiful Loretta. Your mother was the most amazing woman I have ever known and I have missed her so much since she left. I'll tell her all about your adventures in Italy and that you found Lorenzo's family, that will make her very happy to know they have accepted you as their sister. Don't cry Rose, I've had a wonderful full life and I am so pleased that I got to call you my daughter."

Rose bent and kissed his damp forehead. "I'm so lucky that I got to have you as my Father, you have never made me feel anything but your daughter and I don't think I have told you enough how grateful I am for that. I love you Dad and when you see Mum tell her, tell her I love her." Rose caught the sob in her throat; she didn't want Martin's last hours to be sad ones with tears.

"I will honey." Martin looked around at his children and smiled. "I have been blessed with the best kids in the world, you all have made me so proud, don't be sad for too long, be happy that I'm finally going to your mother, I miss her so much. I'm tired now, it's time for me to go. I love you all and I will always be with you in your hearts and your memories." Martin closed his eyes and took his last breath, a peace came across his face and they knew he was on his way home to Loretta.

CHAPTER 39

MARCH 2015

Rose was about to turn seventy in a few days but that didn't stop her doing the gardening and the mowing. She had been out mowing the large lawn when she felt dizzy, her heart had started to beat fast, she felt clammy and could feel the sweat on her face, everything started to spin and she sat on the ground. Tom had seen her from the balcony and came running to her side.

"Rose, are you okay?" Tom knelt beside her.

"No Tom, I think I'm going to pass out and my heart is racing, call the ambulance." Rose lay down on the grass while Tom ran inside and called the ambulance.

Lilly was packing up her caravan getting ready to leave on another trip around Australia she would be leaving in three days' time straight after the birthday party they had organised for their mother when her phone rang. "Hello."

"Lilly, it's Dad, your mum's had a turn, the ambulance is here now and they are taking her up to Kempsey hospital."

"What, is she okay? Was it her heart?" Lilly could feel the tears pricking her eyes, she wouldn't bear it if anything happened to her mother.

"They think she's had a minor heart attack, can you go to the hospital love?"

"I'm on my way Dad, I love you."

"I love you too honey, drive carefully."

"I will Dad, I'll call you when I get there." Lilly tried to stay calm on the forty minute drive to Kempsey, she called her sister and brother and told them what was happening and as soon as she knew more she would call. Lilly was led into the emergency room where her mother was sitting up in the bed grinning sheepishly.

"Mum are you alright?" Lilly burst into tears, she couldn't hold her emotions back.

"Yes honey I'm fine, it's okay." Rose wrapped her arms around her. "I'm going to be alright."

"What happened? Dad said it was your heart."

"I was out mowing the lawn."

"You were what?" Lilly was gobsmacked. "Why are you mowing the lawn for god sake Mum, I know you're healthy but you're not a spring chicken either."

"I always mow the lawn. I got dizzy and my heart was racing so Tom called the ambulance and when they put me on the heart monitor it showed a minor heart attack, so they brought me here to do more tests and my heart is clear it's not a heart attack. They think it's because I was dehydrated and pushing the mower up the hill and the heat made me feel faint. I'm going to be fine. Stop worrying."

"I won't stop worrying and you won't be mowing the lawn again." Lilly stood with her hands on her hips, Rose could see the tears in her eyes and the worry she had caused her.

Rose thought about arguing the point but realised she would not win this fight with her daughter, she nodded faintly, there was really no choice at all. Lilly drove Rose home and gave her a good ear bashing all the way about mowing the lawn at her age. If she didn't organise a man to mow the lawn she would, she made her promise she would not do it again. Rose gave in; she knew not to argue with Lilly and she was sure Ruby would also give her a piece of her mind too when she called.

"Lilly, maybe we should cancel my birthday party."

"Don't think you're getting out of it that easy Mum, I know you don't like a fuss but it's organised and everyone is coming, after giving us all that scare you will be having a party." Lilly was quite firm and Rose knew there would be no changing her mind.

Rose sat with all her children, grandchildren, sisters, brothers and friends at her birthday party, she looked around the table and realised how blessed she was to have such a loving family. Tom caught her eye and gave her a wink and smile. She certainly was blessed and very much loved. As the party finished up, it was time for Lilly to leave and head off to the Northern Territory where she had singing gigs booked for the next few months. Rose worried about her youngest daughter out there on the road alone with just a dog for company, Lilly had had her own share of problems with men over the years and had left Port Macquarie after her abusive marriage ended to travel and find herself again. She was a strong, good hearted girl and she seemed finally happy and at peace and she did love travelling in the outback to remote areas. Rose always enjoyed listening to her stories about the people she had met and the places she had seen each time she phoned.

CHAPTER 40

Rose had been to Italy four times over the years to see her family, on one trip Ruby had travelled with her. Rose was so pleased to be able to introduce Ruby to her Italian family, her Italian language skills were coming along well, she could even translate a little for Ruby. Angelica found it funny that she was Ruby's aunt yet Ruby was older.

They had written many letters, gifts were sent to and from each other. Lilly had also visited Italy to meet and stay with the family.

The last twenty nine years had been the happiest of her life. She had found the love of her life, her soulmate and best friend, her children were happy and had raised their own families, she even had great grandchildren. Ruby worked in an International company travelling the world and lived in Sydney, Fred had built up his earthmoving business and still lived in Port Macquarie and Lilly, well she was still enjoying her single life of adventure and travelling around Australia, towing a caravan with her loyal dog as company, getting various work along the way. Rose was in regular contact with her family in Italy, her life was full and happy.

Tom, Ruby, Fred and Lilly had been keeping a secret from their mother, Angelica and Antonio were coming to Australia to visit her and spend Christmas. This was a big thing for Angelica. She had never flown before and was afraid of flying but her desire to come and see the place where her father had spent years and to spend time with her sister was greater than her fear. Lilly was away working in the remote Northern Territory as a camp cook, five hundred miles up the Tanami Road near the Granites Mine, she had called her mother on the work satellite phone and told her she could not make it back for Christmas, but she too was going to surprise her mother flying in on boxing day.

Ruby picked up Angelica and Antonio from Sydney international airport and they drove the five hours from Sydney to Hat Head. She had called Rose to say she and her partner were coming to stay for a couple of weeks and was bursting with the secret they had kept for the last six months, knowing how happy and surprised their mother would be. Ruby went into the house first and distracted her mother while Angelica and Antonio quietly came up the stairs at the side of the house and stood excitedly at the back door. They knocked on the door, Rose turned around and could not believe her eyes. She was speechless, her Italian family, in Australia, in her house, standing in front of her, it was a shock and a glorious surprise. They all hugged and cried. A few days later Lilly arrived. It had been arranged that Ruby would take Rose, Angelica and Antonio up to Bellingen, where Lorenzo had spent his time in the war, they would visit the old houses and the area where their father had met Rose's mother. They had chosen this day so that Lilly could sneak into the house before they arrived home. Lilly hadn't seen her mother for eleven months and had flown in to surprise her, it had been so hard for her to keep this secret from her mother and she hated lying to her.

Tom was sitting on the lounge smiling, he was trying so hard not to laugh and give the secret away, he could see Lilly hiding behind the open freezer door in the kitchen and he knew he was going to get the blame for the door being open. Ruby came in the back door first followed by Rose.

"Mum, why is the freezer door open?" Ruby tried not to giggle, Lilly had told her what she was going to do.

"Oh I don't know, Tom, did you leave the freezer door open? For god sakes Tom you silly old bugger," she laughed.

Lilly closed the door and stood there grinning at her mother "No, it's me Mum, isn't there anything to bloody eat in this house? I've come a long way for a home cooked meal."

Rose stopped and looked, it took a moment to register that it was Lilly, they grabbed each other and hugged, kissed and cried, Rose held her at arm's length then gave her a smack on the bottom.

"You little bugger, you've been lying to me, that was a great performance you put on yesterday on the phone, crying saying you wished you could be here."

"Sorry Mum, it's all Ruby's fault she made me lie."

Ruby laughed. "Yeah, blame the big sister."

Rose looked around at her family. "There are no more surprises are there? I don't think I could take another one."

"No more surprises Mum we promise." Ruby cuddled her mum and sister. "Merry Christmas Mum."

Lilly could only stay two days; she had to get back to work in the Northern Territory. Angelica and Antonio had another two weeks to spend with Rose, they spent their days on the beach, walking through the national park, sightseeing and just chatting and catching up. Rose was very sad when they had to leave to return to Italy but Angelica promised they would come back again and next time they would stay longer.

CHAPTER 41

THE GAP, HAT HEAD
JANUARY 2017

Rose and Tom stood at The Gap headland watching the sun rise together, it was thirty years today when they first started dating. They stood with their arms around each other, silently watching the beauty and freshness of another day starting. The clouds were brilliant pink, yellow and mauve as the sun started to rise up out of the sea. They'd had an amazing thirty years together so far and were still very much in love, they laughed together every day and had their own private little jokes. They were happy in their world just the two of them, they had ten children, numerous grandchildren and great grandchildren who adored their grandparents. Her children had grown up and were successful and happy, despite their hard childhood, she did sometimes worry about Lilly though, she'd had a few rough times but always managed to pick herself up and get on with it.

They were happy in their retirement, their lives were simple and their days were much the same every day, quiet and calm. They both acted like kids, sometimes pulling pranks on each other and teasing each other about something silly. Every day was bliss for them, they were a perfect match, true, loving soulmates. Together they could conquer the world. Tom looked at this beautiful woman by his side, she was gentle, understanding, caring, giving, tender and sweet. He knew he would do anything in the world to make her happy.

"You know Rose, the best day of my life was the day you agreed to come out on a date with me. It was like I'd won the lottery and you were my prize. I was the luckiest man alive and I still am to have you by my side. I can't tell you how much I love you and I'm grateful every day I get to wake up and look at your beautiful face." Tom bent down and kissed the top of her head. "You're the best thing that ever happened to me."

Rose looked up at this amazing man, he was all she ever wanted and more, he had made her life complete just by loving her, having him by her side was all she needed to be happy. "No Tom, I'm the lucky one, you made me see there is real never ending love, you showed me how to be loved and I'm grateful for every day we have had together and all the ones to come. It's been a long road to happiness but it was worth it to get to you. You're my best friend and I love you Tom."

Tom smiled, wrapped his arms around her, leaned in and kissed her softly on the mouth. "We will always be together my love. Always."

It was just like a fairytale.

SPECIAL DEDICATION

This book is dedicated to the man I have called Dad for the past 31 years.

You were the most loving, caring man I have ever known. You brought so much love, laughter and light to our mother's life, showing her and everyone around you what true love is meant to be. Thank you for making our mother's life so happy and loving us like your own children. Anyone who knew you loved you.

You may no longer be with us but you will always be in our hearts and memories.

You are a legend!

To my mother who is the most amazing woman I know, you are my inspiration and my role model.

I Love You.

AUTHOR BIO

Marianne Delaforce is an adventurous, brave, take-no-prisoners kind of woman with a big heart. Marianne grew up on a dairy farm at Telegraph Point, NSW. She has raised two sons and has four grandchildren.

Marianne will have a go at anything if it interests her and believes if you're not happy and don't like what you're doing, don't whinge about it, change it! She can drive a road train, ride a motorbike, likes skydiving and bungy jumping.

She has worked as a shop assistant, waitress, axeman on the Forest Commission, sales rep, remote camp cook, furniture removalist and truck driver. She has owned and operated a transport company employing forty staff driving twelve trucks out of two depots, one each in NSW and the NT. She has also owned and operated a Mediterranean restaurant on the riverbank of Port Macquarie.

Over the past thirty-five years her real passion has been singing and entertaining. She currently works as a marriage celebrant, entertainer and audiobook narrator.

She sold her company and restaurant in 2014, packed up and took off on the adventure of a lifetime to find herself again on the "Free, Fabulous and 50 Tour".

Marianne has travelled Australia with her trusty blue heeler dog, Elly, by her side. Towing an off-road caravan with her Land Rover, they have made their way around Australia three times, through the Gulf of Carpentaria, up to Cape York, across the Nullarbor, and have traversed both The Gibb River Road and The Outback Way, Australia's longest shortcut.

"Broken Promises" is Marianne's second novel in the series "Promises".

Website: mariannedelaforce.com

THANK YOU

Rosemary my amazing sister. What can I say? You have been a constant support to me, your input and suggestions have been invaluable. Thanks for being my ghost writer, for loving me and encouraging me to follow my passion and my dream. I will keep my promise to you when I'm rich and famous LOL your house on the Riviera and the yacht !!!! Sorry I can't grant your 3rd request. I'm sitting beside George Clooney at the movie premiere and Mum has shot gunned the other side.

Love you Sis. xxx

Michelle Vassallo for your support and help in so many ways. Thank you for letting me camp up in my caravan in your backyard when I venture home from my travels. You are more than a friend, you are family. I treasure our friendship.

Thank you Lesley Owen for sharing your valuable time, your wisdom and polishing my words and story. It's much appreciated.

My amazing nephew-in-law Mark Connors once again thank you for designing and keeping my website up to date.

To my family and friends who have supported me in buying the first book in the series and encouraging me. Thank You.

And lastly to my BFF Jo Everson my life would be very boring without you Wifey. Thank You for your constant love and support over the last 35 years.

NEVER STOP DREAMING

HELP & SUPPORT

Do not suffer in silence if you or anyone you know is being abused please ask for help. There are many organisations out there who can help in so many ways, you are not alone.

WHITE RIBBON AUSTRALIA

White Ribbon Australia is a domestic violence primary prevention campaign – specifically, they work to change the attitudes and behaviours that lead to violence against women.

Please contact the support hotline 1800 737 732, or visit www.whiteribbon.org.au

LIFELINE

Phone: 13 11 14

Relationships Australia

Support groups and counselling on relationships, and for abusive and abused partners.

Phone: 1300 364 277

THE PROMISED LAND
BOOK 1

Loretta was forced into an arranged marriage to a much older man who she did not love, by her strict Italian father. She suffered under his abusive control until World War II intervened and the handsome Italian Prisoner of War arrived on their farm in The Promised Land, NSW, Australia.

Their story of emotional conflict and forbidden love unfolded, and a child was born. When the war ended and he returned to Italy he made her a promise to return for her and the child. But her fairytale did not end the way she had hoped.

This is a story of love, betrayal and courage. Sometimes our destiny has a way of surprising us.

A PROMISE KEPT
BOOK 3

Once upon a time a handsome prince...... that's how fairytales start, and they always end with a happily ever after. With a tough childhood and an abusive father, then several bad choices with men, Lilly's life was far from the fairytale she had always dreamed of.

Lilly felt blessed to have strong women to show her the way, her Grandmother Loretta and her mother Rose. With their love and support she knew she could conquer anything, as long as she believed in herself. Even with that support sometimes she wondered, how do you pick yourself up when someone you love is always trying to drag you down and crush your spirit? Why does she continue to allow this to happen?

What was her purpose in life? Lilly sold everything and headed off, driving around Australia to find herself. Traveling alone to some of the most remote parts of Australia she wondered, would she ever find real love? The kind that her grandparents had shared. Did she have the strength and courage to see this bold journey through alone?

Lilly made herself a promise, but would she be able to keep it?